Jane Eyre Laid Bare

Jane Eyre Laid Bare

The Classic Novel with an Erotic Twist

CHARLOTTE BRONTË

and

EVE SINCLAIR

St. Martin's Griffin
New York

This is a work of fiction. All of the characters, organizations, and events portrayed in this novel are either products of the author's imagination or are used fictitiously.

Printed in the United States of America. For information, address St. Martin's Press, 175 Fifth Avenue, New York, N.Y. 10010.

www.stmartins.com

Library of Congress Cataloging-in-Publication Data

Sinclair, Eve.
Jane Eyre laid bare : the classic novel with an erotic twist / Charlotte Brontë and Eve Sinclair.—1st St. Martin's Griffin ed.
p. cm.
ISBN 978-1-250-03270-6 (trade pbk.) – ISBN 978-1-250-03271-3 (e-book)
1. Young women—England—Fiction. 2. Self-realization in women—Fiction. 3. Boarding schools—England—Fiction. 4. Erotic fiction. 5. Love stories. I. Brontë, Charlotte, 1816–1855. II. Title.
PS3619.I5678J36 2012
813'.6—dc23

2012032383

First published in Great Britain by Pan Books, an imprint of Pan Macmillan, a division of Macmillan Publishers Limited

First St. Martin's Griffin Edition: October 2012

10 9 8 7 6 5 4 3 2 1

For my own Mr R

Acknowledgements

Thank you to all the people who helped make this book happen, in particular Vivienne Schuster and Felicity Blunt, and the team at Curtis Brown. My heartfelt thanks also to the visionary Wayne Brookes and Jeremy Trevathan at Pan Macmillan and their 'can do' team, but most of all to the readers of this book for being prepared to be excited by the amazing and brilliant Charlotte Brontë, but in a different kind of way.

ONE

A new chapter in a novel is something like a new scene in a play, and when I draw up the curtain this time, reader, you must fancy you see a room in the George Inn at Millcote, with such large figured papering on the walls as many inn rooms have, such a carpet, such furniture, such ornaments on the mantelpiece, such prints, including a portrait of George the Third, and another of the Prince of Wales, and a representation of the death of Wolfe.

All this is visible to you by the light of an oil lamp hanging from the ceiling, and by that of an excellent fire, near which I sit in my cloak and bonnet. My muff and umbrella lie on the table and I am warming away the numbness and chill contracted by sixteen hours' exposure to the rawness of this October day. I left Lowton at four o'clock this morning and the Millcote town clock is now just striking eight.

Reader, though I look comfortably accommodated, I am not very tranquil in my mind. I thought when the coach stopped here there would be someone to meet me. I looked anxiously round as I descended the wooden steps, expecting to hear my name pronounced and to see a carriage waiting to convey me to Thornfield Hall.

Nothing of the sort was visible and when I asked a waiter if anyone had been to inquire after a Miss Eyre, I was answered in the negative. So I had no resource but to request to be shown into a private room. And here I am waiting, while all sorts of doubts and fears are troubling my thoughts.

It is a very strange sensation to inexperienced youth to feel itself quite alone in the world, cut adrift from every connection, uncertain whether the port to which it is bound can be reached, and prevented by many impediments from returning to that it has quitted. The charm of adventure sweetens that sensation, the glow of pride warms it, but then the throb of fear disturbs it. And fear with me became predominant when half an hour elapsed and still I was alone. I bethought myself to ring the bell.

'Is there a place in this neighbourhood called Thornfield?' I asked of the waiter who answered the summons.

'Thornfield? I don't know, ma'am. I'll inquire at the bar.' He vanished, but reappeared instantly.

'Is your name Eyre, Miss?'

'Yes.'

'Person here waiting for you.'

I jumped up, took my muff and umbrella, and hastened into the inn-passage. A man was standing by the open door, and in the lamplit street I dimly saw a one-horse conveyance.

'This will be your luggage, I suppose?' said the man rather abruptly when he saw me, pointing to my trunk in the passage.

'Yes.' He hoisted it onto the vehicle, which was a sort of

car, and then I got in. Before he shut me up, I asked him how far it was to Thornfield.

'A matter of six miles.'

'How long shall we be before we get there?'

'Happen an hour and a half.'

He fastened the car door, climbed to his own seat outside, and we set off.

Our progress was leisurely, and gave me ample time to reflect. I was content to be at length so near the end of my journey, and as I leaned back in the comfortable though not elegant conveyance, I pulled the woollen blanket around me.

Before long, in a half doze, as the light faded, the gentle rhythm of the carriage awoke my senses and I found, having slipped downwards on the leather seat, that the underneath seam of my drawers was tugging at me in such a way that I latched onto the familiar sensation which so often had been a prelude to sleep in the dark dormitory at Lowood. In the privacy of the carriage, quite alone for the first time in as long as I could remember, and still on the very verge of sleep, my mind wandered back to the girls at the boarding school that I had just left and their soft embraces.

And as I reflected further, I remembered Bessie and how she had taught me her secret remedy to alleviate the disquiet of the mind, and how her swift fingers and thumb had massaged my young body into its first delight. I shifted beneath the blanket, half asleep and, arching my spine, braced myself against the narrow arm rests, pressing down against the hard leather ridge of the seat. Presently, as we entered a straight stretch of the road, the horse sped up and the carriage jiggled beneath me at such an agreeable speed, that I was brought quickly to a pleasurable release.

Afterwards, feeling more relaxed and quite refreshed from this unexpected turn of events, I rearranged myself and meditated much at my ease.

'I suppose,' I thought, 'judging from the plainness of the servant and carriage, Mrs Fairfax is not a very dashing person. So much the better, for I never lived amongst fine people but once, and I was very miserable with them. I wonder if she lives alone except this little girl, and if so, whether she is in any degree amiable and I will be able to get on with her. I will do my best, although it is a pity that doing one's best does not always answer. At Lowood, indeed, I took that resolution, kept it, and succeeded in pleasing those around me in all manner of ways, but with Mrs Reed, I remember my best was always spurned with scorn and spanking.

'I pray God Mrs Fairfax may not turn out a second Mrs Reed, but if she does, I am not bound to stay with her. Let the worst come to the worst, I can advertise for the position of a governess again. How far are we on our road now, I wonder?'

I let down the window and looked out. Millcote was behind us, and judging by the number of its lights, it seemed a place of considerable magnitude, much larger than Lowton. We were now, as far as I could see, on a sort of common, but there were houses scattered all over the district. I felt we were in a different region to Lowood, more populous, less picturesque and certainly less romantic.

The roads were heavy, the night misty and when my conductor let his horse walk all the way, the hour and a half extended, I verily believe, to two hours. At last he turned in his seat and, knocking on the car, said, 'You're noan so far fro' Thornfield now.'

About ten minutes after, the driver got down and opened a pair of gates. We passed through, and they clashed to behind us. We now slowly ascended a drive, and came upon the long front of a house. Candlelight gleamed from one curtained bow window, but all the rest were dark. The car stopped at the front door. It was opened by a maidservant. I alighted and went in.

'Will you walk this way, ma'am?' said the girl and I followed her across a square hall with high doors all round. She ushered me into a room whose double illumination of fire and candle at first dazzled me, contrasting as it did with the darkness to which my eyes had been for two hours inured. When I could see, however, a cosy and agreeable picture presented itself to my view.

A snug small room, a round table by a cheerful fire and an armchair, wherein sat the neatest imaginable little elderly lady, in widow's cap, black silk gown and snowy muslin apron. Exactly like I had fancied Mrs Fairfax, only less stately and milder looking. She was occupied in knitting, whilst a large cat purred loudly at her feet. Nothing in short was wanting to complete the idyll of domestic comfort. A more reassuring introduction for a new governess could scarcely be conceived. There was no grandeur to overwhelm, no stateliness to embarrass. As I entered, the old lady got up and promptly and kindly came forward to meet me.

'How do you do, my dear? I am afraid you have had a tedious ride. John drives so slowly. You must be cold. Come over to the fire.'

'Not at all. Mrs Fairfax, I suppose?' I said.

'Yes, you are right. Do sit down.'

She conducted me to her own chair, and then began to remove my shawl and untie my bonnet strings. I begged she would not give herself so much trouble.

'Oh, it is no trouble. I daresay your own hands are almost numbed with cold. Leah, make a little hot drink and cut a sandwich or two. Here are the keys of the storeroom.'

And she produced from her pocket a most housewifely bunch of keys, and delivered them to the servant.

'She treats me like a visitor,' I thought. 'I little expected such a reception. I anticipated only coldness and stiffness. This is not at all how I have heard governesses are usually addressed.'

She returned and with her own hands cleared her knitting apparatus and a book or two from the table, to make room for the tray which Leah now brought, and then herself handed me the refreshments.

'Shall I have the pleasure of seeing Miss Fairfax tonight?' I asked, when I had partaken of what she offered me.

'What did you say, my dear? I am a little deaf,' returned the good lady, approaching her ear to my mouth.

I repeated the question more distinctly.

'Miss Fairfax? Oh, you mean Miss Varens! Varens is the name of your future pupil.'

'Indeed! Then she is not your daughter?'

'No, no. I have no family.'

I should have followed up my first inquiry, by asking in what way Miss Varens was connected with her, but I recollected it was not polite to ask too many questions. Besides, I was sure to hear in time.

'I am so glad,' she continued, as she sat down opposite to me, and took the cat on her knee, 'I am so glad you have come. It will be quite pleasant living here now with a companion. To be sure it is pleasant at any time, for Thornfield is a fine old hall, rather neglected of late years perhaps, but still it is a respectable place. Yet you know, in wintertime one feels dreary quite alone in the best quarters. I say alone – Leah is a nice girl to be sure, and John and his wife are very decent people, but then you see they are only servants, and one can't converse with them on terms of equality. One must keep them at due distance, for fear of losing one's authority. It was only at the commencement of this autumn that little Adela Varens came with her nurse. A child makes a house alive all at once, and now you are here I shall be quite gay.'

My heart really warmed to the worthy lady as I heard her talk. I drew my chair a little nearer to her, and expressed my sincere wish that she might find my company as agreeable as she anticipated.

'But I'll not keep you sitting up late tonight. It is on the stroke of twelve now, and you have been travelling all day. You must feel tired. If you have got your feet well warmed, I'll show you your bedroom. I've had the room next to mine prepared for you. It is only a small apartment, but I thought you would like it better than one of the large front chambers. To be sure they have finer furniture, but they are so dreary and solitary, I never sleep in them myself.'

I thanked her for her considerate choice, and as I really felt fatigued with my long journey, expressed my readiness to retire.

She took her candle, and I followed her from the room. First she went to see if the hall door was fastened. Having taken the key from the lock, she led the way upstairs. The steps and banisters were of oak and the staircase window was high and latticed. Both it and the long gallery into which the bedroom doors opened looked as if they belonged to a church rather than a house. A very chill and vault-like air pervaded the stairs and gallery, suggesting cheerless ideas of space and solitude. I was glad, when finally ushered into my chamber, to find it of small dimensions, and furnished in ordinary, modern style.

When Mrs Fairfax had bidden me a kind goodnight, and I had fastened my door, I gazed upon the cheerful aspect of my little room and I remembered that, after a day of bodily fatigue and mental anxiety, I was now at last in safe haven.

The impulse of gratitude swelled my heart and I knelt down at the bedside, and offered up thanks where thanks were due, not forgetting, ere I rose, to implore aid on my further path, and the power of meriting the kindness which seemed so frankly offered me before it was earned. At once weary and content, I slept soon and soundly.

When I awoke it was broad day. The chamber looked such a bright little place to me as the sun shone in between the gay blue chintz window curtains, showing papered walls and a carpeted floor, so unlike the bare planks and stained plaster of Lowood, that my spirits rose at the view.

Externals have a great effect on the young and I thought that a fairer era of life was beginning for me. One that was to have its flowers and pleasures, as well as its thorns and toils and faculties. Roused by the change of scene, my senses seemed all astir.

I stretched, feeling a new delight awaken in my body. So long accustomed to sleeping in the company of others, the soft silence of the room, the trill of birdsong faint beyond the window, made my excitement mount.

I threw back the counterpane, letting the sunlight fall on the thin muslin cloth of my nightgown, and I spread my limbs, sunbathing like a cat. As the steady warmth increased, I felt my hand falling to the soft pillow of my inner thigh.

Unlike yesterday in the carriage, I knew this morning that I had time at my disposal, and with this in mind, I closed my eyes, and found myself remembering Emma Wilby. After my dearest friend, Helen Burns, had died, it had been Emma with whom I had formed a deep attachment and I now reflected on how Emma would have loved this room, this space and solitude. Yet, at the same time I couldn't help remembering how our exploration of one another had only been heightened by the illicitness of our encounters in the public spaces of Lowood.

Now I heard a gentle moan escape unbidden from my lips, as I remembered that first far distant day in the library, Emma's face still etched in my mind, as she'd looked up at me from between my legs, her eyes glittering, as they'd dared me to command her to stop. I'd sat on the edge of that hard teacher's desk, my skirt hitched up around me, naked above my stocking tops, Emma's long red hair tickling my thighs, hardly daring to breathe, knowing how close we were to being caught, but unable to move away. How I had trembled against her like a fluttering bird, but she'd only assured me not to be afraid.

I felt my hand languidly lifting my gown and straying to the place Emma had caressed so often, my fingers feeling my silken wet crevasse, remembering that first flicker of her tongue against my bud. I felt my sex warm in the sunlight through the window, opening like a flower, and my memory pulled me back to Emma and how I had braced against the desk, terrified and yet delighted in the shimmering dart of pleasure that she had ignited within me. How she'd spread me with her fingertips, holding back my damp, coiled pubic hair and lapped at me, and how the sound of my juices against her mouth had excited me beyond all measure, until I had implored her and, grabbing my hips, she'd pressed her mouth against me, sucking me harder, pulling me into her.

In the sunlight now, I pushed my finger inside my sex, feeling the warm, wet opening yielding, then pulling it out again to rub my engorged bud. Bucking up, my thighs tensing,

I gasped, as with the memory of Emma's flickering tongue, my head seemed to explode like a shattered mirror, shards of pleasure spinning with light.

Sated, I rose, my sex still throbbing in the aftermath of my pleasure. I dressed myself with care, although I was obliged to be plain, for I had no article of attire that was not made with extreme simplicity. Even so, I was still by nature solicitous to be neat.

It was not my habit to be disregardful of appearance or careless of the impression I made. On the contrary, I wished to look as well as I could, and to please as much as my want of beauty would permit. I sometimes regretted that I was not handsomer and I sometimes wished to have rosy cheeks, a straight nose and small cherry mouth. I desired to be tall, stately and finely developed in figure, with the kind of buxom full breasts that Emma had so proudly possessed. I felt it a misfortune that I was so little, so pale, and had features so irregular and so marked, although the pertness of my nipples and my buttocks had been held in high regard at Lowood by the other girls.

Why had I these aspirations and these regrets about my womanly faculties? It would be difficult to say. I could not then distinctly say it to myself, yet I had a reason, and a logical, natural reason too. My experience at Lowood was over. Helen, Emma, all the others had gone and I would never be in the company of those girls who had comforted me. I wondered how long I could sustain myself on their memory, for already they seemed to be slipping away like ghosts, leaving me with a new kind of yearning, but for what, I knew not. Cast out into this new adventure, with no experience other than those pale-limbed innocents, I felt unsure of the future and of this adult world to which I now belonged.

I felt confused, too. The bodily pleasures in which we girls had all delighted in the dormitory had been so commonplace as to indicate normalcy, yet in the two moments I alone had enjoyed since my departure from Lowood, the solitary secretiveness of my self-pleasure appeared, in retrospect, more shameful than I expected, and a creeping and unfamiliar sense of wrongdoing came upon me.

However, when I had brushed my hair very smooth, and smoothed the black frock over my slim waist – which, Quakerlike as it was, at least had the merit of fitting to a nicety – and adjusted my clean white tucker, I thought I should do respectably enough to appear before Mrs Fairfax, and that neither she nor my new pupil would ever guess my secret, or recoil from me with antipathy. Having opened my chamber window, and seen that I left all things straight and neat on the toilet table, I ventured forth.

TWO

Traversing the long and matted gallery, I descended the slippery steps of oak to the hall. I halted there a minute and looked at some pictures on the walls (one, I remember, represented a tall man in tight breeches with a riding crop, standing over a supine lady with powdered hair fingering a pearl necklace at her naked breast), at a bronze lamp pendent from the ceiling, at a great clock whose case was of oak curiously carved and ebony black with time and rubbing.

Everything appeared very stately and imposing to me, but then I was so little accustomed to grandeur. The hall door, which was half of glass, stood open and I stepped over the threshold. It was a fine autumn morning. The early sun shone serenely on embrowned groves and still green fields. Advancing onto the lawn, I turned and looked up to survey the front of the mansion.

It was three storeys high, of proportions not vast, though considerable. A gentleman's manor house, not a nobleman's seat. Battlements round the top gave it a picturesque look. Its grey front stood out well from the background of a rookery, whose cawing tenants were now on the wing, and I watched as they flew over the lawn and grounds to alight in a great meadow. Farther off were hills. They were not so lofty as those round Lowood, nor so craggy, nor so like barriers of separation from the living world, but yet quiet and lonely and seeming to embrace Thornfield with a seclusion I had not expected to find.

I was yet enjoying the calm prospect and pleasant fresh air, yet listening with delight to the cawing of the rooks and thinking what a great place it was for one lonely little dame like Mrs Fairfax to inhabit, when that lady appeared at the door.

'What! Out already?' said she. 'I see you are an early riser.' I went up to her, and was received with an affable kiss and shake of the hand.

'How do you like Thornfield?' she asked. I told her I liked it very much.

'Yes,' she said, 'it is a pretty place, but I fear it will be getting out of order, unless Mr Rochester should take it into his head to come and reside here permanently. Or, at least, visit it rather oftener. Great houses and fine grounds require the presence of the proprietor.'

'Mr Rochester!' I exclaimed. 'Who is he?'

'The owner of Thornfield,' she responded quietly. 'Did you not know he was called Rochester?'

Of course I did not. I had never heard of him before. But the old lady seemed to regard his existence as a universally understood fact.

'I thought,' I continued, 'Thornfield belonged to you.'

'To me? Bless you, child. What an idea! To me! I am only the housekeeper and manager. To be sure I am distantly related to the Rochesters by the mother's side, but I never presume on the connection. In fact, it is nothing to me. I consider myself quite in the light of an ordinary housekeeper.'

'And the little girl? My pupil?'

'She is Mr Rochester's ward. He commissioned me to find a governess for her. Here she comes, with her "bonne", as she calls her nurse.'

The enigma then was explained. This affable and kind little widow was no great dame, but a dependant like myself. I did not like her the worse for that. On the contrary, I felt better pleased than ever. The equality between her and me was real and my position was all the freer.

As I was meditating on this discovery, a little girl, followed by her attendant, a pretty young woman with a coil of dark hair, came running up the lawn. I could see the woman's slim ankles as she held her skirt aloft and the softness of her full lips as she called to the child ahead of her.

I looked at my pupil, who did not at first appear to notice me. She was quite a child, perhaps seven or eight years old, slightly built, with a pale, small-featured face, and a redundancy of hair falling in curls to her waist.

'Good morning, Miss Adela,' said Mrs Fairfax. 'Come and speak to the lady who is to teach you, and to make you a clever woman some day.' She approached.

'C'est là ma gouverante!' said she, pointing to me, and addressing her nurse, who answered, 'Mais oui, certainement.'

'Are they foreigners?' I inquired, amazed at hearing the French language.

'The nurse is a foreigner, and Adela was born on the Continent. I believe she never left it till within six months ago. When she first came here she could speak no English. Now she can talk it a little. I don't understand her, she mixes it so with French, but you will make out her meaning very well, I daresay.'

Fortunately I had had the advantage of being taught French by a French lady, and, as I had always made a point of conversing with Madame Pierrot as often as I could, had acquired a certain degree of readiness and correctness in the language. I was not likely to be much at a loss with Mademoiselle Adela.

She came and shook hands with me when she heard that I was her governess, and as I led her in to breakfast, I addressed some phrases to her in her own tongue. She replied briefly at first, but after we were seated at the table, and she had examined me some ten minutes with her large hazel eyes, she suddenly commenced chattering fluently.

'Ah!' cried she, in French. 'You speak my language as well as Mr Rochester does. I can talk to you as I can to him, and so can Sophie. She will be glad. Nobody here understands her, as Madame Fairfax is all English. Sophie is my nurse. She came with me over the sea in a great ship with a chimney that smoked. Oh, how it did smoke! And I was sick, and so was Sophie, and so was Mr Rochester. Mr Rochester lay down in a pretty room called the salon with

Sophie, and I had a little bed in another place. I nearly fell out of mine, it was like a shelf.'

I looked up and saw Sophie staring at me with her cool green eyes, and I imagined that I saw the colour rise in her cheeks. I had no time to contemplate the child's insinuation that her maid and Mr Rochester had openly shared a bed, even if it were just for convenience, and with them both being seasick, as the child had pinned me with her attention.

'And Mademoiselle – what is your name?'

'Eyre. Jane Eyre.'

'Aire? Bah! I cannot say it. Well, our ship stopped in the morning, before it was quite daylight, at a great city. A huge city, with very dark houses and all smoky. Not at all like the pretty clean town I came from. And Mr Rochester carried me in his arms over a plank to the land, and he carried Sophie after, and we all got into a coach, which took us to a beautiful large house, larger than this and finer, called a hotel. We all stayed there in a grand suite for nearly a week. I and Sophie used to walk every day in a great green place full of trees, called the park. And there were many children there besides me, and a pond with beautiful birds in it, that I fed with crumbs.'

'Can you understand her when she runs on so fast?' asked Mrs Fairfax.

I understood her very well, for I had been accustomed to the fluent tongue of Madame Pierrot.

'I wish,' continued the good lady, 'you would ask her a

question or two about her parents. I wonder if she remembers them?'

'Adèle,' I inquired, 'with whom did you live when you were in that pretty clean town you spoke of?'

'I lived long ago with mama, but she is gone to the Holy Virgin. Mama used to teach me to dance and sing, and to say verses. A great many gentlemen and ladies came to see mama, and I used to dance before them, or to sit on their knees and sing to them. I liked it. Shall I let you hear me sing now?'

She had finished her breakfast, so I permitted her to give a specimen of her accomplishments. Then, folding her little hands demurely before her, shaking back her curls and lifting her eyes to the ceiling, she commenced singing a song from some opera.

It was the strain of a forsaken lady, who, after bewailing the perfidy of her lover, calls pride to her aid, desires her attendant to deck her in her brightest jewels and richest robes, and resolves to meet the false one that night at a ball. To prove to him, by the gaiety of her demeanour, how little his desertion has affected her.

The subject seemed strangely chosen for an infant singer, but I suppose the point of the exhibition lay in hearing the notes of love and jealousy warbled with the lisp of childhood. And in very bad taste that point was. At least I thought so.

I saw Sophie, her nurse, sitting very still, her hands clasped in her lap, listening attentively, as if this subject matter were quite normal. As I gazed upon her fine profile, I wondered whether she had also shared a bed with the mysterious Mr Rochester in the hotel that Adèle had spoken of.

Adèle sang the canzonette tunefully enough, and with the naïveté of her age. This achieved, she said, 'Now, Mademoiselle, I will repeat you some poetry.'

Assuming an attitude, she began, 'La Ligue des Rats. Fable de La Fontaine.'

She then declaimed the little piece with an attention to punctuation and emphasis, a flexibility of voice and an appropriateness of gesture, very unusual indeed at her age, and which proved she had been carefully trained.

'Was it your mama who taught you that piece?' I asked.

'Yes, and she just used to say it in this way: "Qu' avez vous donc? Lui dit un de ces rats. Parlez!" Now shall I dance for you?'

'No, that will do. But after your mama went to the Holy Virgin, as you say, with whom did you live then?'

'With Madame Frédéric and her husband. She took care of me, but she is nothing related to me. I think she is poor, for she had not so fine a house as mama. I was not long there. Mr Rochester asked me if I would like to go and live with him in England, and I said yes, for I knew Mr Rochester before I knew Madame Frédéric, and he was always kind to me and gave me pretty dresses and toys. But you see he has not kept his word, for he has brought me to England, and now he is gone back again himself, and I never see him.'

After breakfast, Adèle and I withdrew to the library, which room, it appears, Mr Rochester had directed should be used as the schoolroom. I was briefly reminded of Lowood and that heady moment I had shared with Emma which I had only this morning been hotly reminiscing upon, but as I walked further into the plush library, I put the thought firmly from my mind.

Most of the books bound in red and gold were locked up behind glass doors, but there was one bookcase left open containing everything that could be needed in the way of elementary works, and several volumes of light literature, poetry, biography, travels, a few romances. There was also a collection of classic novels, including the familiar tome of *Pamela* by Samuel Richardson, which, as I picked it up to examine it, disgorged from between its covers a pamphlet entitled *An Apology for the Life of Mrs Shamela Andrews*, which looked most curious, and I resolved to read it at a later date.

I suppose Mr Rochester had considered that these books were all the governess would require for her private perusal. Indeed, they contented me amply for the present, compared with the scanty pickings I had now and then been able to glean at Lowood. In this room, too, there was a cabinet piano, quite new and of superior tone, as well as an easel for painting and a pair of globes.

I found my pupil sufficiently docile, and when I had talked to her a great deal, and got her to learn a little, and when the morning had advanced to noon, I allowed her to return to her nurse. I then proposed to occupy myself till dinner time in drawing some little sketches for her use.

As I was going upstairs to fetch my portfolio and pencils, Mrs Fairfax called to me.

'Your morning school hours are over now, I suppose,' said she.

She was in a room the folding doors of which stood open, and I went in when she addressed me. It was a large, stately apartment, with several purple chaises longues, large chairs and velvet curtains, a Turkey carpet, walnut-panelled walls, one vast window rich in slanted glass, and a lofty ceiling, nobly moulded. Mrs Fairfax was dusting some vases of fine purple spar, which stood on a sideboard.

'What a beautiful room!' I exclaimed, as I looked round, trailing my hand along the soft back of the chair and to the urn of pampas feathers, for I had never before seen any half so sumptuous.

'Yes, this is the dining room. I have just opened the window, to let in a little air and sunshine, for everything gets so damp in apartments that are seldom inhabited. The drawing room yonder feels like a vault.'

She pointed to a wide arch corresponding to the window, and hung like it with a Tyrian-dyed curtain, now looped up. Mounting to it by two broad steps, and looking through, I thought I caught a glimpse of a fairy place, so bright to my novice eyes appeared the view beyond.

It was a pretty drawing room, and within it a boudoir with a huge cushion-covered day bed, and above it a spread of white carpets, on which seemed laid brilliant garlands of flowers and white grapes and vine leaves. Beneath, in rich contrast, were crimson couches and ottomans, some shaded by screens that had been placed in such a way to form private enclosures. On the far wall a giant painting depicted a group of people engaged in some sort of outdoor pursuit – perhaps picnicking – but painted from the most obscure perspective with only glimpses of flesh and hair showing between the leaves.

The pale marble mantelpiece was covered in strange ornaments of sparkling Bohemian glass, ruby red, the same rounded columns with bulbous tops in several sizes. Between the windows large mirrors repeated the general blending of snow and fire.

'In what order you keep these rooms, Mrs Fairfax!' I said. 'No dust, no canvas coverings. Except that the air feels chilly, one would think they were inhabited daily.'

'Why, Miss Eyre, though Mr Rochester's visits here are rare, they are always sudden and unexpected and he sometimes entertains guests in his private soirees. I observed that it put him out to find everything swathed up, and to have a bustle of arrangement on his arrival, so I thought it best to keep the rooms in readiness.'

'Is Mr Rochester an exacting, fastidious sort of man?'

'Not particularly so. He has a gentleman's tastes and habits, and he expects to have things managed in conformity to them.'

'Do you like him? Is he generally liked?'

'Oh, yes. The family have always been respected here. Almost all the land in this neighbourhood, as far as you can see, has belonged to the Rochesters time out of mind.'

'Well, but, leaving his land out of the question, do you like him? Is he liked for himself?'

'I have no cause to do otherwise than like him. I believe

he is considered a just and liberal landlord by his tenants, but he has never lived much amongst them.'

'But has he no peculiarities? What, in short, is his character?'

'He is rather peculiar, perhaps. He has travelled a great deal, and seen a great deal of the world, I should think. I daresay he is clever, but I never had much conversation with him.'

'In what way is he peculiar?'

'I don't know. It is not easy to describe. Nothing striking, but you feel it when he speaks to you, you cannot be always sure whether he is in jest or earnest, whether he is pleased or the contrary. But it is of no consequence, he is a very good master.'

This was all the account I got from Mrs Fairfax of her employer and mine, but in no way did her answer satisfy my curiosity. Mr Rochester was Mr Rochester in her eyes, a gentleman, a landed proprietor and nothing more. She inquired and searched no further, and evidently wondered at my wish to gain a more definite notion of his identity.

When we left the dining room, she proposed to show me over the rest of the house and I followed her upstairs and downstairs, admiring as I went. The large front chambers I thought especially grand, and some of the third-storey rooms, though dark and low, were interesting from their air of antiquity.

The imperfect light entering by their narrow casement showed bedsteads of a hundred years old with iron bars, low-hanging iron chandeliers dripping with old red wax, and engraved chests in oak or walnut. A row of venerable chairs dominated one wall, and one in particular caught my attention. It looked most uncomfortable, with a wooden protuberance jutting up from the middle of the seat and iron cuffs at its arms and base, like the kind a convict might wear. Did someone here ever suffer from a medical ailment of the mind, perhaps, whereby it was necessary that they were restrained?

All these relics gave to the third storey of Thornfield Hall the aspect of a home of the past, a shrine of memory. I liked the hush, the gloom, the quaintness of these retreats in the day, but I by no means coveted a night's repose on one of those wide and heavy beds. Shut in, some of them were, with doors of oak, shaded, others, with wrought old English hangings crusted with thick work portraying effigies of strange flowers, and stranger birds, and the strangest human beings contorted in positions I had never seen.

'Do the servants sleep in these rooms?' I asked.

'No. No one ever sleeps here. One would almost say that, if there were a ghost at Thornfield Hall, this would be its haunt.'

'You have no ghost, then?'

'None that I ever heard of,' returned Mrs Fairfax, smiling.

'Nor any traditions of one? No legends or ghost stories?'

'I believe not. And yet it is said the Rochesters have been rather a violent than a quiet race in their time. Perhaps, though, that is the reason they rest tranquilly in their graves now.'

'Yes – "after life's fitful fever they sleep well",' I muttered.

'Where are you going now, Mrs Fairfax?' for she was moving away.

'On to the leads. Will you come and see the view from thence?'

I followed still, up a very narrow staircase to the attics, and thence by a ladder and through a trapdoor to the roof of the hall. I was now on a level with the crow colony, and could see into their nests. Leaning over the battlements and looking far down, I surveyed the grounds laid out like a map: the bright velvet lawn closely girdling the grey base of the mansion, the field, wide as a park, dotted with its ancient timber, the wood divided by a path visibly overgrown, greener with moss than the trees were with foliage, the church at the gates, the road, the tranquil hills, all reposing in the autumn day's sun. No feature in the scene was extraordinary, but all was pleasing.

When I turned from it and re-passed the trapdoor, I could scarcely see my way down the ladder. The attic seemed black as a vault compared with that arch of blue air to which I had been looking up.

Mrs Fairfax stayed behind a moment to fasten the trapdoor. By groping, I found the outlet from the attic and proceeded to descend the narrow garret staircase. I lingered in the long passage to which this led, separating the front and back rooms of the third storey. Narrow, low and dim, with only one little window at the far end, with its two rows of small black doors all shut, it looked like a corridor in some Bluebeard's castle.

While I paced softly on, the last sound I expected to hear

in so still a region was a laugh and then a noise as if bare flesh struck. Then immediately afterwards another curious laugh which was distinct, formal, mirthless.

I stopped. The sound ceased, only for an instant, then it began again, louder. For at first, though distinct, it was very low. It passed off in a clamorous peal that seemed to wake an echo in every lonely chamber, though it originated but in one, and I could have pointed out the door whence the accents issued.

'Mrs Fairfax!' I called out, for I now heard her descending the great stairs. 'Did you hear that sound? That loud laugh? Who is it?'

'Some of the servants, very likely,' she answered. 'Perhaps Grace Poole.'

'Did you hear it?' I again inquired.

'Yes, plainly. I often hear her. She sews in one of these rooms. Sometimes Leah is with her and they are frequently noisy together.'

The laugh was repeated in its low, syllabic tone, and terminated in an odd exultant murmur.

'Grace!' exclaimed Mrs Fairfax.

I really did not expect any Grace to answer, for the laugh was as preternatural a laugh as any I ever heard.

The door nearest me opened, and a servant came out. She was a woman of between thirty and forty, red-haired and with a hard, plain face. Her cheeks were highly flushed.

'Too much noise, Grace,' said Mrs Fairfax. 'Remember directions!'

Grace curtseyed stiffly and went into the room backwards,

quickly shutting the door once again, so that I could not see inside.

'She is a person we have to sew and assist Leah in her housemaid's work,' continued the widow. 'She is not altogether unobjectionable in some points, but she does well enough. By the bye, how have you got on with your new pupil this morning?'

The conversation, thus turned on Adèle, continued till we reached the light and cheerful region below. Adèle came running to meet us in the hall, exclaiming, 'Mesdames, vous êtes servies!' adding, 'J'ai bien faim, moi!'

We found dinner ready and waiting for us in Mrs Fairfax's room.

THREE

The promise of a smooth career, which my first calm introduction to Thornfield Hall seemed to pledge, was not belied on a longer acquaintance with the place and its inmates. Mrs Fairfax turned out to be what she appeared, a placid-tempered, kind-natured woman, of competent education and average intelligence. My pupil was a lively child, who had been spoilt and indulged and therefore was sometimes wayward, but she soon became obedient and teachable.

She had no great talents, no marked traits of character, no peculiar development of feeling or taste which raised her one inch above the ordinary level of childhood, but neither had she any deficiency or vice which sunk her below it. Her simplicity and efforts to please me inspired a degree of attachment sufficient to make us both content in each other's society.

Now and then, when I took a walk by myself in the grounds, I went down to the gates and looked through them along the road. Sometimes, while Adèle played with her nurse, and Mrs Fairfax made jellies in the storeroom, I climbed the three staircases, raised the trapdoor of the attic, and having reached the leads, looked out afar over field and hill. Then I longed for a power of vision which might overpass the horizon and reach the busy world which was full of the life that I had heard of, but never seen.

I desired with a mounting longing so much more practical experience than I possessed. I wanted more intercourse with my kind, acquaintance with variety of character and in particular with the opposite sex, than was here within my reach in the confines of Thornfield. I valued what was good in Mrs Fairfax, and what was good in Adèle, but I believed in the existence of another more vivid kind of goodness, and what I believed in I wished to behold.

Who blames me? I could not help it. Restlessness was in my nature. It agitated me to pain sometimes and, although I often pleasured myself for relaxation at night as was my habit, a deeper satisfaction eluded me.

Then, my sole relief was to walk along the corridor of the third storey, safe in the silence and solitude of the spot, and allow my mind's eye to dwell on the bright visions in the faded paintings on the wall and the tapestries in the old bedrooms. They depicted couples in all manner of undress, their carnal desires plainly bared. In particular, the tapestry in the largest room caught my attention. It showed a naked god bearing down upon a sea-maiden, his tumultuous member poised between her eager, open legs, her head thrown back in wanton desire. Each time I studied the scene, it ignited my imagination, expanded it with life, with fire and a curiosity for the pleasures of the flesh that had not been in my actual existence.

It is in vain to say human beings ought to be satisfied with tranquillity. They must have action and they will make it if they cannot find it. Millions are condemned to a stiller doom than mine, and millions are in silent revolt against their lot. Nobody knows how many rebellions besides political rebellions ferment in the masses. Women are supposed to be very calm generally, but women feel just as men feel.

When thus alone, I not infrequently heard Grace Poole's laugh. The same peal, the same low, slow 'Ha! Ha!' which, when first heard, had thrilled me. I heard, too, her eccentric murmurs, stranger than her laugh and the strange slapping sound, which jolted me and filled me with a restlessness I could not explain.

There were days when she was quite silent, but there were others when I could not account for the sounds she made, or the sound of chains rattling, or I imagined, the sound of a switch flying through the air. Sometimes I saw her as she came out of her room with a basin, or a plate, or a tray in her hand, and went stiffly down to the kitchen and shortly return, generally (oh, romantic reader, forgive me for telling the plain truth!) bearing a pot of porter.

Her appearance always acted as a damper to the curiosity raised by her oral oddities. Hard-featured and staid, she had no point to which interest could attach. I made some attempts to draw her into conversation, but she seemed a person of few words and a monosyllabic reply usually cut short every effort of that sort.

The other members of the household, John and his wife, Leah the housemaid, and Sophie the French nurse, were decent people, but in no respect remarkable. With Sophie I used to talk French. At first I entertained a fleeting and secret hope that she may be inclined as Emma had been and, such was my loneliness, imagined her in my tangled embrace.

I imagined her too with the mysterious Mr Rochester aboard the ship Adèle had described, and in the hotel suite after, and often, seeing her eat, wondered what her full lips had done and where they had been. Occasionally, when we were alone, the heady French perfume she wore was enough to make me want to blurt my desire and entreat her to join in my fantasies, but I always stopped myself, ashamed of where my mind had taken me. My dalliances at Lowood, those innocent explorations with my fellow young women, belonged to another time. Sophie was a travelled woman and I had no means of communicating my envy at her experience.

Besides, when I tried conversation and asked her questions about her native country, she was not of a descriptive or narrative turn, and generally gave such vapid and confused answers as were calculated rather to check than encourage inquiry. A few weeks after my arrival, when both Mrs Fairfax and Adèle seemed satisfied with my care alone, Sophie returned to France.

October, November, December passed away. One afternoon in January, Mrs Fairfax had begged a holiday for Adèle because she had a cold, and, as Adèle seconded the request with an ardour that reminded me how precious occasional holidays had been to me in my own childhood, I agreed to it.

It was a fine, calm day, though very cold. I was tired of

sitting still in the library through a whole long morning and Mrs Fairfax had just written a letter which was waiting to be posted, so I put on my bonnet and cloak and volunteered to carry it to Hay. The two-mile distance would afford me with a pleasant winter afternoon walk.

The ground was hard, the air was still and my road was lonely. I walked fast till I got warm, and then I walked slowly to enjoy and analyse the species of pleasure brooding for me in the hour and situation. It was three o'clock. The church bell tolled as I passed under the belfry. The charm of the hour lay in its approaching dimness, in the low-gliding and pale-beaming sun. I was a mile from Thornfield, in a lane whose best winter delight lay in its utter solitude and leafless repose.

This lane inclined uphill all the way to Hay, and having reached the middle, I sat down on a stile which led thence into a field. From my seat I could look down on Thornfield. The grey and battlemented hall was the principal object in the vale below me and its woods and dark rookery rose against the west. I lingered till the sun went down amongst the trees, and sank crimson and clear behind them. I then turned eastward.

On the hilltop above me sat the rising moon. Pale yet as a cloud, but brightening momentarily, she looked over Hay, which, half lost in trees, sent up a blue smoke from its few chimneys. It was yet a mile distant, but in the absolute hush I could hear plainly its thin murmurs of life.

A rude noise broke on these fine ripplings and whisperings. A positive tramp, tramp, a metallic clatter. The din was on the causeway. A horse was coming and the windings of the lane yet hid it, but it approached.

I was just leaving the stile, but, as the path was narrow, I sat still to let it go by. In those days I was young, and all sorts of fancies bright and dark tenanted my mind. The memories of nursery stories were there amongst other rubbish, and when they recurred, maturing youth added to them a vigour and vividness beyond what childhood could give.

As this horse approached, and as I watched for it to appear through the dusk, I remembered certain of Bessie's tales, wherein figured a North-of-England spirit called a 'Gytrash', which, in the form of horse, mule or large dog, haunted solitary ways, and sometimes came upon belated female travellers, as this horse was now coming upon me.

It was very near, but not yet in sight, when, in addition to the tramp, tramp, I heard a rush under the hedge, and close down by the hazel stems glided a great dog – a lion-like creature with long hair and a huge head. It passed me, however, quietly enough, not staying to look up with its strange canine eyes, as I half expected it would, or to nuzzle and sniff me.

The horse followed – a tall steed, and on its back a rider. The man, the human being, broke the spell at once. Nothing ever rode the Gytrash. It always came upon fair maidens alone. No Gytrash was this. Only a traveller taking the shortcut to Millcote.

He passed, and I went on a few steps. As I turned, a sliding sound, an exclamation of 'What the deuce is to do now?' and a clattering tumble arrested my attention.

Man and horse were down. They had slipped on the sheet of ice which glazed the causeway. I walked down to the traveller, by this time struggling himself free of his steed. His efforts were so vigorous, I thought he could not be much hurt.

'Are you injured, sir?' I asked.

I think he was swearing, but am not certain. However, he was pronouncing some formula which prevented him from replying to me directly.

'Can I do anything?' I asked again.

'You must just stand on one side,' he answered as he rose, first to his knees, and then to his feet.

I did, whereupon began a heaving, stamping, clattering process, accompanied by a barking and baying which removed me effectually some yards' distance. But I would not be driven quite away till I saw the that the horse was re-established, and the dog was silenced with a 'Down, Pilot!'

The traveller now, stooping, felt his foot and leg, as if trying whether they were sound. Apparently something ailed them, for he halted to the stile whence I had just risen, and sat down.

'If you are hurt, and want help, sir, I can fetch someone either from Thornfield Hall or from Hay.'

'Thank you. I shall do. I have no broken bones, only a sprain,' and again he stood up and tried his foot, but the result extorted an involuntary 'Ugh!'

Something of daylight still lingered, and the moon was waxing bright so that I could see him plainly. His figure was enveloped in a riding cloak, fur collared and steel clasped.

I traced the general points of middle height and considerable breadth of chest. He had a dark face, with stern features and a heavy brow, and his eyes and gathered eyebrows looked ireful and thwarted just now. He was past youth, but had not reached middle age – perhaps he might be thirty-five.

I felt no fear of him, and but little shyness. Had he been a handsome, heroic-looking young gentleman, I should not have dared to stand thus questioning him against his will, and offering my services unasked. I had hardly ever seen a handsome youth and certainly never spoken to one in my life. If even this stranger had smiled and been good-humoured to me when I addressed him, if he had put off my offer of assistance gaily and with thanks, I should have gone on my way and not felt any vocation to renew inquiries. But the frown, when he waved to me, compelled me to speak again.

'I cannot think of leaving you, sir, at so late an hour, in this solitary lane, till I see you are fit to mount your horse.'

He looked at me when I said this. He had hardly turned his eyes in my direction before, but now his dark gaze met mine and I felt my boldness evaporate under his scrutiny.

'I should think you ought to be at home yourself,' he said, 'if you have a home in this neighbourhood. Where do you come from?'

'From just below. I am not at all afraid of being out late when it is moonlight. I will run over to Hay for you with pleasure, if you wish it. Indeed, I am going there to post a letter.'

'You live just below . . . do you mean at that house with the battlements?' pointing to Thornfield Hall, on which the moon cast a hoary gleam, bringing it out distinct and pale from the woods that, by contrast with the western sky, now seemed one mass of shadow.

'Yes, sir.'

'Whose house is it?'

'Mr Rochester's.'

'Do you know Mr Rochester?'

'No, I have never seen him.'

'He is not resident, then?'

'No.'

'Can you tell me where he is?'

'I cannot.'

'You are not a servant at the hall, of course. You are . . .'

He stopped, ran his eye over my dress, which, as usual, was quite simple: a black merino cloak, a black beaver bonnet, neither of them half fine enough for a lady's maid. His gaze made my bare skin unexpectedly flush below the clothes he was studying.

He seemed puzzled to decide what I was, so I helped him.

'I am the governess.'

'Ah, the governess!' he repeated. 'Deuce take me, if I had not forgotten! The governess!' and again as my raiment underwent scrutiny, I felt a deep, incomprehensible tug of my flesh.

He rose from the stile. His face expressed pain when he tried to move.

'I cannot commission you to fetch help,' he said, 'but you may help me a little yourself, if you will be so kind.'

'Yes, sir.'

'You have not an umbrella that I can use as a stick?'

'No.'

'Try to get hold of my horse's bridle and lead him to me. You are not afraid?'

I should have been afraid to touch a horse when alone, although Bessie's stories had long been in my imaginings, but when told to do it, I was disposed to obey. I put down my muff on the stile, went up to the tall steed and endeavoured to catch the bridle, but it was a spirited thing, and would not let me come near its head. I made effort on effort, though in vain, because I was so mortally afraid of its trampling forefeet. The traveller waited and watched for some time, and at last he laughed.

'I see,' he said, 'the mountain will never be brought to Mahomet, so all you can do is to aid Mahomet to go to the mountain. I must beg of you to come here.'

I came.

'Excuse me,' he continued, 'necessity compels me to make you useful.'

He laid a heavy hand on my shoulder, and leaning on me with some stress, limped to his horse. Having once caught the bridle, he mastered it directly and sprang to his saddle, grimacing grimly as he made the effort, for it wrenched his sprain. I felt strangely light in the absence of his weight bearing down upon me.

'Now,' said he, releasing his underlip from a hard bite, 'just hand me my whip. It lies there under the hedge.'

I sought it and found it and handed it to him. He looked

at me once again, as he ran the thin leather through his glove.

'Thank you. Now make haste with the letter to Hay, and return as fast as you can.'

A touch of a spurred heel made his horse first start and rear, and then bound away. The dog rushed in his traces and all three vanished, and I was left staring after them, my heart pounding.

I took up my muff and, pushing my hands inside, walked on. The incident had occurred and was gone, yet it marked with change one single hour of a monotonous life. The new face of this dark stranger was like a new picture introduced to the gallery of my memory, and it was dissimilar to all the others hanging there. Firstly, because it was masculine and, secondly, because it was so strong, and stern. I had it still before me when I entered Hay and slipped the letter into the post office, and I saw it as I walked fast downhill all the way home.

I did not like re-entering Thornfield and this evening I was more reluctant than ever. To pass its threshold was to return to stagnation. To cross the silent hall, to ascend the darksome staircase, to seek my own lonely little room, and then to meet tranquil Mrs Fairfax, and spend the long winter evening with her, and her only, was to quell wholly the excitement wakened by my walk.

I lingered at the gates, I lingered on the lawn, my spirit fevered, as the moonlight bathed the park in silver. My mind was taking me where I knew it must go, where it had been heading on the entire walk back from Hay, and I knew resistance was pointless. Because the strange horseman had been transposed in my dark imagination into the pictures I had studied by candlelight on the third floor.

Moreover, the form of the naked god I had gazed upon in the threadbare tapestry, in truth the only image of a naked man I had ever seen at close hand, now had the face of the man in the woods. And I, who had long cast myself into the role of sea-maiden, was all the more in the grip of the hitherto unformed fantasy, one which, I knew with certainty, would remain unformed, now that the stranger had ridden off into the night.

Little things recall us to earth, however. The clock struck in the hall and broke my spell, and, dressing myself down for my romantic musings, I turned from moon and stars, opened a side door and went in.

The hall was not dark, nor yet was it lit, only by the high-hung bronze lamp, and a warm glow suffused both it and the lower steps of the oak staircase. This ruddy shine issued from the great dining room, whose two-leaved door stood open, and showed a genial fire in the grate, glancing on marble hearth and brass fire irons, and revealing purple draperies and polished furniture, in the most pleasant radiance.

It revealed, too, a group near the mantelpiece. I had scarcely caught it, and scarcely become aware of a cheerful mingling of voices, amongst which I seemed to distinguish the tones of Adèle, when the door closed.

I hastened to Mrs Fairfax's room. There was a fire there

too, but no candle, and no Mrs Fairfax. Instead, all alone, sitting upright on the rug, and gazing with gravity at the blaze, I beheld a great black-and-white long-haired dog, just like the Gytrash of the lane.

It was so like it that I went forward and said, 'Pilot,' and the thing got up and came to me and snuffed me. I caressed him, and he wagged his great tail, but he looked an eerie creature to be alone with, and I could not tell whence he had come. I rang the bell, for I wanted a candle and I wanted, too, to get an account of this visitant. Leah entered.

'What dog is this?'

'He came with master.'

'With whom?'

'With master – Mr Rochester. He is just arrived.'

'Indeed! And is Mrs Fairfax with him?'

'Yes, and Miss Adèle. They are in the dining room, and John is gone for a surgeon, for master has had an accident, his horse fell and his ankle is sprained.'

At her words, a strange flush fell over me and for a moment I felt dizzy. 'Did the horse fall in Hay Lane?'

'Yes, coming downhill. It slipped on some ice.'

'Ah! Bring me a new candle, will you, Leah?'

Leah brought it – one of the new candles Mrs Fairfax had ordered. Then Mrs Fairfax herself entered, repeating the news and adding that Mr Carter the surgeon was come, and was now with Mr Rochester. Then she hurried out to give orders about tea, and I went upstairs to take off my things.

*

My room was freezing, but as I undressed, I realized that I was shivering not from the cold, but from an altogether molten internal heat. When my hand caught the hardness of my nipple as I unfastened my corset, my flesh erupted into even more goosebumps. My fingers were fumbling with the corset strings so ineffectually that I left it on, watching my engorged breast spill over the top of it. I took off my underskirts and pants and was left naked apart from my stockings.

I studied myself in the full-length mirror, the sliver of moonlight through the window illuminating my silhouette. I grasped the fat length of the candle in my fist, intending to turn and replace the spent one in my candleholder, but instead, I lingered, watching myself tremble.

As my eyes met my reflection in the mirror, I let out a whimper, my mind was in such torment.

The dark horse-rider was Mr Rochester himself! My master and employer. I tried to remove him from the fantasy that I had entertained about the stranger in the lane on my return from Hay, but I couldn't. The musings I had tried to leave outside now filled my mind. Somehow, the fact of the discovery of his identity was more shocking and exhilarating than I could account for. I sat down heavily on the bed, my heart pounding.

I was in Mr Rochester's employ. Whatever his character or countenance, I would have to conduct myself in his presence with as demure and detached a stance as befitted my position. Now that he was under the same roof as I, my exploration of the third floor, and musings over those pictures that belonged to Mr Rochester himself, seemed more shameful than ever, especially as I had already connected my employer to them in my mind's eye. I resolved that I must stop and never go to the third storey again.

And yet . . . and yet at the same time, I couldn't help but remember the way his eyes had raked over me on the lane and a dart of pleasure that had made my sex twitch. Before I could help it, I was overtaken by my traitorous mind and I knew I would give in to my desire again. Thus transformed into the sea-maiden, I opened my legs, watching myself in the mirror as I lay back on the bed, submitting myself to the terrible, forbidden fantasy.

The candle was still grasped in my fist and, eyes half closed and unable to stop myself, I pressed the blunt end of it against my moist opening. I felt it slide easily inside me a short way, but such was my need to be filled, I continued, pressing against the hardness, my eyelids heavy, my breathing ragged, as I clenched around the candle and in a moment felt a release so sudden and intense, that I thought I might faint.

FOUR

Mr Rochester, it seems, by the surgeon's orders, went to bed early that night, nor did he rise soon next morning. When he did come down, it was to attend to business, as his agent and some of his tenants had arrived and were eager to speak with him.

Adèle and I had now to vacate the library. It would be in daily requisition as a reception room for callers. A fire was lit in an apartment upstairs, and there I carried our books, and arranged it for the future schoolroom.

I discerned in the course of the morning that Thornfield Hall was a changed place. No longer silent as a church, it echoed every hour or two to a knock at the door, or a clang of the bell. Steps often traversed the hall and new voices spoke in different keys below. A river of life from the outer world was flowing through the house now that it had a master and for my part, I liked it better.

Adèle was not easy to teach that day. She could not apply herself and she kept running to the door and looking over the banisters to see if she could get a glimpse of Mr Rochester.

Then she coined pretexts to go downstairs, in order, as I shrewdly suspected, to visit the library, where I knew she was not wanted.

Then, when I got a little angry, and made her sit still, she continued to talk incessantly of her 'ami, Monsieur Edouard Fairfax de Rochester', as she dubbed him, and to conjecture what presents he had brought her, for it appears he had intimated the night before, that when his luggage came from Millcote, there would be found amongst it a little box in whose contents she had an interest.

My own curiosity was naturally aroused, but dampened by my resolution of the previous evening, which I held at the forefront of my mind. After I had returned the candle to its natural home in its brass holder, I had dressed quickly for bed, throwing a shawl over the mirror. Then I had knelt and prayed earnestly that my evil imagination would cease to haunt me, and I promised solemnly that I would no longer study any of the lascivious art in the dark upstairs of Thornfield, or seek to pleasure myself from those sinful images. And, most importantly of all, never to connect my employer with them ever again.

Indeed, after an exhausted sleep I had awoken in the morning refreshed, and the activity in the house only confirmed to me that a new era had begun and my secret life no longer existed.

As for Mr Rochester, I resolved to be as meek and unobtrusive a governess as was possible. I would pay him as little attention as I felt sure he would pay me. In the light of day, I felt aggrieved that he had tricked me as to his identity and had enjoyed the power of knowing who I was, when I had not been given the chance to introduce myself properly. I was on my guard not to be caught out again.

My pupil and I dined as usual in Mrs Fairfax's parlour. The afternoon was wild and snowy and we passed it in the schoolroom. When it got dark outside I allowed Adèle to put away books and work, and to run downstairs, for, from the comparative silence below, and from the cessation of appeals to the doorbell, I conjectured that Mr Rochester was now at liberty.

Left alone, I walked to the window, but nothing was to be seen. Twilight and snowflakes together thickened the air and hid the shrubs on the lawn. I had just let down the curtain and gone back to the fireside, when Mrs Fairfax came in.

'Mr Rochester would be glad if you and your pupil would take tea with him in the drawing room this evening,' she said. 'He has been so much engaged all day that he could not ask to see you before.'

'When is his teatime?' I inquired.

'Oh, at six o'clock. He keeps early hours in the country. You had better change your frock now. I will go with you and fasten it. Here is a candle.'

'Is it necessary to change my frock?'

'Yes, you had better. I always dress for the evening when Mr Rochester is here.'

This additional ceremony seemed somewhat stately, however, I repaired to my room, and, with Mrs Fairfax's aid, replaced my black stuff dress by one of black silk – the best and the only additional one I had, except one of light grey, which, in my Lowood notions of the toilette, I thought too fine to be worn, except on first-rate occasions.

'You want a brooch,' said Mrs Fairfax.

I had a single little pearl ornament which Miss Temple at Lowood had given me as a parting keepsake and I put it on, bemused by Mrs Fairfax's fussing, which I deemed to be rather unnecessary. I had no desire to draw attention to myself.

Then we went downstairs. Unused as I was to strangers, it was rather a trial to appear thus formally summoned in Mr Rochester's presence. I let Mrs Fairfax precede me into the dining room, and kept in her shade as we crossed that apartment. Then, passing the arch, whose curtain was now dropped, I entered the elegant recess beyond.

Two wax candles stood lighted on the table, and two on the mantelpiece. Basking in the light and heat of a superb fire lay Pilot. Adèle knelt near him.

Half reclined on a couch was Mr Rochester, his foot supported by the cushion. He was looking at Adèle and the dog and the fire shone full on his face. I knew my traveller with his broad forehead, strong eyebrows and the sweep of black hair. I recognized his decisive nose, more remarkable for character than beauty, his full nostrils, his mouth, chin and chiselled jaw. Now he had been divested of his cloak, I perceived that he had a good figure in the athletic sense of the term, broad chested and thin flanked.

Mr Rochester must have been aware of the entrance of

Mrs Fairfax and myself, but he appeared not to notice us, for he never lifted his head as we approached.

'Here is Miss Eyre, sir,' said Mrs Fairfax, in her quiet way.

He bowed, still not taking his eyes from the group of the dog and child.

'Let Miss Eyre be seated,' he said, but there was something in his impatient yet formal tone, which seemed to say, 'What the deuce is it to me whether Miss Eyre be there or not? At this moment I am not disposed to acknowledge her.'

I sat down quite disembarrassed. A reception of finished politeness would probably have confused me, as I could not have returned or repaid it by answering with the necessary grace and elegance on my part. Yet this harsh caprice laid me under no obligation. On the contrary, sitting quietly gave me the advantage. Besides, he was being so deliberately provocative, I felt interested to see what he would do next.

He went on as a statue would. That is, he neither spoke nor moved. Mrs Fairfax seemed to think it necessary that someone should be amiable and she began to talk. Kindly, as usual, and, as usual, rather trite, she condoled with him on the pressure of business he had had all day, on the annoyance it must have been to him with that painful sprain. Then she commended his patience and perseverance in going through with it.

'Madam, I should like some tea,' was the sole rejoinder she got.

She hastened to ring the bell, and when the tray came, she proceeded to arrange the cups and spoons carefully and quickly. I and Adèle went to the table, but the master did not leave his couch.

'Will you hand Mr Rochester's cup?' said Mrs Fairfax to me. 'Adèle might perhaps spill it.'

I did as requested. As he took the cup from my hand, his finger pressed against mine and my eyes sprang to his dark gaze, and in that moment, I realized that he had been quite aware of my presence all along. Just as I had experienced the previous evening under his dark scrutiny, I felt my skin goose-bump, although this time it was so much worse for the proximity between us.

Adèle, thinking the moment propitious for making a request in my favour, cried out, 'N'est-ce pas, monsieur, qu'il y a un cadeau pour Mademoiselle Eyre dans votre petit coffre?'

'Who talks of cadeaux?' said he gruffly, sitting back and breaking contact with me. 'Did you expect a present, Miss Eyre? Are you fond of presents?' and he searched my face with eyes that were so piercing, I felt as if he were looking right into my hidden thoughts. The way his eyes glittered made me think that he was playing some sort of private game and required me to rise to an unknown challenge.

'I hardly know, sir,' I said. 'I have little experience of them, but they are generally thought pleasant things, are they not?'

'Generally thought? But what do you think?'

'I should be obliged to take time, sir, before I could give you an answer worthy of your acceptance. A present has many faces to it, has it not? And one should consider all, before pronouncing an opinion as to its nature.'

'Miss Eyre, you are not so unsophisticated as Adèle. She demands a "cadeau", clamorously, the moment she sees me. You beat about the bush.'

'Because I have less confidence in my deserts than Adèle has. She can prefer the claim of old acquaintance, and the right too of custom, for she says you have always been in the habit of giving her playthings. But if you were to bestow a gift upon me, I should be puzzled, since I am a stranger, and have done nothing to entitle me to an acknowledgement.'

'Oh, don't fall back on over-modesty! I have examined Adèle, and find you have taken great pains with her. She is not bright, she has no talents, yet in a short time she has made much improvement.'

'Sir, you have now given me my "cadeau". I am obliged to you. It is that which teachers most covet. Praise of their pupils' progress.'

'Humph!' said Mr Rochester, and he took his tea in silence, but despite his gruffness I felt a shimmer of triumph.

Later, in the silence, as Mr Rochester stared into the fire, Adèle led me by the hand round the room, showing me the beautiful books and strange ornaments, whilst Mrs Fairfax settled into a corner with her knitting.

The mural on the far wall, on closer inspection, was much more explicit than I had at first realized. Had Mr Rochester commissioned the piece? I wondered. It was less revealing, perhaps, than the painting of the naked lady and gentleman with the riding crop on the stairs in the hallway, but nevertheless, the glimpses of half-naked flesh hinted at several of the couples being suggestively joined and I felt an unexpected arousal as I peered closer at the painting.

Yet I had no time to consider it further, because suddenly the master spoke.

'Come to the fire,' he said.

We obeyed dutifully and returned towards where he was sitting.

Adèle wanted to take a seat on my knee, but she was ordered to amuse herself with Pilot.

'You have been resident in my house three months?'

'Yes, sir.'

'And you came from—?'

'From Lowood school.'

'Ah! A charitable concern. How long were you there?'

'Eight years.'

'Eight years! You must be tenacious of life. I thought half the time in such a place would have done up any constitution! No wonder you have rather the look of another world. I marvelled where you had got that sort of face. When you came on me in Hay Lane last night, I thought unaccountably of fairy tales, and had half a mind to demand whether you had bewitched my horse. I am not sure yet. Who are your parents?'

'I have none.'

'Nor ever had, I suppose. Do you remember them?'

'No.'

'I thought not. And so you were waiting for your people when you sat on that stile?'

'For whom, sir?'

'For the men in green. It was a proper moonlight evening for them. Did I break through one of your rings, that you spread that damned ice on the causeway?'

I shook my head. 'The men in green all forsook England a hundred years ago,' I said, speaking as seriously as he had done. 'And not even in Hay Lane, or the fields about it, could you find a trace of them. I don't think either summer or harvest, or winter moon, will ever shine on their revels more.'

Mrs Fairfax had dropped her knitting, and, with raised eyebrows, seemed wondering what sort of talk this was.

'Well,' resumed Mr Rochester, 'if you disown parents, you must have some sort of kinsfolk. Uncles and aunts?'

'None that I ever saw.'

'And your home?'

'I have none.'

'Where do your brothers and sisters live?'

'I have no brothers or sisters.'

'Who recommended you to come here?'

'I advertised, and Mrs Fairfax answered my advertisement.'

'Yes,' said the good lady, who now knew what ground we were upon, 'and I am daily thankful for the choice Providence led me to make. Miss Eyre has been an invaluable companion to me, and a kind and careful teacher to Adèle.'

'Don't trouble yourself to give her a character,' returned Mr Rochester. 'Eulogiums will not bias me, as I shall judge for myself. She began by felling my horse.'

'Sir?' said Mrs Fairfax.

'I have to thank her for this sprain.' His gaze went from mine to his ankle and I looked down at my hands in my lap. Was he making a joke at my expense? I had no way of telling. It pained me that he blamed me for his fall, and yet such was his manner of speaking that I knew not how to start defending myself.

The widow looked bewildered, but Mr Rochester seemed to let the subject drop and started once again on his assessment of my past.

'Miss Eyre, have you ever lived in a town?'

'No, sir.'

'Have you seen much society?'

'None but the pupils and teachers of Lowood, and now the inmates of Thornfield.'

'Have you read much?'

'Only such books as came in my way, but they have not been numerous or very learned.'

'You have lived the life of a nun. No doubt you are well drilled in religious forms? Brocklehurst, who I understand directs Lowood, is a parson, is he not?'

'Yes, sir.'

'And you girls probably worshipped him, as a convent full of religious nuns would worship their director.'

'Oh, no.'

'You are very cool! No! What! A novice not worship her priest! That sounds blasphemous.'

'I disliked Mr Brocklehurst and I was not alone in the feeling. He is a harsh man and was both pompous and meddling. He cut off our hair and for economy's sake bought us bad needles and thread, with which we could hardly sew.'

'That was very false economy,' remarked Mrs Fairfax, who now again caught the drift of the dialogue.

'And was that the head and front of his offending?' demanded Mr Rochester.

Of course I did not tell him about the despicable acts Brocklehurst had demanded of some of the girls. Ones which I considered myself fortunate enough only to have heard about and not been a part of. Such as how he had once made Mary Keeler stand with her dress pulled up and her breast exposed whilst he had gripped himself under his desk. Or how Mavis Tyler, who had been his favourite for punishment, had been spanked on her bare bottom on more than one occasion, then had been subjected to Brocklehurst's earnest embrace, and how she had had to touch him through the black surplus he wore on Sundays and beg for forgiveness.

'He starved us when he had the sole superintendence of the provision department, before the committee was appointed. He bored us with long lectures once a week, and with evening readings from books about sudden deaths and judgments, which made us afraid to go to bed,' I said.

'What age were you when you went to Lowood?'

'About ten.'

'And you stayed there eight years, so you are now, then, eighteen?'

I assented.

'Arithmetic, you see, is useful. Without its aid, I should

hardly have been able to guess your age. It is a point difficult to fix where the features and countenance are so much at variance as in your case.'

I raised my head up, my colour rising. I was unprepared for his harsh tone and his judgement on my appearance. Did he think I looked strange? Or older than my years? Had my behaviour displeased him? I did not know.

'And now what did you learn at Lowood? Can you play?'

'A little,' I replied.

'Of course. That is the established answer. Go into the library – I mean, if you please. Excuse my tone of command. I am used to saying, "Do this," and it is done. I cannot alter my customary habits for one new inmate. Go, then, into the library and take a candle with you. Leave the door open, sit down to the piano and play a tune.'

I departed, obeying his directions. It was much colder and gloomier in the library and I shivered as I lifted the lid of the piano. I flexed my fingers, keen to show my limited ability in its best light, and began the satisfying harmonies of a hymn.

'Enough!' he called out in a few minutes. 'You play a little, I see, like any other English schoolgirl. Perhaps rather better than some, but not well.'

I closed the piano and returned, more annoyed than I would like that he had found me lacking and that he considered me a schoolgirl.

Mr Rochester continued, 'Adèle showed me some sketches this morning, which she said were yours. I don't know whether they were entirely of your doing. Probably a master aided you?'

'No, indeed!' I interjected.

'Ah! That pricks pride. Well, fetch me your portfolio, if you can vouch for its contents being original. But don't pass your word unless you are certain. I can recognize patch-work.'

'Then I will say nothing, and you shall judge for yourself, sir.'

I brought the portfolio from the library.

'Approach the table,' he said and I wheeled the small table bearing my portfolio to his couch. Adèle and Mrs Fairfax drew near to see the pictures.

'No crowding,' said Mr Rochester. 'Take the drawings from my hand as I finish with them, but don't push your faces up to mine.'

He deliberately scrutinized each sketch and painting. Three he laid aside, and the others, when he had examined them, he swept from him.

'Take them off to the other table, Mrs Fairfax,' said he, 'and look at them with Adèle. You,' he commanded, glancing at me, 'resume your seat, and answer my questions. I perceive those pictures were done by one hand. Was that hand yours?'

'Yes.'

'And when did you find time to do them? They have taken much time, and some thought.'

'I did them in the last two vacations I spent at Lowood, when I had no other occupation.'

'Where did you get your ideas?'

'Out of my head.'

'That head I see now on your shoulders?' Again he looked directly at me and again I noticed the twinkle of challenge in his eyes. Was he meddling with me, like a cat toying with a mouse? I hardly knew, but I was determined to stand my ground and not be cowed by him. I saw his eyes study my nose and my hair and my neck. I tucked a strand of errant hair behind my ear.

'Yes, sir.'

'Has it other ideas of the same kind within?'

'I should think it may have. I should hope better.'

He spread the pictures before him, and again surveyed them alternately.

While he is so occupied, I will tell you, reader, what they are, but first, I must premise that they are nothing wonderful. The subjects had, indeed, risen vividly on my mind. As I saw them with the spiritual eye, before I attempted to embody them, they were striking, but my hand would not second my fancy, and in each case it had wrought out but a pale portrait of the thing I had conceived.

These pictures were in watercolours. The first represented clouds low and livid, rolling over a swollen sea. All the distance was in eclipse, and so, too, was the foreground, or rather, the nearest billows, for there was no land. One gleam of light lifted into relief a half-submerged mast, on which sat a cormorant, dark and large, with wings flecked with foam. Its beak held a gold bracelet set with gems, that I had touched with as brilliant tints as my palette could yield, and as glittering distinctness as my pencil could impart. Sinking below the bird and mast, a drowned corpse glanced through the green water. A fair arm was the only limb clearly visible, whence the bracelet had been washed or torn.

The second picture contained for foreground only the dim peak of a hill, with grass and some leaves slanting as if by a breeze. Beyond and above spread an expanse of sky, dark blue as at twilight, and rising into the sky was a naked woman with ample breasts (which in my mind's eye I had modelled on Emma's) over which I had painted a diaphanous shroud in tints as dusk and soft as I could combine. The dim forehead was crowned with a star, the eyes shone dark and wild, the hair streamed shadowy. On the neck lay a pale reflection like moonlight, the same faint lustre touched the train of thin clouds from which she rose like the Evening Star.

The third showed the pinnacle of a pointed iceberg piercing a polar winter sky, a muster of northern lights along the horizon. In the foreground rose a colossal head, inclined towards the iceberg, the mouth open as if to devour it.

'Were you happy when you painted these pictures?' asked Mr Rochester presently.

'I was absorbed, sir, and yes, I was happy. To paint them, in short, was to enjoy one of the keenest pleasures I have ever known.'

'That is not saying much. Your pleasures, by your own account, have been few. But I daresay you did exist in a kind of artist's dreamland while you created these strange images. Did you sit at them long each day?'

'I had nothing else to do, because it was the vacation, and I sat at them from morning till noon, and from noon till night. The length of the midsummer days favoured my inclination to apply myself.'

'And you felt self-satisfied with the result of your ardent labours?'

'Far from it. I was tormented by the contrast between my idea and my handiwork. In each case I had imagined something which I was quite powerless to realize.'

'Not quite. You have secured the shadow of your thought, but no more, probably. You had not enough of the artist's skill and science to give it full being. Yet the drawings are, for a schoolgirl, peculiar. As to the thoughts, they are elfish. These eyes in the Evening Star you must have seen in a dream. How could you make them look so clear, and yet not at all brilliant? And what meaning is that in their solemn depth? And who taught you to paint wind?' He shook his head as if quite frustrated with the images before him. 'There! Put the drawings away!'

As I took my portfolio I wondered whether my pictures had in some way displeased him. Or whether he had just been humouring me with his appraisal and had become bored of expending his expertise on one as lowly and untalented as I. I had scarce tied the strings of the portfolio, when, looking at his watch, he said abruptly, 'It is nine o'clock. What are you about, Miss Eyre, to let Adèle sit up so long? Take her to bed.'

Adèle went to kiss him before quitting the room. He endured the caress, but scarcely seemed to relish it more than Pilot would have done, nor so much.

'I wish you all goodnight, now,' said he, making a movement of the hand towards the door, in token that he was tired of our company, and wished to dismiss us. He turned his gaze away from me and towards the fire.

Mrs Fairfax folded up her knitting and we curtseyed to him, received a frigid bow in return, and so withdrew.

I put Adèle to bed and then returned to Mrs Fairfax's room, where I found her wiping crumbs off the large oak table and folding the crocheted doilies.

'You said Mr Rochester was not strikingly peculiar, Mrs Fairfax,' I observed.

'Well, is he?'

'I think so. He is very changeful and abrupt.'

'True, no doubt he may appear so to a stranger, but I am so accustomed to his manner, I never think of it. But then, if he has peculiarities of temper, allowance should be made.'

'Why?'

'Partly because it is his nature, and we can none of us help our nature. And partly because he has painful thoughts, no doubt, to harass him, and make his spirits unequal.'

'What about?'

'Family troubles, for one thing.'

'But he has no family.'

'Not now, but he has had, or at least, relatives. He lost his elder brother a few years since.'

'His elder brother?'

'Yes. The present Mr Rochester has not been very long in possession of the property. Only about nine years.'

'Nine years is a tolerable time. Was he so very fond of his brother as to be still inconsolable for his loss?'

'Why, no. Perhaps not. I believe there were some misunderstandings between them. Mr Rowland Rochester was not quite just to Mr Edward, and perhaps he prejudiced his father against him. The old gentleman was fond of money, and anxious to keep the family estate together. Soon after Mr Edward was of age, old Mr Rochester and Mr Rowland combined to bring Mr Edward into what he considered a painful position, for the sake of making his fortune. What the precise nature of that position was I never clearly knew, but his spirit could not brook what he had to suffer in it.

'He is not very forgiving and he broke with his family, and now for many years he has led an unsettled kind of life. I don't think he has ever been resident at Thornfield for a fortnight together, since the death of his brother without a will left him master of the estate, so no wonder he shuns the old place.'

'Why should he shun it?'

'Perhaps he thinks it gloomy.'

The answer was evasive. I should have liked something clearer, but Mrs Fairfax either could not, or would not, give me more explicit information of the origin and nature of Mr Rochester's trials. She implied that they were a mystery to herself, and that what she knew was chiefly from conjecture. It was evident, indeed, that she wished me to drop the subject, which I did accordingly.

And yet, as I walked to my room that night, running my hand along the smooth banister, I felt a curiosity alight within me. Despite Mr Rochester's gruff manner and thorough examination of my character, our conversation had nonetheless been most stimulating compared to all of the others I had had at Thornfield. His dark brooding countenance suggested to me a deep river of knowledge, and I marvelled at his obvious familiarity with art, travel and the world at large, which his house had long suggested to me and yet his presence within it now made so vivid.

I mused, too, that a man such as he, with so many responsibilities, should come home to his castle to relax and rest. Yet, even in repose on the couch, as I had been introduced to him earlier, he seemed inwardly troubled – and I decided that his conversation with me had been a mere trifle to distract him.

Mrs Fairfax's explanation had only inflamed my imagination as to what ailed him. What had his father and brother made him do to turn Edward Rochester into such a restless man?

As I undressed and kneeled in prayer it occurred to me that perhaps this conjecture was of my own making. I had so little knowledge of men, especially of the standing of my employer, that perhaps all of them might behave in a similar manner to Mr Rochester when faced with their ward's governess. Or maybe there was an even simpler explanation. His sprained ankle and the pain it was causing him was the reason for his swift dismissal. I prayed to the good Lord for his swift recovery and His forgiveness, if indeed, as Mr Rochester had suggested, the injury had in some way been my fault.

Much later, as I lay in bed, chaste under the covers and still quite determined to keep my resolution, even though sleep was frustratingly elusive with my mind so active, I stared wide-eyed at the ceiling and wondered whether Mr Rochester was lying awake too. Had he as readily dismissed me from his thoughts as he had from his presence?

When sleep finally came, I dreamt of the mural in the great drawing room coming to life, the naked figures laughing and chasing one another through the trees.

FIVE

For several subsequent days I saw little of Mr Rochester. In the mornings he seemed much engaged with business, and, in the afternoon, gentlemen from Millcote or the neighbourhood called, and sometimes stayed to dine with him. When his sprain was well enough to admit of horse exercise, he rode out a good deal – probably to return these visits, as he generally did not come back till late at night.

During this interval, Adèle was seldom sent for to his presence, and all my acquaintance with him was confined to an occasional meeting in the hall, on the stairs, or in the gallery, when he would sometimes pass me haughtily and coldly, just acknowledging my presence by a distant nod or a cool glance, and sometimes bow and smile with gentlemanlike affability. His changes of mood did not offend me, because I surmised that the ebb and flow depended on causes quite disconnected with me.

One day he had company to dinner, but the gentlemen went away early to attend a public meeting at Millcote, as

Mrs Fairfax informed me, but, the night being wet and inclement, Mr Rochester did not accompany them.

Soon after they were gone he rang the bell and a message came that I and Adèle were to go downstairs. I brushed Adèle's hair and made her neat, and having ascertained that I was myself in my usual Quaker trim, where there was nothing to retouch, we descended. Adèle kept wondering whether the petit coffre was at length come, for, owing to some mistake, its arrival had hitherto been delayed. She was gratified when we entered the dining room and there it stood, a little carton, on the table. She appeared to know it by instinct.

'Ma boite! Ma boite!' exclaimed she, running towards it.

'Yes, there is your "boite" at last. Take it into a corner, you genuine daughter of Paris, and amuse yourself with disembowelling it,' said the deep and rather sarcastic voice of Mr Rochester, proceeding from the depths of an immense easy chair at the fireside. 'And mind,' he continued, 'don't bother me with any details. Let your operation be conducted in silence: tiens-toi tranquille, enfant, comprends-tu?'

Adèle seemed scarcely to need the warning, as she had already retired to a sofa with her treasure, and was busy untying the cord which secured the lid. Having removed this impediment, and lifted certain silvery envelopes of tissue paper, she merely exclaimed, 'Oh ciel! Que c'est beau!' and then remained absorbed in ecstatic contemplation.

'Is Miss Eyre there?' now demanded the master, half rising from his seat to look round to the door, near which I still stood.

'Ah! Well, come forward. Be seated here.'

He drew a chair near his own.

'I am not fond of the prattle of children,' he continued, 'for, old bachelor as I am, I have no pleasant associations connected with their lisp. It would be intolerable to me to pass a whole evening tête-à-tête with a brat. Don't draw that chair farther off, Miss Eyre, sit down exactly where I placed it.' He paused for a second. 'If you please, that is,' he added. 'Confound these civilities! I continually forget them. Nor do I particularly affect simple-minded old ladies. By the bye, I must have mine in mind and it won't do to neglect her. She is a Fairfax, or wed to one, and blood is said to be thicker than water.'

He rang, and despatched an invitation to Mrs Fairfax, who soon arrived, knitting basket in hand.

'Good evening, madam. I sent to you for a charitable purpose. I have forbidden Adèle to talk to me about her presents, but she is bursting to talk to someone. Will you listen to her? It will be one of the most benevolent acts you ever performed.'

Adèle, indeed, no sooner saw Mrs Fairfax, than she summoned her to her sofa, and there quickly filled her lap with the porcelain, the ivory, the waxen contents of her 'boite', explanations and raptures pouring out of her in such broken English as she was mistress of.

'Now I have performed the part of a good host,' pursued Mr Rochester, 'put my guests into the way of amusing each other, I ought to be at liberty to attend to my own pleasure. Miss Eyre, draw your chair still a little farther forward. You are yet too far back. I cannot see you without disturbing my position in this comfortable chair, which I have no mind to do.'

I did as I was bid, though I would much rather have remained somewhat in the shade, but Mr Rochester had such a direct way of giving orders, it seemed a matter of course to obey him promptly.

We were, as I have said, in the dining room, and the candelabras, which had been lit for dinner, filled the room with a festive breadth of light. The large fire was all red and clear, the purple curtains hung rich and ample before the lofty window and loftier arch and everything was still, save the subdued chat of Adèle (she dared not speak loud), and, filling up each pause, the beating of winter rain against the panes.

Mr Rochester, as he sat in his damask-covered chair, looked different to how I had seen him look before. Dressed as he was in a fine coat for dinner, he had loosened his tie and tonight he looked not quite so stern and much less gloomy. Indeed, as I drew close to him, my nostrils filling with the musky smell of his perfume, I swallowed hard and smoothed down my Quaker gown, preparing myself.

There was a smile on his lips, and his eyes sparkled, whether with wine or not, I am not sure, but I think it very probable, for a crystal glass was in his fingertips. He was, in short, in his after-dinner mood. More expanded and genial, and also more self-indulgent than the frigid and rigid temper of the morning. Cushioning his massive head against the swelling back of his chair, the light of the fire fell on his granite-hewn features, and in his great, dark eyes.

He had been looking two minutes at the fire, and I had been looking the same length of time at him, when, turning suddenly, he caught my gaze.

'You examine me, Miss Eyre,' he said. 'Do you think me handsome?'

His attention thus turned fully on me, his eyes still soft, I felt myself flush deeply. I should have replied to this question with something conventionally vague and polite, but instead the answer somehow slipped from my tongue before I was aware.

'No, sir.' Though I confess, as I said it, I could not meet his gaze, as in truth my statement had been a lie.

'Ah! By my word! There is something singular about you,' he exclaimed. 'You have the air of a little nun. You're quaint, quiet, grave and simple, as you sit with your hands before you, and your eyes generally bent on the carpet (except, by the bye, when they are directed piercingly to my face, as just now, for instance), and when one asks you a question, or makes a remark to which you are obliged to reply, you rap out a round reply, which, if not blunt, is at least brusque. What do you mean by it?'

'Sir, I was too plain. I beg your pardon. I ought to have replied that it was not easy to give an impromptu answer to a question about appearances, that tastes mostly differ or that beauty is of little consequence. Something of that sort.'

'You ought to have replied no such thing. Beauty of little consequence, indeed! And so, under pretence of softening the previous outrage, of stroking and soothing me into placidity, you stick a sly penknife under my ear! Go on.

What fault do you find with me, pray? I suppose I have all my limbs and all my features like any other man?'

I felt flustered that he was calling me to account and required me to compare him to other men. I had no experience of other men of his calibre with which to make the comparison.

'Mr Rochester, allow me to disown my first answer. It was only a blunder.'

'Just so and you shall be answerable for it. If you want to criticize me, do so. Does my forehead not please you?'

He lifted up the sable waves of hair which lay horizontally over his brow. His deep brow looked, to my untrained eye, like the one a gentleman should possess.

'Far from it, sir. You would, perhaps, think me rude if I inquired in return whether you are a philanthropist?'

'There again! Another stick of the penknife, when she pretended to pat my head. That is because I said I did not like the society of children and old women. No, young lady, I am not a general philanthropist, but I bear a conscience.'

I pressed my lips together and looked once again at my hands in my lap for a second. Mr Rochester took a long sip of his wine. I saw his fine teeth pull his bottom lip into his mouth to remove a drop of the scarlet liquid. His lip glistened with moisture in the candlelight.

'I once had a tenderness of heart. When I was as old as you, I was a caring kind of fellow, always drawn to the unfledged, unfostered and unlucky. But Fortune has knocked me about since.'

'I see,' I said quietly.

Mr Rochester smiled. 'You looked very much puzzled, Miss Eyre. And though you are not pretty any more than I am handsome, a puzzled air becomes you. Besides, it is convenient, for it keeps those searching eyes of yours away from my face, and busies them with the worsted flowers of the rug, so puzzle on. Young lady, I am disposed to be gregarious and communicative tonight. Let me explain more.'

With this announcement he rose from his chair, and stood, leaning his arm on the marble mantelpiece. In that attitude his shape was seen plainly as well as his face. I am sure most people would have thought him an ugly man, yet there was so much unconscious pride in his port, so much ease in his demeanour, such a look of complete indifference to his own external appearance, that, in looking at him, one inevitably shared his confidence.

I couldn't help but put my faith in his confidence. If he had been foppish or beautiful, I would not have found him half as fascinating, but as it was, I found his indifference to his own personal attractiveness only piqued my interest. My eyes wandered up the length of his legs to the smooth shape of his buttocks in his tight breeches.

'I am disposed to be gregarious and communicative tonight,' he repeated, 'and that is why I sent for you. The fire and the chandelier were not sufficient company for me. Nor would Pilot have been, for none of these can talk. Adèle is a degree better, but still far below the mark. Mrs Fairfax ditto. You, I am persuaded, can suit me if you will. You puzzled me the first evening I invited you down here. I have almost forgotten you since as other ideas have driven yours from my head, but tonight I am resolved to be at ease. It would please me now to draw you out, to learn more of you.'

I smiled, and not a very complacent or submissive smile either. It was a smile of unbidden joy at his permission to entertain him and a frisson of satisfaction that I had roused his curiosity as he had roused mine. My vanity fanned, I felt another unexpected tug of my flesh, as his gaze turned down on me. I bit my lip, smothering my smile, but then he raised his eyebrows at me, a dark shadow of annoyance fleeting across his face.

'I desire you to have the goodness to talk to me a little now, and divert my thoughts, which are galled with dwelling on one point, cankering as a rusty nail. I have battled through a varied experience with many men of many nations, and roamed over half the globe, while you have lived quietly with one set of people in one house, and yet, all that aside, I feel you may be a good person to converse with. Nay, more than that. Perhaps you may make a timely confessor.'

'You have much to confess?'

He smiled sadly, running his finger along one of the marble statues on the mantelpiece.

'Miss Eyre, you have no idea.'

I saw now that the marble statue was that of a naked woman. When he noticed me watching him, his long finger stopped on the curve of her ample white hip. He removed his hand and took a sip of wine. Then he looked down at me again.

'I envy you your peace of mind, your clean conscience,

your unpolluted memory. A memory without blot or contamination must be an exquisite treasure. An inexhaustible source of pure refreshment, is it not?'

I did not confess to the state of my conscience which had only, in truth, been clear for a very short time. I could not confess either to a memory without blot or contamination. Yet my overriding desire was for him to continue. I could not risk repelling him with so much as a hint of my own secrets.

'How was your memory when you were eighteen, sir?'

'It was all right then. Limpid, salubrious. No gush of bilge water had turned it to fetid puddle. I was your equal at eighteen, quite your equal. Nature meant me to be, on the whole, a good man, Miss Eyre. One of the better kind, and you see I am not so. You would say you don't see it, at least I flatter myself I read as much in your eye (beware, by the bye, what you express with that organ as I am quick at interpreting its language). Then take my word for it. I am not a villain. You are not to suppose that. But owing, I believe, rather to circumstances than to my natural bent, I am a commonplace sinner.'

I felt heat rising inside me. Was he referring to the night he spent aboard the paddle steamer from France with Adèle's nurse, Sophie? Or any number of other indiscretions of which I was ignorant? What acts, I wondered, did he consider so sinful?

He put his thumb under his chin and tapped his finger on his full lips, in contemplation.

'Do you wonder that I avow this to you?' he said, glancing down towards me. 'Know, that in the course of your future life you will often find yourself elected the involuntary confidant of your acquaintances' secrets. People will instinctively find out, as I have done, that it is not your forte to tell of yourself, but to listen while others talk of themselves. They will feel, too, that you listen with no malevolent scorn of their indiscretion, but with a kind of innate sympathy, not the less comforting and encouraging because it is very unobtrusive in its manifestations.'

'How do you know? How can you guess all this, sir?'

'I know it well. Therefore I proceed almost as freely as if I were writing my thoughts in a diary.'

I tried to sit as the listener he had perceived me to be. Did I have an innate sympathy, as he had suggested? Or did my demeanour only mask the curiosity I now felt and my desire to know so much more about his troubled soul?

Mr Rochester sighed and shook his head, lost in memory.

'You would say, I should have been superior to circumstances. So I should . . . so I should. But you see I was not. When fate wronged me, I turned desperate. Then I degenerated. I wish I had stood firm. God knows I do! Dread remorse when you are tempted to err, Miss Eyre. Remorse is the poison of life.'

'Repentance is said to be its cure, sir.'

'It is not its cure. Reformation may be its cure. And I could reform. I have strength yet for that – if . . .' here he paused and sighed. 'But where is the use of thinking of it, hampered, burdened, cursed as I am? Besides, since happiness is irrevocably denied me, I have a right to get pleasure out of life. And I will get it, cost what it may.'

'Then you will degenerate still more, sir.'

'Possibly. Yet why shouldn't I, if I can get sweet, fresh pleasure? And I may get it as sweet and fresh as the wild honey the bee gathers on the moor.'

'It will sting. It will taste bitter, sir.'

'How do you know? You never tried it.'

He was right, of course. I had never tasted the life of which he spoke. I wished I had the courage to tell him that I secretly yearned for the kind of experience of which he intimated. That to indulge in sweet, fresh pleasure was a desire I harboured at the core of my soul. But something more than that, too, pricked at my conscience, counterbalancing my inner thoughts with my outer appearance. I could not condone his indulgence in sweet fresh pleasure, if by that, he meant sweet fresh girls, when his experience, his actions had caused him such obvious pain and regret. I was unsure as to why the thought of his desire for pleasure elsewhere bothered me so.

'How very serious, how very solemn you look and yet you are as ignorant of the matter as this cameo head,' he said, taking one from the mantelpiece. 'You have no right to preach to me when you have not passed the porch of life, and are absolutely unacquainted with its mysteries.'

'That may be true, but one thing I can comprehend. You intimated that to have a sullied memory is a perpetual bane. It seems to me, that if you tried hard, you would in time find it possible to become what you yourself would approve of. If from this day you began with resolution to correct your thoughts and actions, you would in a few years have laid up a new and stainless store of recollections, to which you might revert with pleasure.'

I rose, feeling a sense of insecurity, which accompanies a conviction of ignorance as to how to proceed further. I had the feeling I had already said too much and worried that I had given him an unwanted sermon. He saw such innocence in me, but I confess that our exchange had left me deeply conflicted. He had already said he was an expert at reading my eyes and I feared now that if I stayed sitting so, with him so masterfully above me, they may give me away. He may have unburdened himself to me, but I was hardly the saintly confidante he so admired, when his confessions of sin led only to sinful thoughts in myself.

'Where are you going?'

'To put Adèle to bed. It is past her bedtime.'

'You are afraid of me.'

'Your language is enigmatical, sir, but I am certainly not afraid. Only apprehensive as I have no wish to talk nonsense.'

'If you did, it would be in such a grave, quiet manner, I should mistake it for sense.'

He leaned in close to me and, taking me quite by surprise, held my chin in his fingers. His warm touch made my heart race. His eyes were soft pools of dark water as they met mine.

'Do you never laugh, Miss Eyre? Don't trouble yourself to answer, for I see you laugh rarely, but you can laugh very merrily, believe me. You are not naturally austere, any more than I am naturally vicious. The Lowood constraint still clings to you somewhat, controlling your features, muffling your voice and restricting your limbs. You fear in the presence of a man and a brother – or master, or what you will – to smile too gaily, speak too freely, or move too quickly. But, in time, I think you will learn to be natural with me, as I find it impossible to be conventional with you. And then your looks and movements will have more vivacity and variety than they dare offer now. I see at intervals the glance of a curious sort of bird through the close-set bars of a cage. A vivid, restless, resolute captive is there. Were it but free, it would soar cloud-high.'

He stared at me so intently then, that I hardly dared to breathe. I wondered whether he could see into my thoughts. Then, narrowing his eyes and smiling enigmatically, he let me go.

'You are still bent on going?' he asked, putting his hands in his pockets.

'It has struck nine, sir.'

'Never mind. Wait a minute. Adèle is not ready to go to bed yet. My position, Miss Eyre, with my back to the fire, and my face to the room, favours observation. While talking to you, I have also occasionally watched Adèle. I have my own reasons for thinking her a curious study, reasons that I may, nay, that I shall, impart to you some day. About ten minutes ago, she pulled out of her box a little pink silk frock and rapture lit her face as she unfolded it. "Il faut que je l'essaie!" cried she, "Et à l'instant même!" and she rushed out of the room.'

I couldn't help but issue a small laugh at his impersonation. I was relieved, too that our moment of physical intimacy had been broken, but as he leaned in closer to me, talking in a light-hearted and confidential tone, my heartbeat was not calmed by his proximity.

'She is now with Mrs Fairfax and in a few minutes she will re-enter, and I know what I shall see. A miniature of Céline Varens, as she used to appear on the boards at the rising of—'

He stopped himself and rubbed his cheek. Then he sighed. I could tell that he was thinking about Céline Varens, Adèle's mother, and I knew in that instant that she must form some great part of his experience.

'But never mind that. Stay now, to see whether I am right.'

Just then, Adèle's little foot was heard tripping across the hall. She entered, transformed as her guardian had predicted. A dress of rose-coloured satin, very short, and as full in the skirt as it could be gathered, replaced the brown frock she had previously worn. A wreath of rosebuds circled her forehead. Her feet were dressed in silk stockings and small white satin sandals.

'Est-ce que ma robe va bien?' cried she, bounding forwards, 'Et mes souliers? Et mes bas? Tenez, je crois que je vais danser!'

And spreading out her dress, she chasséed across the room till, having reached Mr Rochester, she wheeled lightly round before him on tiptoe, then dropped on one knee at his feet, exclaiming, 'Monsieur, je vous remercie mille fois de votre bonté,' then rising, she added, 'C'est comme cela que maman faisait, n'est-ce pas, monsieur?'

'Pre-cise-ly!' was the answer, and Mr Rochester added to me, 'And, "comme cela", she charmed my English gold out of my British breeches' pocket. I have been green, too, Miss Eyre, grass green, just as you are now. My spring is gone, however, but it has left me that French floweret on my hands,' he said, nodding to Adèle, who was dancing across the floor, 'which, in some moods, I would fain be rid of, but I keep it and rear it rather on the Roman Catholic principle of expiating numerous sins, great or small, by one good work. I'll explain all this some day.'

He held my gaze then for one second, and his eyes in the firelight were like soft black pebbles. For one heady moment, I longed to dive into their depth and discover their beguiling mysteries. I admit that after our exchange this evening I was enthralled by him and longed to hear everything there was to know about Adèle's mother, the woman who had charmed the gold from his pockets.

I contented myself with the fact that he had promised to tell me the story, that he had cast me in the role of his confessor, which could only mean that I would spend more intimate evenings such as this one with him. The thought of it filled me with buoyant feeling I had never experienced before.

Perhaps my eyes gave me away, because abruptly and with no affection in his tone, he said, 'Goodnight, Miss Eyre.'

Then he turned his back on me to refill his wine glass. I ushered Adèle out in order to take her to bed and calm her after the excitement of the evening. I glanced back to see Mr Rochester take a long sip of his wine, but his mood was impenetrable to me. The thought of my little room upstairs, which hitherto in my time in Thornfield had been my sanctuary, now felt like a cold cell to which I had been dismissed. Perhaps I really was the vivid, restless, resolute captive Mr Rochester had described, and, as I shut the door quietly, I wondered if it would be him who knew how to set me free.

SIX

Mr Rochester did eventually explain the mystery of his connection to Adèle's mother, but when I was least expecting it. It was one afternoon, when he chanced to meet me and Adèle in the grounds. While she played with Pilot and her shuttlecock, he asked me to walk up and down a long beech avenue within sight of her.

At the end of the avenue was a bench and we sat down together to watch Adèle. I made a few comments about his ward's progress and, as the afternoon sun came through the bare branches of the great trees, bathing us in an unexpected promise of warmth on the cold winter's day, he started talking about Paris.

I sat demurely, my hands in my muff, remembering how he had found me to be a good listener, and my attention was rewarded when he told me that Adèle was the daughter of a French opera dancer, Céline Varens, towards whom he had once cherished what he called a 'grande passion'. This passion Céline had professed to return with even superior ardour. He thought himself her idol, ugly as he was. He believed, as he said, that she preferred his 'taille d'athlète' to the elegance of the Apollo Belvidere.

'And, Miss Eyre, so much was I flattered by this preference of the Gallic sylph for her British gnome, that I installed her in a hotel, gave her a complete establishment of servants, a carriage, cashmeres, diamonds, etc. In short, I began the process of ruining myself in the received style, like any other spoony.

'I had not, it seems, the originality to chalk out a new road to shame and destruction, but trod the old track with stupid exactness not to deviate an inch from the beaten centre. I had, as I deserved to have, the fate of all other spoonies.

'Happening to call one evening when Céline did not expect me, I found her out. But it was a warm night, and I was tired with strolling through Paris, so I sat down in her boudoir, happy to breathe the air consecrated so lately by her presence. No, I exaggerate. I never thought there was any consecrating virtue about her. It was rather a sort of pastille perfume she had left, a scent of musk and amber, than an odour of sanctity. But as I said, it was warm, and the fumes of conservatory flowers and sprinkled essences made it necessary to open the window, and I stepped out onto the balcony.

'It was moonlight and gaslight besides, and very still and serene. The balcony was furnished with a chair or two, and I sat down, and took out a cigar. I will take one now, if you will excuse me.'

Here ensued a pause, filled up by the producing and lighting of a cigar. I noticed his manicured long fingers and the fullness of his lips as he rolled the cigar between them. He breathed a trail of Havana incense on the freezing air, and went on.

'I liked bonbons too in those days, Miss Eyre, and I ate a chocolate sweet as I smoked, watching the carriages that rolled along the fashionable streets towards the neighbouring opera house. Then an elegant close carriage drawn by a beautiful pair of English horses, and distinctly seen in the brilliant city night, I recognized the "voiture" I had given Céline as it slowed down. She was returning.

'Of course my heart thumped with impatience against the iron rails I leant upon. The carriage stopped, as I had expected, at the hotel door. My flame, my true love alighted, though muffed in a cloak – an unnecessary encumbrance, by the bye, on so warm a June evening – but I knew her instantly by her little foot, seen peeping from the skirt of her dress, as she skipped from the carriage-step. Bending over the balcony, I was about to murmur "Mon ange" – in a tone, of course, which should be audible to the ear of love alone – when a figure jumped from the carriage after her, cloaked also, but with a spurred heel, which had rung on the pavement, and a hatted head which now passed under the arched porte cochère of the hotel.

'You never felt jealousy, did you, Miss Eyre? Of course not. I need not ask you, because you never felt love. You have both sentiments yet to experience. Your soul sleeps. The shock is yet to be given which shall waken it. You think all existence lapses in as quiet a flow as that in which your youth has hitherto slid away. Floating on with closed eyes and muffled ears, you neither see the rocks bristling not far off in the bed of the flood, nor hear the breakers boil at their base. But I tell you – and you may mark my words – you will come some day to a craggy pass in the channel, where the whole of life's stream will be broken up into whirl and tumult, foam and noise. Either you will be dashed to atoms on crag points, or lifted up and borne on by some master-wave into a calmer current, as I am now.

'I like this day. I like that sky, the sternness and stillness of the world under this frost. I like Thornfield, its antiquity, its retirement, its old crow-trees and thorn-trees, its grey façade, and lines of dark windows, and yet how long have I abhorred the very thought of it, shunned it like a great plague-house? How I do still abhor. If you only knew—'

He ground his teeth and was silent. He struck his boot against the hard ground. Some hated thought seemed to have him in its grip, and to hold him so tightly that he could not advance.

The hall was before us at the end of the long avenue of trees. Lifting his eye to its battlements, he cast over them a glare such as I never saw before or since. Pain, shame, ire, impatience, disgust, detestation, seemed momentarily to hold a quivering conflict in the large pupil dilating under his ebony eyebrows. Wild was the wrestle which should be paramount, but another feeling rose and triumphed. Something hard and cynical, self-willed and resolute.

Adèle suddenly ran before him with her shuttlecock, breaking his dark reverie. 'Away!' he cried harshly. 'Keep at a distance, child, or go inside.'

He stood and started walking, but I sensed he wished me

to follow. Descending the path of beech trees, we walked together in silence. I ventured to recall him to the point whence he had abruptly diverged from his recollection.

'Did you leave the balcony, sir,' I asked, 'when Mademoiselle Varens entered?'

I almost expected a rebuff for this hardly well-timed question, but, on the contrary, waking out of his scowling abstraction, he turned his eyes towards me, and the shade seemed to clear off his brow.

'Oh, I had forgotten Céline! Well, to resume. When I saw my charmer thus come in accompanied by a cavalier, I seemed to hear a hiss, and the green snake of jealousy, rising on undulating coils from the moonlit balcony, glided within my waistcoat, and ate its way in two minutes to my heart's core. Strange!' he exclaimed, suddenly starting again from the point and stopping on the path. 'Strange that I should choose you for the confidant of all this, young lady. And strange that you should listen to me quietly, as if it were the most usual thing in the world for a man like me to tell stories of his opera mistresses to a quaint, inexperienced girl like you!

'But the last singularity explains the first, as I intimated once before. You, with your gravity, considerateness and caution were made to be the recipient of secrets. Besides, I know what sort of a mind I have placed in communication with my own. I know it is one not liable to take infection. It is a peculiar mind. It is a unique one. Happily I do not mean to harm it, but, if I did, it would not take harm from me. The more you and I converse, the better. You are so innocent, so green that I cannot blight you, whereas you may refresh me.'

'I hope so, sir.'

I felt a small dance go on in my stomach, as he smiled down at me. Then with a draw on his cigar, he walked on.

'I remained in the balcony. "They will come to her boudoir, no doubt," I thought. "Let me prepare an ambush."

'So putting my hand in through the open window, I drew the curtain over it, leaving only an opening through which I could take observations. Then I closed the casement, all but a chink just wide enough to furnish an outlet to lovers' whispered vows. Then I stole back to my chair and as I resumed it the pair came in. My eye was quickly at the aperture. Céline's chambermaid entered, lit a lamp, left it on the table and withdrew.

'The couple were thus revealed to me clearly. Both removed their cloaks, and there was "the Varens", shining in satin and jewels, my gifts of course, and there was her companion in an officer's uniform. I knew him for a young vicomte – a brainless and vicious youth whom I had sometimes met in society, and had never thought of hating because I despised him so absolutely. On recognizing him, the fang of the snake Jealousy was instantly broken, because at the same moment my love for Céline sank under an extinguisher. A woman who could betray me for such a rival was not worth contending for. She deserved only scorn. Less, however, than I, who had been her dupe.

'They began to talk and their conversation eased me completely. It was frivolous, mercenary, heartless and senseless, rather calculated to weary than enrage a listener. A card of mine lay on the table and, this being perceived, brought my name under discussion. Neither of them possessed energy or wit to belabour me soundly, but they insulted me as coarsely as they could in their little way, especially Céline, who even waxed rather brilliant on my personal defects – deformities she termed them. It had been her custom to launch out into fervent admiration of what she called my "beauté mâle," wherein she differed diametrically from you, who told me point blank, at the second interview, that you did not think me handsome. The contrast struck me at the time and—'

Adèle here came running up again.

'Monsieur, John has just been to say that your agent has called and wishes to see you.'

I mentally shook myself. So enraptured had I been in his story, I imagined myself, as him, looking in on his lover. I wanted to contradict him, convinced as he was that I thought him not handsome, but this was not the moment, nor, I thought, would there ever be a moment to change his mind.

He had assumed me to be completely innocent of jealousy, but now a strange hiss seemed to gather around my heart as I stared on Adèle. I felt furious with her for disturbing the story I had so longed to hear. Yet Mr Rochester seemed unperturbed.

'Ah! In that case I must abridge,' he said. 'Where was I? Yes, so opening the window, I walked in upon them. They were, by this time, in each other's arms and lying on the bed. The vicomte had his face buried in Céline's ample décolletage. Seeing them so, I liberated Céline from my protection and gave her notice to vacate her hotel. I offered her a purse for immediate exigencies, disregarded screams, hysterics, prayers, protestations, convulsions, and made an appointment with the vicomte for a meeting at the Bois de Boulogne. The next morning I had the pleasure of encountering him and left a bullet in one of his arms, and then thought I had done with the whole crew.

'Unluckily for me, however, the Varens, six months before, had given me this fillette Adèle, who, she affirmed, was my daughter. Perhaps she may be, though I see no proofs of such grim paternity written in her countenance. Pilot is more like me than she. Some years after I had broken with the mother, she abandoned her child, and ran away to Italy with a musician or singer. I acknowledged no natural claim on Adèle's part to be supported by me, nor do I now acknowledge any, for I am not her father. Yet hearing that she was quite destitute, I took the poor thing out of the slime and mud of Paris, and transplanted it here, to grow up clean in the wholesome soil of an English country garden.

'Mrs Fairfax found you to train it, but now you know that it is the illegitimate offspring of a French opera girl, you will perhaps think differently of your post and protégée? Will you be coming to me some day with notice that you have found another place? That you beg me to look out for a new governess, eh?'

'No,' I answered quickly. 'Adèle is not answerable for either her mother's faults or yours. Now that I know she is, in a sense, parentless – forsaken by her mother and disowned by you, sir – I shall cling closer to her than before. How could I possibly prefer the spoilt pet of a wealthy family, who would hate her governess as a nuisance, to a lonely little orphan, who leans towards her as a friend?'

'Oh, that is the light in which you view it! Well, I must go in now, and you too. It darkens.'

But I stayed out a few minutes longer with Adèle and Pilot. I ran a race with her, and played a game of battledore and shuttlecock. When we went in, and I had removed her bonnet and coat, I took her on my knee and kept her there an hour, allowing her to prattle as she liked. I didn't rebuke the little trivialities to which she was apt and which betrayed in her a superficiality of character, concluding that they were inherited probably from her mother.

Still, she had her merits, and I was disposed to appreciate all that was good in her to the utmost. I sought in her countenance and features a likeness to Mr Rochester, but found none. No trait, no turn of expression announced their relationship. It was a pity. If she could but have been proved to resemble him, he would have thought more of her.

It was not till after I had withdrawn to my own chamber for the night, that I steadily reviewed my afternoon encounter with Mr Rochester, examining it from every angle. There was something decidedly strange in the paroxysm of emotion which had suddenly seized him when he was in the act of expressing the present contentment of his mood, and his newly revived pleasure in the old hall and its environs. He seemed as if some aspect of the hall had vexed him most deeply, that there was something about it that made his innermost soul uneasy.

I meditated wonderingly on this incident, but gradually quitted it, as I found it for the present inexplicable, and I turned to the consideration of my master's manner to myself. The confidence he had thought fit to repose in me seemed a tribute to my discretion. I regarded and accepted it as such and was indeed flattered that he trusted me as his confessor.

Yet now that I was alone and no longer observed in the manner of a nun, I fell upon the details of the tale Mr Rochester had told me and devoured them. With seemingly perfect recall, I filled in the sketch he had given me with the vivid colours of my imagination. I conjured Paris in the summer, the carriages on the gaslit streets and the apartment of Céline Varens, the smell of her perfume and the flowers he had described.

I relived his grande passion, fleshing out his affair with the great French beauty. I saw him in her boudoir, looking at her in the glass as he bestowed a diamond necklace upon her, and her delight as she fingered the jewels around her neck, standing to embrace him, running her hands through his thick hair, kissing his strong jaw and likening him, in her flirtatious French accent, to a Greek god.

He had described himself as a spoony, yet I was beguiled by the romance of it all, as I pictured Mr Rochester escorting his lover to the opera, kissing her gloved hands, his dark eyes soft with love. Céline Varens must have been a hard-hearted and self-regarding kind of woman, but in trying to imagine her trifling with Mr Rochester, I could only think how I might feel, having been given all he had described.

And as I progressed through everything I imagined the affair to have involved, I finally reached the scene of Rochester on the balcony, his face wreathed in cigar smoke, his tongue caressing a chocolate bonbon. I saw him watching his lover arriving in the carriage and I saw, too, the young officer whom Mr Rochester had considered so far beneath him.

I pictured them entering Céline Varens's chamber and Mr Rochester peeping through the curtains and seeing the vicomte – whom I imagined as young and blonde – his fingers inside the front of Céline's dress, kissing her breasts as they spoke of Mr Rochester.

Somehow my mind could not move beyond that fleeting moment of sensuality which Mr Rochester had so matter-of-factly described in his tale. The hint towards the carnal life of which he had so clear and full a knowledge – even in describing someone else – had set my imagination on fire. With such an intimate scene drawn, the colours and scents, the sounds and the two other characters besides Mr Rochester fully fleshed in my imagination, I found myself lost in the moment, as if studying a moving picture.

What would have happened if Mr Rochester had not been so adamant, or the snake of jealousy had not extinguished his ardour so fully? What if he had continued to be beguiled by the beautiful opera singer and, rather than rushing through the curtain and challenging her other lover to a duel, another scenario had occurred?

What if Rochester had found the vicomte – my vicomte, as I now saw him – in more attractive and less threatening terms, as I regarded him now. What if Céline Varens, skilled seductress as she was, had managed to soothe this Mr Rochester of my fantasy and had entreated him to join her and the officer on her bed?

The thought seemed like a lightning bolt to a secret place within me. And it was so much more powerful knowing that Mr Rochester had told me this story expressly because he knew it would not stain my mind. Yet that is exactly what it had done, and I was in the delightful grip of the corruption, as it spread like ink on blotting paper.

I closed my eyes, knowing that I would not be free until I had taken this scene to its conclusion. I gave in and cast myself as Céline Varens, the beautiful, voluptuous singer, and it was me the two men were undressing, both equally eager to prove their worth.

Such a fully formed fantasy was different to anything I had experienced before. The naked figures I had seen in the tapestries upstairs, and which I had not visited since Mr Rochester's arrival at the hall, were at odds with these two men in my imaginary embrace, who were so real, so tantalizingly within my grasp. I could almost feel their breath, smell their scent.

I felt as if the vision were reducing, the details around the room retreating, as I focused in on the scene on the bed and was overtaken with a sensuality I had not imagined before. Daring myself to watch, I saw both men in my mind's eye undoing my bodice, and each of them pulling my breasts from their constraints. I felt one man at each nipple, nuzzling, fondling, sucking. I saw each one smiling up as me, as each of my nipples hardened beneath their tongues, their hands running over my body, over my stomach, down my legs and up again, drawing up my skirts. Two hands caressing their way separately above the tops of my stockings to my sex.

I imagined pulling the young officer up towards me and entreating him to kiss me, knowing how jealous this would make Rochester. How the vicomte and I showed him our kiss, our tongues colliding, Mr Rochester's face so close, his dark eyes boring into me as he observed from my breast.

I had no way of knowing whose hand it was that touched me beneath my skirts – Mr Rochester's or the officer's – but as I closed my eyes, holding this image in my mind, the sensation became as real as if I were actually experiencing the scene.

I kissed the vicomte again and this time Rochester's face was level with my own, and I turned slightly to receive his kiss too.

I tried to stop myself, to linger poised there at the top of my fantasy, but my imagination was too powerful, and as I felt two sets of fingers exploring my eager, wet opening, I felt a sudden physical rush that I knew, even as it was happening, would wash away the scene.

Ashamed, I fell back on the pillow, my spent body trembling beneath the bedclothes, as Céline Varens and her two lovers disappeared. Then the candle by my bedside stuttered and extinguished itself in the draught, leaving me panting in the dark.

SEVEN

Over the following weeks, Mr Rochester's deportment changed towards me. Whenever he met me unexpectedly, the encounter always seemed welcome. He had always a word and sometimes a smile for me and when summoned by formal invitation to his presence, I was honoured by a cordiality of reception that made me feel I really possessed the power to amuse him, and that these evening conferences were sought as much for his pleasure as for my benefit.

I, indeed, talked comparatively little, but I heard him talk with relish. He liked to open to a mind unacquainted with the world glimpses of its scenes and ways. I do not mean its corrupt scenes and wicked ways, as I had interpreted myself from his descriptions, but the general scale and characteristics of life. I had a keen delight in receiving the new ideas he offered, in imagining the new pictures he portrayed. He did not refer back to Céline Varens and I did not encourage him to speak of his time with her in Paris, but his stories took me all over Europe and I had the impression that his

French mistress had been just one of the many that had made him a man of the world.

So happy, so gratified did I become with this new interest in my life, that I ceased to pine after other kindred. My thin crescent-destiny seemed to enlarge, the blanks of existence were filled up and my bodily health improved. I gathered flesh and strength.

Was Mr Rochester now ugly in my eyes? No, reader. Gratitude, and many associations, all pleasurable, made his face the object I best liked to see. His presence in a room was more cheering than the brightest fire.

Yet I had not forgotten his faults. Indeed, I could not, for he brought them frequently before me. He was proud, sardonic, harsh to inferiority of every description. I knew that his great kindness to me was balanced by unjust severity to many others. He was moody, too – unaccountably so. More than once when he sent for me to read to him I found him sitting in his library alone, with his head bent on his folded arms. When he looked up, a morose, almost a malignant, scowl blackened his features.

But I believed that his moodiness, his harshness, and his former faults of morality (I say former, for now he seemed corrected of them) had their source in some cruel cross of fate, which I gathered was in some way connected with Thornfield itself, although I could not fathom an explanation for this belief.

Yet I determined that he was naturally a man of better tendencies, higher principles and purer tastes than such as circumstances had developed, education instilled, or destiny encouraged. I thought there were excellent materials in him, though for the present they hung together somewhat spoiled and tangled and I cannot deny that I grieved for his grief, whatever that was, and would have given much to assuage it.

One night I had lain down in bed, but I could not sleep for thinking of his look when he paused in the avenue and stared up at Thornfield, and to the several allusions to the pain he felt here that he had mentioned since.

'What is it that alienates him from the house?' I wondered. Then, another more worrying thought occurred to me. 'Will he leave it again soon? Mrs Fairfax said he seldom stayed here longer than a fortnight at a time, and he has now been resident eight weeks. If he does go, the change will be doleful. Suppose he should be absent spring, summer and autumn. How joyless sunshine and fine days will seem!'

I hardly know whether I had slept or not after this musing. At any rate, I started wide awake on hearing a vague murmur, peculiar and lugubrious, which sounded, I thought, just above me. I wished I had kept my candle burning. The night was drearily dark and my spirits were depressed. I rose and sat up in bed, listening. The sound was hushed.

I tried again to sleep, but my heart beat anxiously, my inward tranquillity broken. The clock, far down in the hall, struck two. Just then it seemed my chamber door was touched, as if fingers had swept the panels in groping a way along the dark gallery outside. I said, 'Who is there?' Nothing answered. I was chilled with fear.

All at once I remembered that it might be Pilot, who, when the kitchen door chanced to be left open, not infrequently found his way up to the threshold of Mr Rochester's chamber. I had seen him lying there myself in the mornings. The idea calmed me somewhat and I lay down.

Silence composes the nerves, and as an unbroken hush now reigned again through the whole house, I began to feel the return of slumber. But it was not fated that I should sleep that night. A dream had scarcely approached my ear, when it fled affrighted, scared by a marrow-freezing incident enough.

This was a demoniac laugh, low, suppressed and deep, and uttered, it seemed, at the very keyhole of my chamber door. The head of my bed was near the door, and I thought at first the goblin-laugher stood at my bedside, or rather, crouched by my pillow. I rose, looked round, and could see nothing, while, as I still gazed, the unnatural sound was reiterated. I knew it came from behind the panels. My first impulse was to rise and fasten the bolt, my next, again to cry out, 'Who is there?'

Something laughed and moaned.

Ere long, steps retreated up the gallery towards the third-storey staircase. A door had lately been made to shut in that staircase. I heard it open and close, and all was still.

'Was that Grace Poole? And is she possessed with a devil?' I thought.

Impossible now to remain longer by myself, I reasoned that I must go to Mrs Fairfax.

I hurried on my shawl, withdrew the bolt and opened the door with a trembling hand.

There was a candle burning just outside, and on the matting in the gallery. I was surprised at this circumstance, but still more was I amazed to perceive the air quite dim, as if filled with smoke. While looking to the right hand and left, to find whence these blue wreaths issued, I became further aware of a strong smell of burning.

Something creaked. It was a door ajar. And that door was Mr Rochester's, the smoke rushing out in a cloud from thence.

I thought no more of Mrs Fairfax. I thought no more of Grace Poole, or the laugh. In an instant, I was within the chamber.

Tongues of flame darted round the bed. The curtains were on fire. In the midst of blaze and vapour, Mr Rochester lay stretched motionless, in deep sleep. In the burning light, I could see his form beneath the thin sheets, the spread of his loins, the bulge between them and for one fleeting second, I thought that Céline Varens hadn't been wrong. Unencumbered by clothes, he was like a Greek god.

'Wake! Wake!' I cried. I shook him, but he only murmured and turned. The smoke had stupefied him.

Not a moment could be lost. The very sheets were kindling, and I rushed to his basin and ewer. Fortunately, one was wide and the other deep, and both were filled with water. I heaved them up, deluged the bed and its occupant, flew back to my own room, brought my own water-jug, baptized the couch afresh, and, by God's aid, succeeded in extinguishing the flames which were devouring it.

The hiss of the quenched element, the breakage of a pitcher which I flung from my hand when I had emptied it, and, above all, the splash of the shower-bath I had liberally bestowed, roused Mr Rochester at last.

Though it was now dark, I knew he was awake, because I heard him muttering at finding himself lying in a pool of water.

'Is there a flood?' he cried.

'No, sir,' I answered, 'but there has been a fire. Get up. You are drenched now. I will fetch you a candle.'

'In the name of all the elves in Christendom, is that Jane Eyre?' he demanded. 'What have you done with me, witch, sorceress? Who is in the room besides you? Have you plotted to drown me?'

'I will fetch you a candle, sir. In heaven's name, get up. Somebody has plotted something. You have to find out who and what it is.'

'There! I am up now. Fetch a candle yet. Now run!'

I did run. I brought the candle which still remained in the gallery. He took it from my hand, held it up and surveyed the bed, all blackened and scorched, the sheets drenched, the carpet round swimming in water.

'What is it? And who did it?' he asked.

I briefly related to him what had transpired. The strange laugh I had heard in the gallery. The step ascending to the third storey. The smoke, the smell of fire which had conducted me to his room and in what state I had found matters there. And how I had deluged him with all the water I could lay hands on.

He listened very gravely as I went on, but his face expressed more concern than astonishment. He did not immediately speak when I had concluded. I watched his shoulders tense beneath the thin wet cloth of his nightshirt.

'Shall I call Mrs Fairfax?' I asked.

'Mrs Fairfax? No, what the deuce would you call her for? What can she do? Let her sleep.'

'Then I will fetch Leah, and wake John and his wife.'

'Not at all. Just be still. You have a shawl on. If you are not warm enough, you may take my cloak. Here, wrap it about you, and sit down in the armchair. There, I will put it on you. Now place your feet on the stool, to keep them out of the wet. I am going to leave you a few minutes. I shall take the candle. Remain where you are till I return. Be as still as a mouse. I must pay a visit to the upstairs storey. Don't move, remember, or call anyone.'

He went. I watched the light withdraw. He passed up the gallery very softly, unclosed the staircase door with as little noise as possible, shut it after him, and the last ray vanished. I was left in total darkness.

I listened for some noise, but heard nothing. A very long time elapsed. I grew weary. It was cold, in spite of the cloak, and then I did not see the use of staying, as I was not to rouse the house. I was on the point of risking Mr Rochester's displeasure by disobeying his orders, when the light once more gleamed dimly on the gallery wall, and I heard his unshod feet tread the matting.

'I hope it is he,' I thought, 'and not something worse.'

He re-entered, pale and very gloomy. 'I have found it all out,' said he, setting his candle down on the washstand. 'It is as I thought.'

'How, sir?'

He made no reply, but stood with his arms folded, looking on the ground. At the end of a minute he inquired in rather a peculiar tone, 'I forget whether you said you saw anything when you opened your chamber door.'

'No, sir, only the candlestick on the ground.'

'But you heard an odd laugh? You have heard that laugh before, I should think, or something like it?'

'Yes, sir. There is a woman who sews here, called Grace Poole. She laughs in that way. She is a strange person.'

'Just so. Grace Poole – you have guessed it. She is, as you say, strange – very. Well, I shall reflect on the subject. Meantime, I am glad that you are the only person, besides myself, acquainted with the precise details of tonight's incident. You are no talking fool. Say nothing about it. I will account for this state of affairs' (pointing to the bed), 'and now return to your own room. I shall do very well on the sofa in the library for the rest of the night. It is near four. In two hours the servants will be up.'

'Goodnight, then, sir,' I said, departing.

He seemed surprised – very inconsistently so, as he had just told me to go.

'What!' he exclaimed, stepping towards me. 'Are you quitting me already, and in that way?'

'You said I might go, sir.'

'But not without taking leave. Not without a word or two of acknowledgement and goodwill. Not, in short, in that brief, dry fashion. Why, you have saved my life! Snatched me from a horrible and excruciating death! And you walk past me as if we were mutual strangers! At least shake hands.'

He held out his hand. I gave him mine. He took it first in one, then in both his own. Then, to my astonishment, he kissed my fingertips. A ripple of desire seemed to run from the place where his lips had made contact with my flesh, right through me.

'You have saved my life, Jane. I have a pleasure in owing you so immense a debt. I cannot say more.'

He paused, gazed at me, and I was drawn in, magnetized by his eyes.

'Goodnight again, sir,' I said, but my voice was no more than a whisper. 'You do not owe me a debt.'

'I knew,' he continued, holding my palm now against his lips, 'you would do me good in some way, at some time. I saw it in your eyes when I first beheld you. Their expression and smile did not,' again he stopped, closing in, 'did not strike delight to my very inmost heart so for nothing.'

I felt the great overcoat he had given me slide from my shoulders to the floor, but I did not feel the loss of heat, because my whole body seemed flushed with a new kind of warmth.

'I have heard of good genii and I believe there are grains of truth in the wildest fable, for you are mine. My cherished preserver.'

Strange energy was in his voice, strange fire in his look.

You are mine. His words swept into my heart, like the luxurious chord of a harp, but my reason dampened the music. 'He cannot mean it,' I thought.

'I am glad I happened to be awake,' I said, but my knees were trembling and weak. Closer and closer, his eyes drew me in.

Fear overtook me then. Not fear of him, but fear of myself, of the inner life I'd held privately for so long, my desire, my carnal longings, all threatening to rise to the surface and engulf me.

I quickly turned to go. I could not trust myself to stay. I could not trust myself to stare into his eyes and what they suggested.

'What! You will go?' he said, reaching out and drawing me back to him.

'I am cold, sir,' I lied.

'Cold? Yes and standing in a pool! Go, then, Jane, go!'

His voice sounded as if he meant it, but he still retained my hand, and I could not free it. I looked from his grip to his eyes. They burned even brighter now.

And then he was gently pulling me towards him, as if he still expected me to take flight. In the soft, dim light of the candle, his face filled my vision.

'You cannot leave me like this,' he breathed.

I was trembling uncontrollably, but I could not pull away.

He stared down at me, drawing me further towards his warm embrace. Closer, closer he came, daring me to buckle and move away, but I was hopelessly, blissfully trapped and borne away on those dark seas I had glimpsed in his eyes for so long, leaving the shores of everything I knew to be right to sail into this unchartered water.

Then his arms were around me and then, even before the

soft gasp could leave my mouth, his lips were on mine. The simple fusion, in the split second after it had happened, seemed so obvious that surely it been destined all along. Quiet, tentative, we stood together suspended in a golden sacred moment. I knew then that I had the choice, that even now it wasn't too late. I could break away, I could still step back onto the shore.

But I couldn't. There was not enough reason or willpower left within me to resist him. My whole being only wanted this moment to go on and on, and I surrendered to it, melting against him. Then, with a low, delicious groan, he seemed to let something go too, the sound of his surrender igniting something within me as surely as the room itself had been aflame earlier.

Oh, reader. The kiss. How many poems, how many novels I had read, and yet nothing had ever come close to describing this feeling. So simple, so lauded and documented, but yet so entirely new to me, and so different to how I had imagined. I had kissed Emma, of course, but it had not been anything like this. How could I compare a girl with a man? They were incomparable.

As I was engulfed in him, the very exotic maleness of him, he kissed me more passionately, his tongue probing into my mouth to find my tongue. And I was lost. His kiss seemed to open my very soul and bare me naked before him.

I felt my feet lift from the ground as he held me, and then his firm, hard body pressing against my own, two thin nightgowns separating us, and I was desperate for his flesh.

'Oh, Jane, Jane,' he murmured, kissing my neck, his hands

cupping my buttocks, squeezing them, pulling me towards him.

I gasped as I felt the hardness of his member against my stomach. I wanted to lift my legs up around his waist and feel him enter me, so consumed was I with the need to fuse and mesh with him.

My hands clasped his hair, my mouth opening, my tongue yielding to him.

Then a noise in the corridor made us freeze.

'I think I hear Mrs Fairfax move,' I whispered.

Silently, I felt my toes touch the sodden carpet and the spell was broken, the all-consuming passion doused with the water of reality, as surely as I had doused the flames myself earlier.

'You must leave me,' he breathed, and relaxed his grip on me. 'Go. You must go.'

I nodded once and, trembling all over, ran from his room.

EIGHT

I both wished and feared to see Mr Rochester on the day which followed this sleepless night. I wanted to hear his voice again, yet feared to meet his eye. I could barely comprehend what had happened between us, or what might have happened if I had stayed. What could possibly occur now in the aftermath of such fire? What would Mr Rochester, my master, no – more than that – my friend, think of me now? Would he consider my pure spirit to be utterly corrupted – even though it had been he himself the corrupter? Would he denounce me? Dismiss me? Be angry with me? Because he could, if he chose to, ruin me.

And yet, as my heart wrestled with such fear, another part of me, still intoxicated, reasoned that the kiss had surely been born of mutual desire? As my fingertips fluttered against my lips, I went over every detail. It was he who had requested me to stay, was it not? He who had overwhelmed me? He who had kissed me, who had opened my soul.

But what now? Would he pretend nothing had happened, or would he want more from me? And what would more mean? I might have started something I could barely begin to think I could control.

During the early part of the morning, I momentarily expected him to come to see me, for though he was not in the frequent habit of entering the schoolroom, he had, on occasion, stepped in for a few minutes.

But the morning passed just as usual. Nothing happened to interrupt the quiet course of Adèle's studies. Only soon after breakfast, I heard some bustle in the neighbourhood of Mr Rochester's chamber, Mrs Fairfax's voice and Leah's, and the cook's – that is, John's wife – and even John's own gruff tones.

There were exclamations of 'What a mercy master was not burnt in his bed!' 'It is always dangerous to keep a candle lit at night.' 'How providential that he had presence of mind to think of the water jug!' 'I wonder he waked nobody!' 'It is to be hoped he will not take cold with sleeping on the library sofa.'

This was all followed by the sound of scrubbing and setting to rights. And when I passed the room, in going downstairs to dinner, I saw through the open door that all was again restored to complete order. Only the bed was stripped of its hangings.

Leah stood up in the window seat, rubbing the panes of glass dimmed with smoke. I was about to address her, for I wished to know what account had been given of the affair, but, on advancing, I saw a second person in the chamber. A woman was sitting on a chair by the bedside sewing rings to new curtains. That woman was no other than Grace Poole.

There she sat, staid and taciturn-looking, as usual, in her brown stuff gown, her check apron, white handkerchief and cap. She was intent on her work, in which her whole thoughts seemed absorbed. On her hard forehead, and in her commonplace features, was nothing either of the paleness or desperation one would have expected to see marking the countenance of a woman who had attempted murder, and whose intended victim had followed her last night to her lair, and (as I believed), charged her with the crime she wished to perpetrate.

After what had passed between Mr Rochester and me last night, I felt a new secret sense of propriety towards him. Her devilish act seemed altogether more outrageous, now my feelings towards him were heightened so. What if she had succeeded in her evil plan? I pondered. What if Mr Rochester had been seriously harmed, or even – my heart lurched at the mere thought – burned to death in his bed?

I was amazed – confounded by her attitude. She looked up, while I still gazed at her. No start, no increase or failure of colour betrayed any emotion, consciousness of guilt, or fear of detection. She said, 'Good morning, Miss,' in her usual phlegmatic and brief manner and, taking up another ring and more tape, went on with her sewing.

'I will put her to some test,' I thought.

'Good morning, Grace,' I said. 'Has anything happened here? I thought I heard the servants all talking together a while ago.'

'Only master had been reading in his bed last night. He fell asleep with his candle lit, and the curtains caught on fire. But, fortunately, he woke up before the bedclothes or the woodwork caught, and contrived to quench the flames with the water in the ewer.'

'A strange affair!' I said, in a low voice. Then, looking at her fixedly, said, 'Did Mr Rochester wake nobody? Did no one hear him move?'

She again raised her eyes to me, and this time there was something of consciousness in their expression. She seemed to examine me warily, then she answered, 'The servants sleep so far off, you know, Miss, they would not be likely to hear. Mrs Fairfax's room and yours are the nearest to master's, but Mrs Fairfax said she heard nothing. When people get elderly, they often sleep heavy.' She paused, and then added, in a marked and significant tone, 'But you are young, Miss, and I should say a light sleeper. Perhaps you may have heard a noise?'

'I did,' I said, dropping my voice, so that Leah, who was still polishing the panes, could not hear me, 'and at first I thought it was Pilot. But Pilot cannot laugh and I am certain I heard a laugh, and a strange one.'

She took a new needle and carefully threaded it with a steady hand. Then she observed, with perfect composure, 'It is hardly likely master would laugh, I should think, Miss, when he was in such danger. You must have been dreaming.'

'I was not dreaming,' I said, with some warmth, for her brazen coolness provoked me. Again she looked at me and with the same scrutinizing and conscious eye.

'Have you told master that you heard a laugh?' she inquired.

'I have not had the opportunity of speaking to him this morning.'

'You did not think of opening your door and looking out into the gallery?'

She appeared to be cross-questioning me, attempting to draw from me information unawares. The idea struck me that if she discovered I knew or suspected her guilt, she would be playing of some of her malignant pranks on me, and I thought it advisable to be on my guard. I also, with a tremor of horror, wondered whether there was any way she could know what had passed between Mr Rochester and me. Could she have followed him back to his room and spied on us together?

'On the contrary,' I said, 'I bolted my door.'

'Then you are not in the habit of bolting your door every night before you get into bed?'

'Fiend! She wants to know my habits, that she may lay her plans accordingly!' Indignation again prevailed over prudence and I replied sharply, 'Hitherto I have often omitted to fasten the bolt because I did not think it necessary. I was not aware any danger or annoyance was to be dreaded at Thornfield Hall, but in future,' I said, stressing my words, 'I shall take good care to make all secure before I venture to lie down.'

'It will be wise to do so,' was her answer. 'This neighbourhood is as quiet as any I know, and I never heard of the hall being attempted by robbers since it was a house, though there are hundreds of pounds' worth of plate in the plate-closet, as is well known. And you see, for such a large house, there are very few servants, because master has never lived here much and when he does come, being a bachelor, he needs little waiting on. But I always think it best to err on the safe side. A door is soon fastened, and it is as well to have a drawn bolt between one and any mischief that may be about.'

I still stood absolutely dumbfounded at what appeared to me her miraculous self-possession and most inscrutable hypocrisy, when the cook entered.

'Mrs Poole,' said she, addressing Grace, 'the servants' dinner will soon be ready. Will you come down?'

'No. Just put my pint of porter and bit of pudding on a tray, and I'll carry it upstairs.'

'You'll have some meat?'

'Just a morsel, and a taste of cheese, that's all.'

The cook here turned to me, saying that Mrs Fairfax was waiting for me, so I departed.

I hardly heard Mrs Fairfax's account of the curtain conflagration during dinner, so much was I occupied in puzzling my brains over the enigmatical character of Grace Poole, and still more in pondering the problem of her position at Thornfield and questioning why she had not been given into custody that morning, or, at the very least, dismissed from her master's service.

He had almost as much as declared his conviction of her criminality last night, so what mysterious cause withheld him from accusing her? Why had he enjoined me, too, to secrecy? It was strange. He was such a bold gentleman, but he seemed somehow to be in the power of one of the meanest of his dependants, so much in her power, that even when she lifted her hand against his life, he dared not openly charge her with the attempt, much less punish her for it.

Had Grace been young and handsome, I should have been tempted to think that tenderer feelings than prudence or fear influenced Mr Rochester in her behalf, but, hard-favoured and matronly as she was, the idea could not be admitted. 'Yet,' I reflected, 'she has been young once. Her youth would be contemporary with her master's. Mrs Fairfax told me once, she had lived here many years. I don't think she can ever have been pretty, but, for all I know, she may possess originality and strength of character to compensate for the want of personal advantages. What if a former caprice (a freak very possible to a nature so sudden and headstrong as his) has delivered him into her power, and she now exercises over his actions a secret influence, the result of his own indiscretion, which he cannot shake off, and dare not disregard?'

But, having reached this point of conjecture, Mrs Poole's square, flat figure and dry, even coarse face, recurred so distinctly to my mind's eye, that I thought, 'No, impossible! My supposition cannot be correct. Yet,' suggested the secret voice which talks to us in our own hearts, 'you are not beautiful either, and perhaps Mr Rochester approves of you anyway. You have often felt as if he did, none more so than last night. Remember his words, remember his look, remember his voice. Remember that embrace! That kiss . . .'

I well remembered it all. His language, glance and tone seemed at the moment vividly renewed. I was now in the schoolroom and Adèle was drawing and I bent over her and directed her pencil. She looked up with a sort of start.

'Qu' avez-vous, mademoiselle?' said she. 'Vos doigts tremblent comme la feuille, et vos joues sont rouges, mais, rouges comme des cerises!'

'I am hot, Adèle, with stooping!' I said, patting my pink cheeks to which she referred with my trembling hand.

She went on sketching as I went on thinking.

I hastened to drive from my mind the hateful notion I had been conceiving respecting Grace Poole – that there may be something secret between her and Mr Rochester. The thought disgusted me. I compared myself with her, and found we were quite different, but I couldn't shake the discomfort of us both being in Mr Rochester's employ and both being his to choose from.

I reminded myself of Bessie. She had said once that I was quite a lady and she spoke truth. I was a lady. And now I looked much better than I did when Bessie saw me. I had more colour and more flesh, more life, more vivacity, because I had brighter hopes and keener enjoyments.

'Evening approaches,' I said to myself, as I looked towards the window. 'I haven't heard Mr Rochester's voice or step in the house today, but surely I shall see him before night. I feared the meeting in the morning, but now I desire it, because expectation has been so long baffled that it is grown impatient.'

When dusk actually closed, and when Adèle left me to go

and play in the nursery, I did most keenly desire it. I listened for the bell to ring below and I listened for Leah coming up with a message. I fancied sometimes I heard Mr Rochester's own tread, and I turned to the door, expecting it to open and admit him.

I imagined him striding across the room to hold me like he had held me last night. I thought of the hurried excuses he would whisper in my ear, which would not matter to me at all, as the relief I would feel would make my spirit soar with happiness.

Yet the door remained shut. Darkness came in through the window. Still it was not late. He often sent for me at seven and eight o'clock, and it was yet but six. Surely I should not be wholly disappointed tonight, when I had so many things to say to him! I wanted again to introduce the subject of Grace Poole, and to hear what he would answer. I wanted to ask him plainly if he really believed it was she who had made last night's hideous attempt on his life and, if so, why he kept her wickedness a secret.

But most of all, I wanted to know what he thought of what had passed between us, whether he regretted it. Or thought less of me, or whether that kiss had altered him as much as it had altered me. And what, if anything, would happen between us now. I felt my hand stray to the front of my gown, remembering the sensation on my stomach of his flesh pressing against mine through the thin fabric and, though I knew it was hopeless, I felt weak with desire.

A tread creaked on the stairs at last. Leah made her appearance, but it was only to tell me that tea was ready in Mrs

Fairfax's room. I was glad to go downstairs. At least, I imagined, I would be closer to Mr Rochester's presence.

'You must want your tea,' said the good lady, as I joined her. 'You ate so little at dinner. I am afraid,' she continued, 'you are not well today. You look flushed and feverish.'

'Oh, quite well! I never felt better.'

'Then you must prove it by having a good appetite. Will you fill the teapot while I knit off this needle?'

Having completed her task, she rose to draw down the blind, which she had hitherto kept up, by way, I suppose, of making the most of daylight, though dusk was now fast deepening into total obscurity.

'It is fair tonight,' said she, as she looked through the panes, 'though not starlight. Mr Rochester has, on the whole, had a favourable day for his journey.'

'Journey! Has Mr Rochester gone somewhere? I did not know he was out.'

'Oh, he set off the moment he had breakfasted! He is gone to the Leas, Mr Eshton's place, ten miles on the other side Millcote. I believe there is quite a party assembled there. Lord Ingram, Sir George Lynn, Captain Dent and others.'

'Do you expect him back tonight?'

'No, nor tomorrow either. I should think he is very likely to stay a week or more. When these fine, fashionable people get together, they are so surrounded by elegance and gaiety, so well provided with all that can please and entertain, they are in no hurry to separate. Gentlemen especially are often in request on such occasions and Mr Rochester is so talented and so lively in society, that I believe he is a general favourite.

The ladies are very fond of him, although you would not think his appearance calculated to recommend him particularly in their eyes, but I suppose wealth and good blood make amends for any little fault of look.'

I tried to keep my voice level as I next spoke. 'Are there ladies at the Leas?'

'Oh, yes. There are Mrs Eshton and her two daughters. Very elegant young ladies they are indeed. And there are the Honourable Blanche and Mary Ingram, the most beautiful women, although I haven't seen Blanche for six or seven years since she was a girl of eighteen. She came here to a Christmas ball and party Mr Rochester gave. You should have seen the dining room that day – how richly it was decorated, how brilliantly lit up! I should think there were fifty ladies and gentlemen present, all of the first county families, and Miss Ingram was considered the belle of the evening.'

'How did you get to see her?'

'As it was Christmastime, the servants were allowed to assemble in the hall, to hear some of the ladies sing and play. Mr Rochester asked me to come in, and I sat down in a quiet corner and watched them. I never saw a more splendid scene. The ladies were magnificently dressed, and most of them – at least most of the younger ones – looked handsome, but Miss Ingram was certainly the queen.'

'And what was she like?'

'Tall, fine bust, sloping shoulders, long, graceful neck and an olive complexion, dark and clear. I'd say her eyes were rather like Mr Rochester's: large and black, and as brilliant as her jewels. And then she had such a fine head of hair, raven-black and so becomingly arranged, a crown of thick plaits behind, and in front the longest, the glossiest curls I ever saw. She was dressed in pure white, an amber-coloured scarf was passed over her shoulder and across her breast, tied at the side, and descending in long, fringed ends below her knee. She wore an amber-coloured flower, too, in her hair, which contrasted well with the jetty mass of her curls.'

'She was greatly admired, of course?'

'Yes, indeed. And not only for her beauty, but for her accomplishments. She was one of the ladies who sang. A gentleman accompanied her on the piano. She and Mr Rochester sang a duet.'

'Mr Rochester? I was not aware he could sing.'

'Oh! He has a fine bass voice, and an excellent taste for music.'

'And Miss Ingram. What sort of a voice had she?'

'A very rich and powerful one. She sang delightfully. It was a treat to listen to her. Oh, and she played afterwards. I am no judge of music, but Mr Rochester is, and I heard him say her execution was remarkably good.'

'Not an average schoolgirl, then,' I thought, remembering how I had tried to impress him with my rendition of a hymn.

'And this beautiful and accomplished lady, she is not yet married?'

'It appears not. I fancy neither she nor her sister have very large fortunes. Old Lord Ingram's estates were chiefly entailed, and the eldest son came in for everything almost.'

'But I wonder no wealthy nobleman or gentleman has

taken a fancy to her. Mr Rochester, for instance. He is rich, is he not?'

'Oh! Yes. But you see there is a considerable difference in age. Mr Rochester is nearly forty and she is but twenty-five.'

'What of that? More unequal matches are made every day.'

'True, yet I should scarcely fancy Mr Rochester would entertain an idea of the sort. When he weds, no doubt he will make a fine match.'

I busied myself with my napkin, worrying the corner. My fingers were trembling, but I took pains for Mrs Fairfax not to see my inner turmoil. And what inner turmoil, dear reader, for I had but one thought: surely no greater fool than Jane Eyre had never breathed the breath of life.

'You,' I said to myself, 'a favourite with Mr Rochester? You gifted with the power of pleasing him? You of importance to him in any way? Cover your face and be ashamed! He said something in praise of your eyes, did he? Blind puppy! Open their lids and look on your own stupidity. It does good to no woman to be flattered by her superior, who cannot possibly intend to marry her, and it is madness in all women to let a secret love kindle within them, which, if unreturned and unknown, must devour the life that feeds it. Or, if discovered and responded to, must lead into a certain course of ruin from which there is no extrication.'

'But you eat nothing, Miss Eyre,' said Mrs Fairfax, interrupting my thoughts. 'You have scarcely tasted anything since you began tea.'

'I am too thirsty to eat. Will you let me have another cup?'

I was about again to torture myself and revert to the probability of a union between Mr Rochester and the beautiful Blanche, but Adèle came in, and the conversation was turned into another channel.

NINE

A week passed, and no news arrived of Mr Rochester. Ten days, and still he did not come. Mrs Fairfax said she should not be surprised if he were to go straight from the Leas to London, and thence to the Continent, and not show his face again at Thornfield for a year to come. He had not infrequently quitted it in a manner quite as abrupt and unexpected. When I heard this, I was beginning to feel a strange chill and failing at the heart.

I was in a perpetual and sickening sense of disappointment, but I forced myself to concentrate on the practical truth of the matter. When I gazed upon my reflection in the glass, plaiting my hair before bed, I counselled myself with reason.

'You have nothing to do with the master of Thornfield, further than to receive the salary he gives you for teaching his protégée, and to be grateful for such respectful and kind treatment as, if you do your duty, you have a right to expect at his hands. Be sure that is the only tie he seriously acknowledges between you and him, so don't make him the object of your fine feelings, your raptures, agonies and so forth. He is not of your order. Keep to your caste and be too self-respecting to lavish the love of the whole heart, soul and strength, where such a gift is not wanted and would be despised.'

I went on with each day's business in outward tranquillity, but vague suggestions kept wandering across my brain of reasons why I should quit Thornfield, and I kept involuntarily framing advertisements and pondering conjectures about new situations.

Mr Rochester had been absent upwards of a fortnight, when the post brought Mrs Fairfax a letter at breakfast time.

'It is from the master,' she said.

I involuntarily spilt half the contents of my cup into my saucer.

'Mr Rochester is not likely to return soon, I suppose?'

'Indeed he is. In three days, he says. That will be next Thursday. And not alone either. I don't know how many of the fine people at the Leas are coming with him, but he sends directions for all the best bedrooms to be prepared and the library and drawing rooms are to be cleaned out. I am to get more kitchen hands from the George Inn, at Millcote, and from wherever else I can. The ladies will bring their maids and the gentlemen their valets, so we shall have a full house of it.' And Mrs Fairfax swallowed her breakfast and hastened away to commence operations.

The next three days were, as she had foretold, a frenzy of activity. I had thought all the rooms at Thornfield beautifully clean and well arranged, but it appears I was mistaken.

Three women were got to help and such scrubbing, such brushing, such washing of paint and beating of carpets, such taking down and putting up of pictures, such polishing of mirrors and lustres, such lighting of fires in bedrooms, such airing of sheets and feather beds on hearths, I never beheld, either before or since.

Adèle ran quite wild in the midst of it. From school duties she was exonerated. Mrs Fairfax had pressed me into her service, and I was all day in the storeroom, helping (or hindering) her and the cook, learning to make custards and cheesecakes and French pastry, to truss game and garnish dessert dishes.

The party were expected to arrive on Thursday afternoon, in time for dinner at six. During the intervening period I had no time to nurse my feelings and I believe I was as active and gay as anybody – Adèle excepted. Still, now and then, I received a damping check to my cheerfulness and was, in spite of myself, thrown back on the region of doubts and portents, and dark conjectures.

This was when I chanced to see the third-storey staircase door (which of late had always been kept locked) open slowly, and give passage to the form of Grace Poole, in prim cap, white apron and handkerchief. I watched her glide along the gallery, her quiet tread muffled in her slippers. She would thus descend to the kitchen once a day, eat her dinner, smoke a moderate pipe on the hearth and go back, carrying her pot of porter with her, for her private solace, in her own gloomy, upper haunt.

The strangest thing of all was that not a soul in the house, except me, noticed her habits, or seemed to marvel at them. No one discussed her position or employment, no one pitied her solitude or isolation. I once, indeed, overheard part of a dialogue between Leah and one of the charwomen, of which Grace formed the subject. Leah had been saying something I had not caught, and the charwoman remarked, 'She gets good wages, I guess?'

'Yes,' said Leah. 'I wish I had as good, not that mine are to complain of as there's no stinginess at Thornfield, but they're not one fifth of the sum Mrs Poole receives.'

'She is a good hand, I daresay,' said the charwoman.

'She understands what she has to do. Nobody better,' rejoined Leah significantly, 'and it is not everyone could fill her shoes – not for all the money she gets.'

But here Leah turned and perceived me, and she instantly gave her companion a nudge.

'Doesn't she know?' I heard the woman whisper.

Leah shook her head, and the conversation was of course dropped. All I had gathered from it amounted to this: that there was a mystery at Thornfield from which I was being purposely and deliberately excluded.

Thursday came at last, and after a long wait (with both Adèle and Mrs Fairfax worrying the curtains by the windows as they waited for movement on the long drive – and positively driving me to distraction) four equestrians galloped up towards the hall, and after them came two open carriages.

Fluttering veils and waving plumes adorned the vehicles. Two of the cavaliers were young, dashing-looking gentlemen, and the third was Mr Rochester, on his black horse, Mesrour, Pilot bounding before him. My heart fluttered at the sight of him, and it was all I could do not to put my hand out to wave, but then I saw that at his side rode a lady, and he and she were the first of the party. Her purple riding habit almost swept the ground, her veil streamed long on the breeze, and mingling with its transparent folds, and gleaming through them, shone rich raven ringlets.

'Miss Ingram!' exclaimed Mrs Fairfax, and away she hurried to her post below.

The cavalcade, following the sweep of the drive, quickly turned the angle of the house, and I lost sight of it. Adèle now petitioned to go down, but I took her on my knee, and gave her to understand that she must not on any account think of venturing in sight of the ladies, either now or at any other time, unless expressly sent for. That Mr Rochester would be very angry if she misbehaved. She shed tears on being told this, but as I began to look very grave, she consented at last to wipe them.

A joyous stir was now audible in the hall. Gentlemen's deep tones and ladies' silvery accents mixed harmoniously together, and distinguishable above all, though not loud, was the sonorous voice of the master of Thornfield Hall, welcoming his fair and gallant guests under its roof. Then light steps ascended the stairs and there was a tripping through the gallery, and soft cheerful laughs, and opening and closing doors, and, for a time, a hush.

Presently the chambers gave up their fair tenants one after another. Each came out gaily and airily, with dresses that gleamed in the light of the huge chandelier on the landing. For a moment they stood grouped together at the other extremity of the gallery, conversing in a key of sweet subdued vivacity, then they descended the staircase almost as noiselessly as a bright mist rolls down a hill. Their collective appearance had left on me an impression of high-born elegance, such as I had never before received.

I found Adèle peeping through the schoolroom door, which she held ajar. 'What beautiful ladies!' cried she in English. 'Oh, I wish I might go to them! Do you think Mr Rochester will send for us after dinner?'

'No, indeed, I don't. Mr Rochester has something else to think about. Never mind the ladies tonight. Perhaps you will see them tomorrow. Here is your dinner.'

I beckoned her over to the table, to where I had laid out the chicken and tarts I had foraged from the kitchen. Whilst she was distracted, I went to the door, pretending to shut it, but using the opportunity to observe the ladies myself.

There were two, I noticed, who lingered last to go down the stairs. Both were young and sweet, with the careless elegance I had long associated with the very wealthy, but had never seen at close hand before. Their skin was glowing, their blue and yellow taffeta gowns, respectively, were frilled and decorated in what I assumed was the latest fashion, their soft rounded breasts pushed out at the front, and they carried about them a knowingness of their beauty which quite enhanced it.

One of them – the blonde one in yellow dress – skipped along the carpet and stopped in front of the glass to admire her reflection. The other, her friend in the blue dress, stood slightly behind her, putting her chin on her shoulder so that their two faces could be admired side by side.

From where I was standing, looking through the chink in the door, I could see what a charming picture they made. They were certainly self-regarding, admiring one other and touching each other's perfect curls, the dark-haired girl inserting her little finger into a blonde ringlet in such an affectionate and intimate way that it captivated my attention.

I was about to force myself to turn away, reminding myself to mind my own business, when the girl in the blue dress kissed the cheek of the girl in the yellow dress, who turned so that the next kiss landed on her mouth. They stayed for a second kissing in a way that made heat rise unbidden in my cheeks.

And as I watched this private moment of intimacy, I suddenly recalled the girls at Lowood and how Emma and I had once kissed in such a way. But our exploratory kisses had seemed innocent and young, and yet these two eligible ladies caressed one another in a way that seemed to suggest something altogether more knowing – even something similar to the kiss I had shared with their host. Despite my very best efforts to put it out of my mind, my kiss with Mr Rochester flooded my memory, making my sex ache with longing as I watched the two beauties across the landing.

Then the one in the blue dress pinched the nipple of the girl in the yellow through the silk material of her dress. She let out a laugh and, in turn, pinched the bottom of the blue girl, reaching out to slap her playfully with her fan, as she ran out of sight towards the stairs.

I shut the door hastily, returning my attention to Adèle, and yet the image of the two ladies stayed with me, making my pulse race. I found myself wondering, what kind of guests had Mr Rochester invited to Thornfield?

I allowed Adèle to sit up much later than usual, for she declared she could not possibly go to sleep while the doors kept opening and shutting below, with people bustling about. Besides, she added, a message might possibly come from Mr Rochester when she was undressed, 'et alors quel dommage!'

I told her stories as long as she would listen to them and then, for a change, I took her out into the gallery. The hall lamp was now lit, and it amused her to look over the balustrade and watch the servants passing backwards and forwards. When the evening was far advanced, a sound of music issued from the drawing room, whither the piano had been removed.

Adèle and I sat down on the top step of the stairs to listen. Presently a voice mixed with the rich tones of the instrument. It was a lady who sang, and very sweet her notes were. The solo over, a duet followed, and then a joyous conversational murmur filled up the intervals. I listened long and suddenly I discovered that my ear was wholly intent on analysing the mingled sounds, and trying to discriminate amidst the confusion of accents those of Mr Rochester, and when it caught them, which it soon did, it found a further task in framing the tones, rendered by distance inarticulate, into words.

The clock struck eleven. I looked at Adèle, whose head leant against my shoulder. Her eyes were waxing heavy, so I took her up in my arms and carried her off to bed. It was near one before the gentlemen and ladies sought their chambers. I waited, hoping for Mr Rochester to knock on mine, but hours passed and I was left alone.

TEN

The next day was as fine as its predecessor. It was devoted by the party to an excursion to some site in the neighbourhood. They set out early before noon, some on horseback, the rest in carriages, and I witnessed both the departure and the return. Miss Ingram, as before, was the only lady equestrian and, as before, Mr Rochester galloped at her side. The two rode a little apart from the rest. I pointed out this out to Mrs Fairfax, who was standing at the window with me.

'You said it was not likely they should think of being married,' I said, 'but you see Mr Rochester evidently prefers her to any of the other ladies.'

'Yes, I daresay. There's no doubt he admires her.'

'And she him,' I added. 'Look how she leans her head towards him as if she were conversing confidentially. I wish I could see her face. I haven't had a glimpse of it yet.'

'You will see her this evening,' answered Mrs Fairfax. 'I happened to remark to Mr Rochester how much Adèle wished to be introduced to the ladies, and he said, "Oh! let her come into the drawing room after dinner. And request Miss Eyre to accompany her."'

It was with some trepidation that I perceived the hour approach when I was to go with my charge to the drawing room. Adèle had been in a state of ecstasy all day, after hearing she was to be presented to the ladies in the evening, and it was not until she commenced the operation of dressing that she sobered down.

Then the importance of the process quickly steadied her, and by the time she had her curls arranged in well-smoothed, drooping clusters, her pink satin frock put on, her long sash tied, and her lace mittens adjusted, she looked as grave as any judge. When she was dressed, she sat demurely down in her little chair, taking care previously to lift up the satin skirt for fear she should crease it, and assured me she would not stir until I was ready.

This I quickly was. My best dress (the silver-grey one, purchased for Miss Temple's wedding, and never worn since) was soon put on, my hair was soon smoothed, my sole ornament, the pearl brooch, soon attached to my dress. We descended.

Fortunately there was another entrance to the drawing room than that through the saloon where they were all seated at dinner. We found the apartment vacant, a large fire burning silently on the marble hearth, and wax candles shining in bright solitude, amid the exquisite flowers with which the tables were adorned. The crimson curtain hung before the arch. Slight as was the separation this drapery formed from the party in the adjoining saloon, they spoke in so low a key that nothing of their conversation could be distinguished beyond a soothing murmur.

A soft sound of rising now became audible as the curtain was swept back from the arch. Through it appeared the dining room, with its lit lustre pouring down light on the silver and glass of a magnificent dessert service covering a long table. A band of ladies stood in the opening. They entered and the curtain fell behind them.

There were but eight, yet somehow, as they flocked in, they gave the impression of a much larger number. Some of them were very tall. Many were dressed in white and all had a sweeping amplitude of array that seemed to magnify their persons as a mist magnifies the moon. I rose and curtseyed to them. One or two bent their heads in return, the others only stared at me.

They dispersed about the room, reminding me, by the lightness and buoyancy of their movements, of a flock of white plumy birds. Some of them threw themselves in half-reclining positions on the sofas and ottomans and the cushion-covered day bed. The rest gathered in a group round the fire and all talked in a low but clear tone which seemed habitual to them.

I heard a muffled laugh. With a little movement of my head and a tilt backwards, I could see around the edge of a screen to where a velvet couch was hidden from view from the other ladies. Two women were reclining on the couch together and, although they were differently dressed, I recognized them as the two I had seen kissing last night.

One plucked a peacock feather from a jar and began

tickling the arm and neck of the other. Even here, were they so brazen as to risk discovery by the group? Yet, as they giggled in their private enclosure, kicking off their slippers, none of the other women seemed to heed them any attention.

My eyes were now drawn to the fireplace, to where two ladies were standing and, when they were addressed by one of their friends, I realized that they were Blanche and Mary Ingram. Mary was too slim for her height, but Blanche was moulded like a goddess. I regarded her, of course, with special interest. First, I wished to see whether her appearance accorded with Mrs Fairfax's description, and second, whether I thought she was likely to suit Mr Rochester's taste.

As far as person went, she answered point for point to Mrs Fairfax's description. The noble bust, the sloping shoulders, the graceful neck, the dark eyes and black ringlets were all there. Her face had high features and had a self-conscious air of pride and, although some might call her beautiful, I knew instinctively that I neither liked nor trusted her.

And did I now think Miss Ingram such a choice as Mr Rochester would be likely to make? I could not tell. I did not know his taste in female beauty. If he liked the majestic, she was the very type of majesty and she was accomplished, sprightly. Most gentlemen would admire her, I thought. And that he did admire her, I already seemed to have obtained proof. To remove the last shade of doubt, it remained but to see them together.

You are not to suppose, reader, that Adèle has all this time been sitting motionless on the stool at my feet. No, when the ladies entered, she rose, advanced to meet them, made a stately reverence, and said with gravity, 'Bonjour, Mesdames.'

And Miss Ingram had looked down at her and exclaimed, 'Oh, what a little poppet!'

One of the ladies I was later to know as Lady Lynn remarked, 'It is Mr Rochester's ward, I suppose – the little French girl he was speaking of.'

Amy and Louisa Eshton, two more of the party, cried out simultaneously, 'What a love of a child!'

And then they had called her to a sofa, where she now sat, ensconced between them, chattering alternately in French and broken English, absorbing the young ladies' attention and getting spoilt to her heart's content.

For the last few months, I had grown in affection towards Adèle and I hoped that it was a mutual admiration, for certainly our days passed together happily. I had felt a kinship forming, taking into account, of course, that I was her superior – in that I was her governess. Yet amongst these ladies, I saw that I was far from her superior. She was Mr Rochester's ward and as such enjoyed a privilege that separated us entirely in rank. Without a glance backwards, Adèle took to the ladies' company like a cygnet gliding amongst swans.

At last coffee is brought in, and the gentlemen are summoned. I sit in the shade amongst the shadows, behind the window curtain which half hides me. Again the arch yawns and they come. My heart pounds so hard in my breast, for I know he must approach.

The collective appearance of the gentlemen, like that of

the ladies, is very imposing. They are all costumed in black. Most of them are tall and all of them young and handsome. Henry and Frederick Lynn are very dashing sparks indeed and Captain Dent is a fine soldierly man. Mr Eshton, the young magistrate of the district, is gentleman-like, his eyebrows and whiskers dark, which gives him something of the appearance of a 'père noble de théâtre'. Lord Ingram, like his sisters, is very tall, and like them, also, he is handsome, but he shares Mary's apathetic look. He seems to have more length of limb than vivacity of blood or vigour of brain.

And where is Mr Rochester?

He comes in last. I am not looking at the arch, yet I see him enter. I try to concentrate my attention on the crochet work I have in my hands, to see only the silver beads and silk threads that lie in my lap, but I distinctly behold his figure, and I inevitably recall the moment when I last saw it, just after he had kissed me.

What had occurred since, his visit to his friends, and now their presence in his house, had all calculated to change his and my relative positions so utterly in my mind. And now, how distant, how far estranged we were! So far estranged, that I did not expect him to come and speak to me. I did not wonder, when, without looking at me, he took a seat at the other side of the room, and began conversing with some of the ladies.

Most true is it that 'beauty is in the eye of the gazer'. My master's olive face, square brow, broad and jetty eyebrows, deep eyes, strong features, firm mouth were not beautiful, according to rule, but they were more than beautiful to me. They were full of an interest and an influence that quite mastered me, that took my feelings from my own power and fettered them in his. I had not intended to love him. The reader knows I had wrought hard to extirpate from my soul the germs of love there detected. Yet now, at the first renewed view of him, he made me love him without looking at me.

When I saw Mr Rochester smile, his stern features softened, his eye grew both brilliant and gentle, its ray both searching and sweet. He was talking, at the moment, to Louisa and Amy Eshton. I expected their eyes to fall, their colour to rise under that look, yet I was glad when I found they were in no sense moved.

'He is not to them what he is to me,' I thought, 'he is not of their kind. I believe he is of mine. I am sure he is. I feel akin to him. I understand the language of his countenance and movements, and though rank and wealth sever us widely, I have something in my brain and heart, in my blood and nerves, that assimilates me mentally to him. While I breathe and think, I must love him.'

Coffee is handed. The ladies, since the gentlemen entered, have become lively as larks, the conversation is brisk and merry. Mr Frederick Lynn has taken a seat beside Mary Ingram, and is showing her the engravings of a splendid volume. She looks, smiles now and then, but apparently says little, although occasionally she gasps and put her hand to her mouth in shock. I wonder what the engravings express in order to be so absorbing and for the colour to rise in her cheeks so.

Lord Ingram has taken possession of an ottoman at the feet of the two ladies behind the screen, who I now know are Lady Fulbright and Miss Dupret. He is fully in view of the whole party, although the ladies are still partially hidden. From my vantage point, I see a stockinged foot of one of the ladies spider up his neck. He turns to the ladies and says something soft. I hear laughter. Then he takes the toe in his mouth and pretends to bite it.

Flustered, I turn my attention to Adèle, who is next to the dashing Captain Dent. He is trying to talk French with her, but Louisa, who is next to him, laughs at his blunders. Behind the back of Adèle, I see her put her arm around his neck and whisper something in his ear. Of this intimate moment, Adèle is either unaware, or, I realize when she turns to look at them, she is entirely comfortable.

Was this the kind of atmosphere that Céline Varens conjured in her parlour, I wondered? Is that why Adèle seems to fit in so easily? I remembered now with clarity, the first time I had met her and the suggestive song she had sung for me. Was this the intimate, warm atmosphere that people of Mr Rochester's standing were used to? Nothing could be further from the stiff, religious, formal evenings at my Aunt Reed's house in my youth. Whereas there everything had been cold and dead, here the room before me seemed to be pulsing with life.

With whom will Blanche Ingram pair? She is standing alone at the table, bending gracefully over an album, her hips swaying suggestively. She flicks her tongue back and forth along the top bow of her lip. She seems waiting to be sought, but she will not wait too long. She herself selects a mate.

Mr Rochester, having quitted the Eshtons, stands on the hearth as solitary as she stands by the table. She confronts him, taking her station on the opposite side of the mantelpiece.

'Mr Rochester, I thought you were not fond of children?'

'Nor am I.'

'Then, what induced you to take charge of such a little doll as that?' (pointing to Adèle). 'Where did you pick her up?'

'I did not pick her up. She was left on my hands.'

'You should have sent her to school.'

'Schools are so dear.'

'Why, I suppose you have a governess for her. I saw a person with her just now. Is she gone? Oh, no! There she is still, behind the window-curtain. You pay her, of course. I should think it quite as expensive, more so, for you have them both to keep in addition.'

I feared – or should I say, hoped? – the allusion to me would make Mr Rochester glance my way, and I involuntarily shrank farther into the shade, but he never turned his eyes.

'I have not considered the subject,' he said indifferently, looking straight before him.

'No, you men never do consider economy and common sense. Mary and I have had, I should think, a dozen governesses at least in our day. Half of them detestable and the rest ridiculous. Do you remember Madame Joubert, Theodore?'

Lord Ingram, engaged with the two ladies behind the screen, extricated himself to answer. His cheeks were flushed.

'Governesses? Why yes, dear sister. I had the lot of them.'

Blanche's laugh was loud. 'So you did, you wicked boy. And that is why, Tedo, Mama procured that whey-faced tutor, Mr Vining. He and Miss Wilson, our maidservant, took the liberty of falling in love with each other – at least Tedo and I thought so, and when we caught them together, we used it to get them out of the house.'

'So we did, so we did. But, speaking from experience, there are a thousand reasons why liaisons between governesses and tutors should never be tolerated for a moment in any well-regulated house,' Lord Ingram said. Again I noticed one of the ladies' toes tickling him, threatening to put him off his speech. The others were watching, smiling at his discomfort, but none of them seemed to find it in any way unusual, or any break with decorum.

'That is so typically hypocritical, Tedo,' Mary said.

'Well, I am in a position to know, wouldn't you say? In hindsight, I can say such liaisons are a very bad idea. My governesses were a terrible example to the innocence of childhood.'

Blanche laughed again, as her brother was pulled in by the two ladies assaulting him, and he disappeared behind the screen.

'He is right in some part. Liaisons of such a nature cause distractions and consequent neglect of duty on the part of the attached – mutual alliance and reliance, confidence thence resulting, insolence accompanying, mutiny and general blow-up,' Blanche said, clapping her hands together like two cymbals.

Amy Eshton, not hearing or not heeding this dictum, joined in with her soft, infantine tone. 'Louisa and I used to like our governess. She was such a good creature, she would bear anything. Nothing put her out. She was never cross with us, was she, Louisa?'

'No, never. We might do what we pleased and she was so good-natured, she would give us anything we asked for. Anything at all. We were like Tedo – in a different sort of way—'

'I suppose, now,' said Miss Ingram, curling her lip, 'we shall have an abstract of the memoirs of all the governesses past and the sordid details of their corruption. I again move the introduction of a new topic. Mr Rochester, do you second my motion?'

'Madam, I support you on this point, as on every other.'

'Are you in voice tonight?'

Miss Ingram seated herself with proud grace at the piano and, spreading out her snowy robes in queenly amplitude, commenced a brilliant prelude, talking all the while. Both her words and her air seemed intended to excite not only the admiration, but the amazement of her auditors. She was evidently bent on striking them as something very dashing and daring indeed.

'Oh, I am so sick of the young men of the present day!' she exclaimed, rattling away at the instrument. 'Poor, puny things, not fit to stir a step beyond papa's park gates, nor to go even so far without mama's permission! Creatures so absorbed in care about their pretty faces, and their white hands, and their small feet, as if a man had anything to do with beauty! As if loveliness were not the special prerogative of woman – her legitimate right! I grant an ugly woman is a blot on the fair face of creation, but as to the gentlemen, let them be solicitous to possess only strength, valour and virility. Let their motto be: Hunt, shoot, fight and fornicate. Such should be mine, were I a man.'

'Whenever I marry,' she continued after a pause, filled with the others laughing and gathering round the piano (of her lewd language, there seemed to be nothing but approval from the titillated assembly, and a baffling disregard for it falling on the ears of a child, but Adèle was smiling too), 'I am resolved my husband shall not be a rival, but a foil to me. I will suffer no competitor near the throne. I shall exact an undivided homage. His devotions shall not be shared between me and the shape he sees in his mirror. His attention shall be all mine and he shall devote himself solely to pleasing me in whichever ways I see fit. Every way I see fit,' she added, pointedly. 'Now sing, Mr Rochester, and I will play for you.'

'I am all obedience,' was the response, and I felt a sharp stab of pain as I watched him touch the bare skin of her neck.

He was no more going to acknowledge my presence than love me back. I could see this so plainly now, laid out before me, as he beheld the beautiful Blanche with her swelling breasts and nimble fingers. Compared to one so sensual and strident as she, what a green schoolgirl he must consider me to be. He had even told me so, on more than one occasion, but fool that I was, I had not listened.

'Sing!' said she, and again touching the piano, she commenced an accompaniment in spirited style.

'Now is my time to slip away,' I thought.

But the tones that then severed the air arrested me. Mrs Fairfax had said Mr Rochester possessed a fine voice. He did – a mellow, powerful bass, into which he threw his own feeling, his own force, finding a way through the ear to the heart, and there waking sensation strangely. I waited till the last deep and full vibration had expired, till the tide of talk, checked an instant, had resumed its flow, then I quitted my sheltered corner and made my exit by the side door, which was fortunately near.

Thence a narrow passage led into the hall. In crossing it, I perceived my sandal was loose. I stopped to tie it, kneeling down for that purpose on the mat at the foot of the staircase. I heard the dining room door unclose. A gentleman came out and, rising hastily, I stood face to face with him. It was Mr Rochester.

'How do you do, Miss Eyre?' he asked. All evening, he had not so much as looked in my direction whilst he had been in company, but now that we were alone, I felt his eyes devouring me.

'I am very well, sir.'

'Why did you not come and speak to me in the room?'

'I did not wish to disturb you, as you seemed engaged, sir.'

'What have you been doing during my absence?'

'Nothing in particular. Teaching Adèle as usual.'

'And getting a good deal paler than you were, as I saw at first sight. What is the matter?'

'Nothing at all, sir.'

'Did you take any cold that night you half drowned me?'

'Not in the least.'

He stepped in closer towards me and, lowering his voice, said, 'You were not alarmed by what passed between us?'

That he had dared to mention our moment of passion – that he even remembered it – set my heart racing. I could not begin to divine his own feelings on the matter and yet his concern for my feelings once again ignited the flame of hope, that only a few moments previously had been thoroughly extinguished upon seeing him sing with Blanche.

He put his finger under my chin and forced me to look at him.

'No, sir.'

'Then return to the drawing room. You are deserting too early.'

'I am tired, sir.'

He looked at me and I felt myself drowning in those sparkling, enticing black pools. All the pent-up frustration of the last weeks without him, and now I was a step away from him. The intoxication of him was too much to bear, when I couldn't throw myself into his arms.

'And a little depressed,' he said. 'What about? Tell me.'

'Nothing – nothing, sir. I am not depressed.'

'Oh, but I think you are. So much depressed that a few more words would bring tears to your eyes – indeed, they are there now, shining and swimming, and a bead has slipped from the lash and fallen. If I had time, and was not in mortal dread of some prig of a servant passing, I would know what all this means.'

He took my shoulders and looked desperately about us.

'Well, tonight I excuse you, but understand that so long as my visitors stay, I expect you to appear in the drawing room every evening. It is my wish. I wish to see you whenever I can. Don't neglect it. Now go, and send Mrs Fairfax for Adèle. Goodnight, my . . . my Jane.'

Then, without warning, he planted a quick, tender kiss on my lips.

ELEVEN

Merry days were these at Thornfield Hall, and busy days too. There was life everywhere, movement all day long. You could not now traverse the gallery, once so hushed, nor enter the front chambers, once so tenantless, without encountering a smart lady's maid or a dandy valet. And it was two such servants that I happened to observe together quite by accident on Wednesday morning.

I had released Adèle from her morning's lessons, as Miss Louisa Eshton had appealed on her behalf to Mr Rochester, who had relented and allowed Adèle to join the party for a game of paille-maille on the lawn.

I had gone to Adèle's room in order to find her better shoes, Mrs Fairfax being far too busy to fulfil such a request, and was lingering at the window watching the ladies in fine summer hats and the gentlemen in fawn trousers hitting the ball with a mallet through the iron hoops that had been set into the perfect green turf far below.

I took the moment of solitude to reflect upon my confused feelings towards Mr Rochester. Staring down at him from

Adèle's open window, his laugh wafting distantly to me on the breeze, he seemed so tantalizingly near, and yet so far apart from my influence.

For nearly a week since his hurried kiss, he had hardly acknowledged me, although I had spent an hour each evening after dinner in the drawing room with Adèle as requested, watching Blanche spin her coquetry around him like a cocoon. At a certain point in the evening, however, Adèle and I were always asked to withdraw.

I put Adèle to bed, then stayed in my chamber, my ears straining to hear any clues at to what Mr Rochester and his guests were doing in the candlelit drawing room far below. I was too agitated to sleep, and yet I had always dozed off by the time the drawing-room door finally opened in the small hours, when I awoke suddenly, hearing the guests tiptoeing to bed. Then I stood by my door, willing Mr Rochester to come to me, but he never did. In fact, I rarely heard him enter his own chamber.

I have told you, reader, that I had learned to love Mr Rochester. I could not un-love him now, merely because I found that since our second furtive kiss, he had all but ceased to notice me. I might pass hours in his presence, and he would never once turn his eyes in my direction, because I saw all his attentions appropriated by a great lady, who scorned to touch me with the hem of her robes as she passed, and who, if ever her dark and imperious eye fell on me by chance, would withdraw it instantly as from an object too mean to merit observation.

I could not un-love him, even though I felt sure he would

soon marry this very lady – because I read daily in her a proud security in his intentions respecting her, and because I witnessed hourly in him a style of courtship which, if careless and choosing rather to be sought than to seek, was yet, in its very carelessness, captivating, and in its very pride, irresistible.

There was nothing to cool or banish love in these circumstances, though much to create despair. Much too, you will think, reader, to engender jealousy, if a woman, in my position, could presume to be jealous of a woman in Miss Ingram's.

But I was not jealous. Or very rarely. The nature of the pain I suffered could not be explained by that word. Miss Ingram was a mark beneath jealousy. She was too inferior to excite the feeling. Pardon the seeming paradox, but I mean what I say.

She was very showy, but she was not genuine. She had a fine person, many brilliant attainments, but whilst she excelled at exhibitionism, her mind was poor and her heart barren by nature. She was not good and she was not original. She often repeated phrases from books I had read, passing them off as her own. She advocated a high tone of sentiment, but she did not know the sensations of sympathy and pity. Tenderness and truth were not in her.

Too often she betrayed this, by the spiteful antipathy she had conceived against little Adèle, pushing her away with some nasty comment if she happened to approach her, sometimes ordering her from the room, and always treating her with coldness. Other eyes besides mine watched these manifestations of character – watched them closely, keenly, shrewdly. Yes, the future bridegroom, Mr Rochester himself, exercised over his intended a ceaseless surveillance, and it was from this obvious absence of passion in his sentiments towards her, that my ever-torturing pain arose. Even as I thought this, I beheld from the window, Mr Rochester observing Blanche as she squealed with affected delight at hitting her ball through a hoop.

I saw he was going to marry her, for family, perhaps political reasons, because her rank and connections suited him. Yet I knew that he had not given her his love, and that her qualifications were ill adapted to win from him that treasure. This was the point. This was where the nerve was touched and teased. This was where the fever was sustained and fed. She could not charm him.

If he had kissed her like he had kissed me, or even looked at her in the same way, I should have covered my face, turned to the wall and (figuratively) have died to them. If Miss Ingram had been a good and noble woman, endowed with force, fervour, kindness, sense, I should have had one vital struggle with two tigers – jealousy and despair. Then, my heart torn out and devoured, I should have admired her and acknowledged her excellence, and been quiet for the rest of my days.

'But why can she not influence him more, when she is privileged to draw so near to him?' I asked myself. 'Surely she cannot truly like him, or not like him with true affection! If she did, she need not coin her smiles so lavishly, flash her glances so unremittingly, manufacture airs so elaborate, graces so multitudinous.'

I could not blame Mr Rochester or indeed Miss Ingram for marrying for interest and connections. These were ideas and principles instilled into them, doubtless, from their childhood. All their class held these principles. It seemed to me that, were I a gentleman like him, I would take to my bosom only such a wife as I could love, but there must be arguments against the general adoption of this motive, of which I was quite ignorant. Otherwise I felt sure all the world would act as I wished to act.

But in other points, as well as this, I was growing very lenient towards my master. I was forgetting all his faults, for which I had once kept a sharp lookout. It had formerly been my endeavour to study all sides of his character, to take the bad with the good. Now I saw no bad.

In my protracted musings, I had strayed to Adèle's closet, where her clothes and shoes and hatboxes were neatly arrayed on shelves and hangers, and it was on the rearranging of these shoeboxes that I heard a muffled laugh and voices coming from the next-door chamber, which I knew to be occupied by Lady Fulbright.

I moved the boxes and put my ear to the wall, but as I did so, I noticed the sound was entering the closet through a grate behind one of the hatboxes on a shelf below me.

Gently I removed it and, kneeling down, peered through the iron mesh into the splendid sun-filled chamber next door.

Standing next to the large four-poster bed, smoothing down a pink silk coverlet and arranging the many lace cushions, was Lady Fulbright's maid. Standing behind her was one of the butlers I had passed briefly, but until this moment had not realized was so tall and strikingly good-looking. He grabbed her, twirling her in his arms.

'We will get caught,' the maid whispered, with a laugh in her voice, as he kissed her neck.

'Annie,' he said, pursuing his embrace. 'Lady Fulbright is out on the lawn. Nobody will find us. Come here. I want you.'

She laughed and then he kissed her, deeply this time.

'Here, then,' she said, obviously relenting and glancing at the door.

More fervently they kissed now. My heart thundered against my ribs, as she suddenly withdrew and sat on the edge of the bed in front of him. I watched her slowly unbutton his breeches. I knew what I would see next and I knew I should look away, but I could not. She pulled his stiffening member from the confines of the cloth and gripped it in her fist, running her tongue slowly across her lower lip, as she began to move her hand, pumping it up and down. I watched as it grew further engorged, its tip glistening and wet. As she continued to squeeze, he let out a carnal moan, which made my own sex throb.

Releasing him, she tipped back on the bed, clamouring backwards, raising her skirts and looking at him, biting her lip.

'I like doing it in here,' he said, hurriedly taking off his jacket and unhitching his shirt, then removing it altogether to reveal his broad, muscular torso. 'It reminds me of your mistress, although I don't know which one I'd have first. Fulbright or Dupret.'

I was shocked to hear them talking of Mr Rochester's guests in such terms, but transfixed by the scene I was witnessing.

'You couldn't have either, Jack,' the maid said, pushing herself back on the bed. 'It is not men they desire. I told you. They suck each other's cunnies all night long. Especially if Lord Ingram is there. He likes to watch them together. You'd like that too, wouldn't you? I've seen him touch himself as he watches them, but he is not as big as you.'

She hoisted up her skirts further, to reveal that she was naked below. She put her hand between her legs, parting the dark hair, still looking up boldly at Jack.

He made a primal kind of grunt and fell on top of her. As he thrust inside her, she let out a delighted gasp, drawing her legs up around him and clasping her arms around his neck.

I could see her heels as she pushed down his trousers and then saw his smooth taut buttocks, and her hands gripping them, pulling him deeper into her. Her desire for him matched equally his desire for her, and it was this, her forthright manner, that shocked me the most. That she knew how and what to do with him made my own innocence and lack of skill so obvious to me. I had never even seen a gentleman's member before, but now that I had, I craved to be able to touch one myself, and not only to touch, but to pull deeper and deeper inside me, over and over again, just as Annie was doing now.

My mind flew also to the topic they had been discussing. The two ladies – Lady Fulbright and Miss Dupret – were lovers, just as I had suspected when I had first seen them kissing. Was I now to believe that the seemingly forbidden sapphic passion that Emma and I had once secretly shared was a common practice in society as a whole, or in Mr Rochester's close circle, at least?

My attention was once more seized by the maid and her lover on the bed now. They had coupled so naturally, so easily. This act that I had dreamt of, that I had fantasized about, was happening right before my eyes and I felt my legs become leaden as they filled with blood, and my loins prickled with desire.

His panting became more ragged now, as he continued to thrust into her, now groping at her firm half-exposed breasts.

'Wait,' she breathed. 'Not yet.'

She wriggled out from underneath him. Then she stood leaning over the bed and flipped up her skirts above her waist so I could now see her glistening pink sex. She bent over further, her hand shaking beneath her, pulling her sex wider apart. She turned to look back at him, over her shoulder, her eyes hungry for more.

Now I saw the butler. He was holding his quivering member in one hand. With the other he smoothed his palm over the glistening end. I let out an involuntary gasp, remembering Mr Rochester's hardness against me as we'd kissed. I had been so close to seeing his naked flesh, as I was now observing the butler's in all its fully erect glory.

I could not help myself. In a moment, my hand was inside my own skirt, delving beneath my drawers to find my own sex wet with longing. I rubbed my fingers over my bud, as Bessie had done, and I had solicitously tried to avoid doing in the past few weeks, but it was hopeless. My body held a greater force than the constraints of decorum could place on it.

I watched through the grate, as the butler stood behind the maid and slowly entered her once more. I could see her own fingers feverishly rubbing herself and I rubbed myself too, imagining that it was me, not her being filled by him. Gripping her shoulder and neck, he thrust faster into her, his panting turning into gasps, until finally his whole body shuddered in spasm.

'Shhh,' she said. 'You will get us discovered.'

Her skirts fell as she stood. She smoothed herself down, tucking her loose hair back beneath her maid's cap. She acted for a moment as if nothing had happened, and yet, as she turned to Jack, and helped him refasten his buttons, her eyes were sparkling with mischief.

'And you,' he told her, gripping her in an embrace, 'I will marry one day.' He kissed her, pressing kisses into her cheeks and neck as if he couldn't make enough for the ardour he felt.

'Of course you will,' she laughed. 'Why else would I let you do that to me?'

My throat ran dry as my body tipped into a silent fountain of ecstasy. I pulled away from the grate, in fear of discovery. My heart was pounding, my neck covered in a thin sheen of perspiration. As I stared back at the grate, I remembered Mr Rochester's description of me, that I was a restless bird in a cage. Looking at the metal grille, I felt more certain than ever that I wanted to be free.

I stood up, remembering why I had come into the closet and fearful now that I had been gone too long. Adèle's white shoes were on the shelf ahead of me. I grabbed them and slipped out into the corridor, hopeful that the maid and butler would not see me.

But as I descended the stairs, passing the painting of the naked woman toying with the pearl necklace on her breast, I stopped still, noticing for the first time the knowing expression in her eyes, one I had seen in Miss Ingram's eyes also and in the maid's just now as she had bent over the bed and turned to look at her lover.

Had I been blind all this time? Was I a fool to seek out love, when the whole house, it now seemed, was living in such decadence? Mr Rochester had himself told me that all he wanted was the pleasure of sweet young flesh and I realized now that it was this currency that Blanche was using to buy Mr Rochester's favour. I felt sure of it. But if they were already lovers, how could I compete? My purse was full of the currency my love desired. I had it all to give, and yet how could I, when he presumed me to be so innocent?

TWELVE

That afternoon, the good weather broke, and continuous rain set in for some days, but no damp seemed cast over enjoyment of the party. Indoor amusements only became more lively and varied, in consequence of the stop put to outdoor gaiety.

I wondered what the party were going to do that evening, when a change of entertainment was proposed. They spoke of 'playing charades', but in my ignorance I did not understand the term. The servants were called in, the dining-room tables wheeled away, the lights otherwise disposed, the chairs placed in a semicircle opposite the arch. While Mr Rochester and the other gentlemen directed these alterations, the ladies were running up and downstairs ringing for their maids, although in all the commotion, I did not see Lady Fulbright's maid.

Mrs Fairfax was summoned to give information respecting the resources of the house in shawls, dresses, draperies of any kind, and certain wardrobes of the third storey were ransacked and brought down in armfuls by the maidservants, then a selection was made, and such things as were chosen were carried to the boudoir within the drawing room.

It was late by this time and Adèle and I were coming to the end of our evening in the company of Mr Rochester, but whilst I was trying to find an appropriate moment to extricate ourselves, Mr Rochester had summoned the ladies round him, and was selecting certain of their number to be of his party.

'Miss Ingram is mine, of course,' he said and afterwards he named the two Misses Eshton, and Miss Dent. He looked at me as I happened to be near him.

'Will you play, Miss Eyre?' he asked, but I shook my head. In truth, I could not meet his eye, shaken as I was by what I had witnessed between the maid and the butler earlier in the day and how much my longing for him had added to my secret shame.

He did not insist, which I rather feared he would have done, and he allowed me to return quietly to my usual seat.

'Stay for a moment and see the first charade, then, if it pleases you,' he said.

He and his aids now withdrew behind the curtain. The other party, which was headed by Captain Dent, sat down on the crescent of chairs. One of the gentlemen, Mr Eshton, observing me, seemed to propose that I should be asked to join them, but Miss Mary Ingram instantly shook her head.

'No,' I heard her say. 'She looks too stupid for any game of the sort.'

I bit my lip, busying myself with my sewing, so that they could not observe my flushed cheeks. I opened the casement window behind me a fraction to let the evening breeze cool me.

Before long a bell tinkled, and the curtain drew up. Within the arch, the bulked-out figure of Sir George Lynn, whom Mr Rochester had likewise chosen, was seen enveloped in a white sheet. Before him, on a table, lay open a large book and at his side stood Amy Eshton, draped in Mr Rochester's cloak, and holding a book in her hand.

Somebody, unseen, rang the bell merrily, then Adèle (who had insisted on being one of her guardian's party), bounded forward, scattering round her the contents of a basket of flowers she carried on her arm.

Then appeared the magnificent figure of Miss Ingram, clad in white, a long veil on her head, and a wreath of roses round her brow. By her side walked Mr Rochester, and together they drew near the table. They knelt, while Miss Dent and Louisa Eshton, dressed also in white, took up their stations behind them. A ceremony followed, in dumb show, in which it was easy to recognize the pantomime of a marriage. At its termination, Captain Dent and his party consulted in whispers for two minutes, then the Captain called out, 'Bride!'

Mr Rochester bowed, and the curtain fell.

Two minutes later, Adèle came running in through a side door. 'That is it for us, Mademoiselle,' she told me. 'Mr Rochester wishes us to retire. He told me to tell you.'

I put away my sewing and said our quick 'good evenings', then took her out of the room. I heard the great doors lock quietly behind us as we left. Out in the corridor, Mrs Fairfax was passing and Adèle implored her to take her to the kitchen on account of the fact that she was starving. Mrs Fairfax shook her head in exasperation at me, shooing Adèle in front of her down the far corridor.

Once she was out of sight, I looked back at the locked door, hearing soft laughter on the other side. My curiosity was so aroused, my suspicion so great, that before I had time to censor myself, I had formed a plan. I had to know what I was being excluded from.

In a moment, I had slipped out through the door and, tiptoeing across the front gravel, made it to the casement window I had unlocked, without being discovered. There, I slipped unseen back into the drawing room, hidden from view by the curtains, which were now drawn.

Peeping through the gap, I could see that in the few moments since Adèle and I had left, the atmosphere of the room had changed. Rather than sitting formally apart, the guests now clustered together in amiable companionship, the girls draping their arms across the men's shoulders, the men having dispatched with their jackets and loosened their ties. Both the men and women of the party were smoking and drinking and laughing merrily together.

A considerable interval elapsed before the curtain again rose. Its second rising displayed a more elaborately prepared scene than the last. The drawing room, as I have before observed, was raised two steps above the dining-room, and on the top of the upper step, placed a yard or two back within the room, appeared a large marble basin – which I recognized as an ornament of the conservatory – where it usually stood, surrounded by exotics, and tenanted by gold fish – and whence it must have been transported with some trouble, on account of its size and weight.

Seated on the carpet, by the side of this basin, was seen Mr Rochester, costumed in shawls, with a turban on his head. His dark eyes and swarthy skin suited the costume exactly. He looked the very model of an Eastern mogul.

Miss Ingram came into view. She, too, was attired in oriental fashion, a crimson scarf tied sash-like round the waist, an embroidered handkerchief knotted about her temples, her beautifully moulded arms bare, one of them upraised in the act of supporting a pitcher, poised gracefully on her head. Both her cast of form and feature, her complexion and her general air, suggested the idea of some princess and such was doubtless the character she intended to represent.

But as she turned fully now to face the audience, what shocked me and made me gasp aloud was that her breasts were naked, but for the thinnest gossamer veils – which, more shockingly still, she now unfastened and allowed to shimmer to the floor, as if blown from her body by an Arabic breeze.

Instead of the shame and mortification one would have expected from a lady of her station thus exposed, she rather seemed to delight in flaunting her luxuriously large breasts with their dusky pink nipples. There was a smattering of applause, which she did not acknowledge, staying steadfastly in the role of her character.

She approached the basin, and bent over it as if to fill

her pitcher, before once more lifting it above her head, and in doing so, her buxom breasts swung magnificently together. The personage – Mr Rochester – on the well-brink now seemed to accost her, to make some request. She hasted, let down her pitcher on her hand, and gave him to drink, pouring water from the pitcher directly into his mouth, so that it spilled over his chin.

From the bosom of his robe he then produced a casket, opened it and showed magnificent bracelets and earrings. She acted astonishment and admiration, kneeling as he laid the treasure at her feet. Incredulity and delight were expressed by her looks and gestures. The stranger fastened the bracelets on her arms and the rings in her ears and clipped beads around her neck.

I could not help but feel faint as I saw Mr Rochester's fingers linger at Miss Ingram's breasts. His familiarity with them, his lack of shock at their presence so near him, or this display of intimacy in front of his guests, showed plainly that this was not the first time he had beheld them.

My heart pounded. I could not believe my eyes and the scene before me. And yet, I reminded myself that for my eyes this had not been intended. My mind told me I should be outraged by the spectacle I was witnessing, and yet my heart? My heart only yearned to see more, to learn more, to be worthy of being included in their world of shared sensuality.

The divining party again laid their heads together, but apparently they could not agree about the word or syllable the scene illustrated. Miss Ingram seemed in no hurry to leave her seated position, her breasts so close to Mr Rochester, who had drawn apart a little way. She toyed with the beads, now nestling between her cleavage, attempting to draw his glance back to her. When he did look at her, she put the tip of her tongue on her teeth and deliberately looked into his lap. Mr Rochester raised his eyebrows at her.

The others seemed oblivious to this suggestive and lascivious exchange, as Captain Dent, their spokesman, was demanding 'the tableau of the whole' whereupon the curtain again descended.

On its third rising only a portion of the drawing room was disclosed, the rest being concealed by a screen, hung with some black gauze material. Behind it, a candelabra full of red candles made the whole scene flicker. It was possible to make out the silhouette of a man being forced into a chair by a woman. I noted, with an intoxicating mixture of horror and enthralment, from the silhouette of the woman that she was most certainly naked, for there was no clothing to mask her fine silhouette. The man in the chair seemed naked, too, although it was difficult to know for certain as the candles cast such a low light on the scene.

The woman seemed to be chaining the man's ankles and feet to the chair and I wondered whether it was the chair that I had seen on the third floor when I had first arrived. As he moved, seemingly in distress at his fate, I heard a chain clank.

Behind the screen, the woman, whom I assumed must be Miss Ingram, mounted the occupant of the chair, kneeling astride him. What was I to believe? That the naked man was

Mr Rochester and Miss Ingram was impaling herself on him, letting him enter her, just as the butler had coupled with the maid earlier?

A fury of jealousy began to possess me, yet just as my breath stayed caught in my throat, she leant back and, raising her hand, struck the face of her captive in an exaggerated gesture, and I reminded myself that this was merely play-acting and only a charade.

'Easy!' called out Captain Dent, with a chuckle. 'Mason!'

The others in the party shrugged at each other, obviously not understanding his reference, but Captain Dent induced the others into merry applause. 'Very good, very good.'

I saw the female form bend down and kiss the man in the chair, their foreheads touching – and again felt the nip of the serpent of jealousy that was coiling around me. Then once again, the curtain fell.

A sufficient interval elapsed for the performers to resume their ordinary costume, before they re-entered the dining room. Mr Rochester led in Miss Ingram. She was complimenting him on his acting. I withdrew even further into my hiding place.

'Do you know,' said she, 'that, of the three characters, I liked you in the last best? You play the part of a submissive well.'

'Well, whatever I am, remember you are my wife. We were married an hour since, in the presence of all these witnesses and you have been quick to consummate the union, have you not?'

She giggled, and her colour rose. I felt my breath catch

again, and tried to remind myself once again to chain the serpent. Surely, he must be toying with her, still play-acting in front of the crowd.

'Now, Dent,' continued Mr Rochester, 'it is your turn.' And as the other party withdrew, he and Miss Ingram took two of the vacated seats.

Miss Ingram placed herself at her leader's right hand, the other diviners filling the chairs on each side of him and her. I did not now watch the actors. I no longer waited with interest for the curtain to rise. My attention was absorbed by the spectators, and in particular Mr Rochester, whose arm was around Miss Ingram's waist, her head touching his shoulder, the very picture of conspiratorial closeness.

Then Lady Fulbright and Miss Dupret came. They were both in black corsets which barely covered their nipples, with nothing below apart from stockings on their legs. Some garters banded their legs above their knees. Feathered plumes rose from their piled-up hair.

I confess my shock at seeing them dressed so scantily and outrageously was numbed in the aftermath of Miss Ingram's show. Even so, I stared, incredulous as they both proceeded to dance with each other, stepping out of the shadows and kicking up their legs in quite a skilled formation. But as they did so, I saw that they were both naked beneath their corsets, each high kick revealing a flash of thick pubic hair and what lay beneath.

My heart pounded as they finished the dance and joined in an embrace, then, undoing each other's corsets, revealed their naked breasts which they set about touching, rubbing their erect nipples against one another's, before kissing each other deeply and lingeringly before the audience, forcibly reminding me what the maid and butler had said about them earlier, as my blood pounded hotly in my ears.

'Paris,' called out Miss Ingram. 'I'm right, am I not? But do carry on.'

I felt myself becoming hopelessly, pitifully aroused. Pitifully, because I saw now so clearly that, as I had begun to suspect, my innocence was my curse. I could never be part of this world, the world that Mr Rochester had told me repulsed him and tortured his soul with guilt. And yet, here he was, enjoying the spectacle he had foretold he would.

Feeling my heart in my throat, I watched Mr Rochester turn to Miss Ingram, and Miss Ingram to him. I saw her incline her head towards him, till the jetty curls almost touched his shoulder, as she took his hand in her own, and, looking him directly in the eye, took his long finger in her mouth to suck it.

And I saw too, that they were not the only ones to have been aroused. Lord Ingram and Captain Dent were both now deeply kissing the Misses Eshton and, fearful of my own discovery and the heated desire rising in me so furiously, I shrank behind the curtain and slipped back out into the dark night.

THIRTEEN

I hardly slept that night, so feverous were my thoughts, and when my dreams did come, they were occupied by the manifestations of the scene in the drawing room, which I knew, even as I went to bed, had almost certainly been happening behind the closed doors since Mr Rochester's guests had arrived. No wonder he had hardly noticed me. I had been moping around like a lovesick fool, and all the time he was enjoying the pleasures of the flesh he had so ashamedly confided in me were his vice.

I ought to have been shocked, repelled even, but such were my feelings towards him that it only made me want to be accepted by him all the more. His flesh was weak, although his spirit was noble, and in this regard, I felt that we were more similar than he would ever know. I should, I knew, have felt guilty for spying on him and his guests, but the scene I had observed had only made me hungry to witness more.

I felt that I had looked through a secret door into a heady world which made everything else seem dull by comparison, while the conventions of society that I had been taught were of the utmost sanctity, had now been revealed as stifling in their rigidity. So much so, that now I wondered whether they had been rendered invalid in the face of my yearnings for a spiritual and, yes, physical awakening.

No wonder these ladies and gentlemen were in no hurry to leave Thornfield, I mused, still incredulous about everything I had seen. No wonder they were so happy. And it was Mr Rochester who was the instigator of it all. What would happen if he ever were to radiate his talent for pleasure in my direction once again? The very thought made me weak. I knew I would capitulate, reader. So weak was I with longing, I knew that I would not be able to resist him.

It was on the afternoon of the following day that I was summoned downstairs by a message. Someone wanted me in Mrs Fairfax's room. On repairing thither, I found a man waiting for me, having the appearance of a gentleman's servant. He was dressed in deep mourning, and the hat he held in his hand was surrounded with a black band.

'I daresay you hardly remember me, Miss,' he said, rising as I entered, 'but my name is Leaven. I lived coachman with your aunt Mrs Reed when you were at Gateshead, eight or nine years since, and I live there still.'

My mind was wrenched away from its constant musings over the secret charades I had seen, to the reality before me. Remembering my manners, I extended my hand.

'Oh, Robert! How do you do? I remember you very well. You used to give me a ride sometimes on Miss Georgiana's bay pony.' I shook his hand. 'Are the family well at the house, Robert?'

'I am sorry I can't give you better news of them, Miss. They are very bad at present.'

'I hope no one is dead,' I said, glancing at his black dress.

He too looked down at the black band round his hat and replied, 'Mr John died yesterday was a week, at his chambers in London.'

'Mr John?' I recalled my cruel cousin, who had teased me and hit me and caused me to get into trouble with my aunt.

'Yes.'

'And how does his mother bear it?'

'Why, you see, Miss Eyre, it is not a common mishap. His life has been very wild, and these last three years he gave himself up to strange ways. He ruined his health and his estate amongst the worst men and the worst women. He got into debt and into jail. His mother helped him out twice, but as soon as he was free, he returned to his old companions and habits. He came down to Gateshead about three weeks ago and wanted Missis to give up all to him, but Missis refused. So he went back again, and the next news was that he was dead. How he died, God knows! They say he killed himself.'

I was silent.

'Missis had been out of health herself for some time. The loss of money and fear of poverty were quite breaking her down. The information about Mr John's death brought on a stroke. She was three days without speaking, but last Tuesday she seemed rather better, and finally when she could speak, she said, "Bring Jane. Fetch Jane Eyre." I left Gateshead yesterday, and if you can get ready, Miss, I should like to take you back with me early tomorrow morning.'

I was surprised by this news and vexed that he had asked me to go with him, but even so, I felt a family duty rising. I had not expected to hear from my Aunt Reed ever again, but the fact that she had sent for me gave me some indication of her suffering. She was an old woman by now, I calculated, and despite my resolve to dismiss her from my thoughts, I felt a shiver of pity for her now.

'Yes, Robert, I shall be ready. It seems to me that I ought to go.'

'I think so too, Miss. But I suppose you will have to ask leave before you can get off?'

'Yes, and I will do it now.'

Having directed him to the servants' hall, and recommended him to the care of John's wife, and the attentions of John himself, I went in search of Mr Rochester, only to discover that he had been summoned to Millcote on business, and was not likely to return till late.

The afternoon was wet and the party seemed subdued and flat without Mr Rochester. I had readily agreed to go in the morning with Robert, but I was most agitated to be called away on such an errand. I had not liked living with my aunt, who had been a cruel woman and her desire to see me now, when she had caste me out of her house was most vexing.

Furthermore, the thought of leaving Thornfield and going back alone to that barren house to tend a dying woman filled me with dread. I did not want to leave Thornfield. Not whilst Mr Rochester was here. I had not had time to understand my confused feelings towards the secret activities of my master and his guests, but now I had discovered them, the thought of being ripped away from discovering more made me feel feverous with anxiety. And then another, even more worrying thought occurred. What if he left before I returned?

Whether it was my own perception, or something real, I knew not, but the whole house seemed to have an agitated, restless atmosphere that afternoon. A walk the party had proposed to take to see a gipsy camp, lately pitched on a common beyond Hay, was deferred due to the weather. Some of the gentlemen were gone to the stables, some, together with the younger ladies, were playing billiards in the billiard room.

Blanche Ingram had first murmured over some sentimental tunes and airs on the piano, and then, having fetched a novel from the library, had flung herself in haughty listlessness on a sofa, and prepared to beguile, by the spell of fiction, the tedious hours of Mr Rochester's absence.

I stared at her, without her noticing me. I had watched her with Mr Rochester last night, and yet, in the light of day, she seemed so calm, so demure and ladylike. How could she be so normal, when she had enjoyed him all to herself the night before? I could not fathom it.

It was verging on dusk, and the clock had already given warning of the hour to dress for dinner, when little Adèle, who knelt by me in the drawing-room window seat, suddenly exclaimed, 'Voilà, Monsieur Rochester, qui revient!'

I turned, and Miss Ingram darted forwards from her sofa. The others, too, looked up from their several occupations, for at the same time a crunching of wheels and a splashing tramp of horse-hoofs became audible on the wet gravel. A post-chaise was approaching.

'What can possess him to come home in that style?' said Miss Ingram. 'He rode Mesrour (the black horse), did he not, when he went out? And Pilot was with him. What has he done with the animals?'

As she said this, she approached her tall person and ample garments so near the window, that I was obliged to bend back almost to the breaking of my spine. In her eagerness she did not observe me at first, but when she did, she curled her lip and moved to another casement. The post-chaise stopped, the driver rang the doorbell and a gentleman alighted attired in travelling garb. But it was not Mr Rochester. It was a tall, fashionable-looking man. A stranger.

'How provoking!' exclaimed Miss Ingram. 'You tiresome monkey!' she said to Adèle. 'Who perched you up in the window to give false intelligence?' And she cast on me an angry glance, as if it were my fault.

Some voices were audible in the hall, and soon the newcomer entered. He bowed to Miss Ingram.

'It appears I come at an inopportune time, madam,' said he, 'when my friend, Mr Rochester, is away from home, but I arrive from a very long journey, and I think I may presume so far on old and intimate acquaintance as to install myself here till he returns.'

His manner was polite, and his accent, in speaking, struck

me as being somewhat unusual. Not precisely foreign, but still not altogether English. His age might be about Mr Rochester's, between thirty and forty, and he was a fine-looking man, at first sight especially.

The sound of the dressing-bell dispersed the party. It was not till after dinner that I saw him again, when he seemed quite at his ease. For a handsome and friendly-looking man, he repelled me exceedingly in comparison to Mr Rochester. There was no power in that smooth-skinned face of a full oval shape, no firmness in that aquiline nose and small cherry mouth, there was no thought on the low, even forehead, no command in that blank, brown eye.

As I sat in my usual nook, and looked at him with the light of the girandoles on the mantelpiece beaming full over him – for he occupied an armchair drawn close to the fire – I compared him less and less favourably with Mr Rochester.

Two or three of the gentlemen sat near him, and I caught at times scraps of their conversation across the room. At first I could not make much sense of what I heard, for the discourse of Louisa Eshton and Mary Ingram, who sat nearer to me, confused the fragmentary sentences that reached me at intervals. These last were discussing the stranger. They both called him 'a beautiful man'. Louisa said he was 'a love of a creature', and she 'adored him'. And Mary insisted that his 'pretty little mouth, and nice nose' were her ideal of the charming.

'And what a sweet-tempered forehead he has!' cried Louisa. 'So smooth. None of those frowning irregularities I dislike so much, and such a placid eye and smile!'

And then, to my great relief, Mr Henry Lynn summoned them to the other side of the room, to settle some point about the deferred excursion to Hay Common.

I was now able to concentrate my attention on the group by the fire, and I presently gathered that the newcomer was called Mr Mason. The name seemed familiar. Had Mason not been mentioned during the secret charades I had witnessed? Captain Dent had referred to Mason, as if it signified some secret kind of code. But now I reasoned that it could not be the same man, especially when I learned that he was but just arrived in England, and that he came from some hot country.

Presently the words Jamaica, Kingston, Spanish Town, indicated the West Indies as his residence and it was with no little surprise I gathered, ere long, that he had there first seen and become acquainted with Mr Rochester. He spoke of his friend's dislike of the burning heats, the hurricanes and rainy seasons of that region. I knew Mr Rochester had been a traveller as Mrs Fairfax had said so, but I thought the continent of Europe had bounded his wanderings. Till now I had never heard a hint given of visits to more distant shores.

I was pondering these things, when an incident, and a somewhat unexpected one, broke the thread of my musings. Mr Mason, shivering as someone chanced to open the door, asked for more coal to be put on the fire, which had burnt out its flame, though its mass of cinder still shone hot and red. The footman who brought the coal, in going out, stopped near Mr Eshton's chair, and said something to him in a low voice, of which I heard only the words, 'old woman, quite troublesome'.

'Tell her she shall be put in the stocks if she does not take herself off,' replied the magistrate.

'No, stop!' interrupted Captain Dent. 'Don't send her away, Eshton, we better consult the ladies.' And speaking aloud, he continued, 'Ladies, you talked of going to Hay Common to visit the gipsy camp. Sam here says that one of the old Mother Bunches is in the servants' hall at this moment, and insists upon being brought in before "the quality", to tell them their fortunes. Would you like to see her?'

'Surely, Captain,' said Mary Ingram, 'you would not encourage such a low impostor? Dismiss her.'

'But I cannot persuade her to go away, my lady,' said the footman, 'nor can any of the servants. Mrs Fairfax is with her just now, entreating her to be gone, but she has taken a chair in the chimney-corner, and says nothing shall stir her from it till she gets leave to come in here.'

'What does she want?' asked Miss Eshton.

'"To tell the gentry their fortunes," she says, ma'am. And she swears she must and will do it.'

'What is she like?'

'A shockingly ugly old creature, miss.'

'Why, she's a real sorceress!' cried Frederick Lynn. 'Let us have her in, of course.'

'To be sure,' rejoined his brother, 'it would be a thousand pities to throw away such a chance of fun.'

'I have a curiosity to hear my fortune told. Therefore, Sam, order her forward,' Blanche said.

'Yes, yes, yes!' the others all chimed in. 'Let her come. It will be excellent sport!'

The footman still lingered. 'She looks such a rough one,' said he.

'Go!' said Miss Ingram, and the man went.

Excitement instantly seized the whole party. A running fire of jests was proceeding when Sam returned.

'She won't come now,' said he. 'She says it's not her mission to appear before the "vulgar herd" (them's her words). I must show her into a room by herself, and then those who wish to consult her must go to her one by one.'

'Show her into the library, of course,' said Blanche. 'It is not my mission to listen to her before the vulgar herd either. I mean to have her all to myself. Is there a fire in the library?'

'Yes, ma'am.'

Again Sam vanished and mystery, animation, expectation rose to full flow once more.

'She's ready now,' said the footman, as he reappeared. 'She wishes to know who will be her first visitor.'

'I think I had better just look in upon her before any of the ladies go,' said Captain Dent.

'Tell her, Sam, a gentleman is coming.'

Sam went and returned.

'She says, sir, that she'll have no gentlemen. They need not trouble themselves to come near her,' he added, with difficulty suppressing a titter, 'she only wants to converse with the young and single ladies.'

'By Jove, she has taste!' exclaimed Henry Lynn.

Miss Ingram rose solemnly. 'I'll go first,' she said, sweeping past her in stately silence. She passed through the door which Captain Dent held open, and we heard her enter the library.

A comparative silence ensued. Amy and Louisa Eshton tittered under their breath, and looked a little frightened.

The minutes passed very slowly. Fifteen were counted before the library door again opened. Miss Ingram returned to us through the arch.

Would she laugh? Would she take it as a joke? All eyes met her with a glance of eager curiosity, and she met all eyes with one of rebuff and coldness. She looked neither flurried nor merry. She walked stiffly to her seat, and took it in silence.

'Well, Blanche?' said Lord Ingram.

'What did she say, sister?' asked Mary.

'What did you think? How do you feel? Is she a real fortune teller?' demanded the Misses Eshton and Lady Fulbright, who had recently joined the group.

'Now, now, good people,' returned Miss Ingram, 'don't press upon me. I have seen a gipsy vagabond. She has practised in hackneyed fashion the science of palmistry and told me what such people usually tell. My whim is gratified and now I think Mr Eshton will do well to put the hag in the stocks tomorrow morning, as he threatened.'

Miss Ingram took a book, leant back in her chair and so declined further conversation. I watched her for nearly half an hour, during which time she never turned a page, and her face grew darker, more dissatisfied and disappointed. She had obviously not heard anything to her advantage and it seemed to me, from her prolonged fit of gloom that she herself, notwithstanding her professed indifference, attached undue importance to whatever revelations had been made her.

Meantime, Mary Ingram, Amy and Louisa Eshton, declared they dared not go alone and yet they all wished to go. A negotiation was opened through the medium of the ambassador, Sam, and after much pacing to and fro, till, I think, the said Sam's calves must have ached with the exercise, permission was at last, with great difficulty, granted for the three to wait upon her in a body.

Their visit was not so still as Miss Ingram's had been. We heard hysterical giggling and little shrieks proceeding from the library and, at the end of about twenty minutes, they burst the door open, and came running across the hall, as if they were half scared out of their wits.

'I am sure she is something not right!' they cried, one and all. 'She told us such things! She knows all about us!' and they sank breathless into the various seats the gentlemen hastened to bring them.

Pressed for further explanation, they declared she had told them of things they had said and done when they were mere children, described books and ornaments they had in their boudoirs at home, keepsakes that different relations had presented to them. They affirmed that she had even divined their thoughts, and had whispered in the ear of each the name of the person she liked best in the world, and informed them of what they most wished for.

Here the gentlemen interposed with earnest petitions to be further enlightened on these two last-named points, but they got only blushes, ejaculations, tremors and titters, in return for their importunity.

In the midst of the tumult, and while my eyes and ears were fully engaged in the scene before me, I heard someone close at my elbow. I turned and saw Sam.

'If you please, miss, the gipsy declares that there is another young unmarried lady in the room who has not been to her yet, and she swears she will not go till she has seen all. I thought it must be you. There is no one else for it. What shall I tell her?'

'Oh, I will go by all means,' I answered. I was glad of the unexpected opportunity to gratify my much-excited curiosity. I slipped out of the room, unobserved by any eye – for the company were gathered in one mass about the trembling trio just returned – and I closed the door quietly behind me.

'If you like, miss,' said Sam, 'I'll wait in the hall for you. If she frightens you, just call and I'll come in.'

'No, Sam, return to the kitchen. I am not in the least afraid.' Nor was I, but I was a good deal interested and excited.

FOURTEEN

The library looked tranquil enough as I entered it, and the fortune teller was seated snugly enough in an easy chair at the chimney corner. She had on a red cloak and a black bonnet. Or rather, a broad-brimmed gipsy hat, tied down under her chin.

An extinguished candle stood on the table. She was bending over the fire, and seemed reading in a little black book, like a prayer book, by the light of the blaze. She muttered the words to herself, as most old women do, while she read. She did not desist immediately on my entrance as it appeared she wished to finish a paragraph.

I stood on the rug and warmed my hands, which were rather cold with sitting at a distance from the drawing-room fire. I felt now as composed as ever I did in my life. There was nothing indeed in the gipsy's appearance to trouble one's calm. She shut her book and slowly looked up. Her hat brim partially shaded her face, yet I could see, as she raised it, that it was a strange one. It looked all brown and black. Wiry hair bristled out from beneath a white band which passed under her chin, and came half over her cheeks, or rather jaws. Her eye confronted me at once, with a bold and direct gaze.

'Well, and you want your fortune told?' she said, in a voice as harsh as her features.

'I don't care about it. You may please yourself, but I ought to warn you, I have no faith.'

'It is just like you to be so impudent. I expected it of you. I heard it in your step as you crossed the threshold.'

'Did you? You've a quick ear.' How the old crone could glean that from my tread, I had no idea.

'I have. And a quick eye and a quick brain.'

'You need them all in your trade.'

'I do, especially when I've customers like you to deal with. Why don't you tremble?'

'I'm not cold.'

'Why don't you turn pale?'

'I am not sick.'

'Why don't you consult my art?'

'I'm not silly.'

The old crone sniggered under her bonnet. She then drew out a short black pipe, and, lighting it, began to smoke. Having indulged a while, she raised her bent body, took the pipe from her lips, and while gazing steadily at the fire, said very deliberately, 'You are cold. You are sick and you are silly.'

'Prove it,' I rejoined.

'I will, in few words. You are cold, because you are alone. No contact strikes the fire from you that is in you. You are sick, because the best of feelings, the highest and the sweetest given to man, keeps far away from you. You are silly, because, suffer as you may, you will not beckon it to approach, nor will you stir one step to meet it where it waits you.'

She again put her short black pipe to her lips, and renewed her smoking with vigour. In honesty, her words struck a chord within me, but I was determined not to get drawn in.

'You might say all that to almost anyone who you knew lived as a solitary dependant in a great house.'

'I might say it to almost anyone, but would it be true of almost anyone?'

'In my circumstances.'

'Yes. Just so, in your circumstances. But find me another precisely placed as you are.'

'It would be easy to find you thousands.'

'You could scarcely find me one. If you knew it, you are peculiarly situated. Very near happiness. Yes, within reach of it. The materials are all prepared. There only wants a movement to combine them.'

'I don't understand.'

'If you wish me to speak more plainly, show me your palm.'

'And I must cross it with silver, I suppose?'

'To be sure.'

I gave her a shilling, which she put into an old stocking that she took out of her pocket, and having tied it round and returned it, she told me to hold out my hand. I did. She approached her face to the palm, and pored over it without touching it.

'It is too fine,' she said. 'I can make nothing of such a hand as that. It is almost without lines. Besides, what is in a palm? Destiny is not written there.'

'I believe you,' I said.

'No,' she continued, 'it is in the face. On the forehead, about the eyes, in the lines of the mouth. Kneel, and lift up your head.'

I knelt within half a yard of her. She stirred the fire, so that a ripple of light broke from the disturbed coal. The glare, however, as she sat, only threw her face into deeper shadow. Mine, it illumined.

'I wonder with what feelings you came to me tonight,' she said, when she had examined me a while. 'I wonder what thoughts are busy in your heart during all the hours you sit in yonder room with the fine people flitting before you like shapes in a magic lantern. Just as little sympathetic communion passing between you and them as if they were really mere shadows of human forms, and not the actual substance.'

'I feel tired often, sleepy sometimes, but seldom sad.'

'Then you have some secret hope to buoy you up and please you with whispers of the future?'

'No, not I. The utmost I hope is to save money enough out of my earnings to set up a school some day in a little house rented by myself.'

'A mean nutriment for the spirit to exist on and sitting in that window seat (you see I know your habits)—'

'You have learned them from the servants.'

'Ah! You think yourself sharp. Well, perhaps I have. To

speak truth, I have an acquaintance with one of them, Mrs Poole—'

I started to my feet when I heard the name.

'You have, have you?' I thought. 'There is devilry in the business after all, then!'

'Don't be alarmed,' continued the strange being. 'She's a safe hand is Mrs Poole. Close and quiet. Anyone may have confidence in her. But, as I was saying. Sitting in that window seat, do you think of nothing but your future school? Have you no present interest in any of the company who occupy the sofas and chairs before you? Is there not one face you study? One figure whose movements you follow with at least curiosity?'

'I like to observe all the faces and all the figures.'

'But do you never single one from the rest. Or it may be, two?'

'I do frequently when the gestures or looks of a pair seem telling a tale. It amuses me to watch them.'

'What tale do you like best to hear? What scenes do you best like to see?'

My mind wandered back to the secret charades I had witnessed, but I could not confess to the gipsy any of what I had seen. I had no desire to bring Mr Rochester's household into disrepute or reveal myself as the voyeur I was.

'Their conversations generally run on the same theme – courtship and the promise to end in the same catastrophe. Marriage.'

'And do you find that a monotonous theme?'

'I don't care about it. It is nothing to me.'

'Nothing to you? When a lady, young and full of life and health, charming with beauty and endowed with the gifts of rank and fortune, sits and smiles in the eyes of a gentleman you—'

'I what? I don't know the gentlemen here. I have scarcely interchanged a syllable with one of them and as to thinking well of them, I consider some respectable, and others young, dashing, handsome and lively, but certainly they are all at liberty to be the recipients of whose smiles they please, without my feeling disposed to consider the transaction of any import to me.'

'You don't know the gentlemen here? You have not exchanged a syllable with one of them? Will you say that of the master of the house!'

'He is not at home.'

'A profound remark! A most ingenious quibble! He went to Millcote this morning, and will be back here tonight or tomorrow. Does that circumstance exclude him from the list of your acquaintance? Blot him, as it were, out of existence?'

'No, but I can scarcely see what Mr Rochester has to do with the theme you had introduced.'

'I was talking of ladies smiling in the eyes of gentlemen and of late so many smiles have been shed into Mr Rochester's eyes that they overflow like two cups filled above the brim. Have you never remarked that?'

'Mr Rochester has a right to enjoy the society of his guests.'

'No question about his right, but have you never observed that, of all the tales told here about matrimony, Mr Rochester has been favoured with the most lively and the most continuous, has he not? And, looking forward, you have seen him married, and beheld his bride happy?'

'Humph! Not exactly. Your witch's skill is rather at fault sometimes.'

'What the devil have you seen, then?'

'Never mind. I came here to inquire, not to confess. Is it known that Mr Rochester is to be married?'

'Yes. To the beautiful Miss Ingram.'

'Shortly?'

'Appearances would warrant that conclusion and, no doubt (although, with an audacity that wants chastising out of you, you seem to question it), they will be a superlatively happy pair. He must love such a handsome, noble, witty, accomplished lady and probably she loves him, or, if not his person, at least his purse. I know she considers the Rochester estate eligible to the last degree, though (God pardon me!) I told her something on that point about an hour ago which made her look wondrous grave. The corners of her mouth fell half an inch. I would advise her suitor to look out. If another comes, with a longer or clearer rent-roll, he's out.'

I found this piece of news most interesting, as it somewhat explained Blanche's countenance upon her return from the library, yet I refused to be drawn by the old hag into making some kind of mistake.

'I did not come to hear Mr Rochester's fortune. I came to hear my own and you have told me nothing of it.'

'Your fortune is yet doubtful. When I examined your face, one trait contradicted another. Chance has meted you a measure of happiness. That I know. I knew it before I came here this evening. She has laid it carefully on one side for you. I saw her do it. It depends on yourself to stretch out your hand, and take it up, but whether you will do so, is the problem I study. Kneel again on the rug.'

'Don't keep me long. The fire scorches me.'

She did not stoop towards me, but only gazed, leaning back in her chair as I knelt.

'The flame flickers in the eye and the eye shines like dew. It looks soft and full of feeling. It smiles at my jargon although an unconscious sadness weighs on the lid which signifies melancholy resulting from loneliness. It turns from me as it will not suffer further scrutiny as it seems to deny, by a mocking glance, the truth of the discoveries I have already made, yet despite such pride, the eye is favourable.

'As to the mouth, it delights at times in laughter, though I daresay it would be silent on much the heart experiences. Mobile and flexible, it was never intended to be compressed in the eternal silence of solitude. It is a mouth which should speak much and smile often, and have much human affection and kisses bestowed upon it.

'I see no enemy to a fortunate issue but in the brow. To me, that brow professes to say, "I can live alone, if self-respect, and circumstances require me so to do. I need not sell my soul to buy bliss. I have an inward treasure born with me, which can keep me alive if all extraneous delights should be withheld, or offered only at a price I cannot afford to give."'

The old woman shifted.

'I think I rave in a kind of exquisite delirium,' she

continued. 'I should wish now to protract this moment ad infinitum, staring at your face, but I dare not. So far I have governed myself thoroughly. I have acted as I inwardly swore I would act, but going further might try me beyond my strength. Rise, Miss Eyre, the play is played out.'

The old woman's voice had changed and, alarmed, I was up on my knees. Suddenly, her accent, her gesture, and all were familiar to me as my own face in a glass, as the speech of my own tongue. I got up.

The flame illuminated her hand stretched out and I at once noticed that hand. It was no more the withered limb of old lady than my own. It was a rounded supple member, with smooth fingers, symmetrically turned, a broad ring flashed on the little finger, and stooping forward, I looked at it, and saw a gem I had seen a hundred times before. Again I looked at the face, which was no longer turned from me.

'Well, Jane, do you know me?' asked the familiar voice.

'Only take off the red cloak, sir, and then—'

'But the string is in a knot. Help me.'

'Break it, sir.' I watched him pull at the tight knot beneath his hood.

'There, then. It's off.' And Mr Rochester stepped out of his disguise.

'It is true. I could stare upon your face all night,' he said. Then, stepping towards me, he pressed my cheeks in his hands and all the passion I had been storing up threatened to overwhelm me as I stared into his eyes. I longed for him to kiss me like he had in his room.

'I am sorry, Jane, dearest Jane,' he said, stopping and stroking my hair away from my face. 'I had to think of a conceit to get you alone.'

My heart soared with his confession. 'What a strange idea!'

'But well carried out, eh? Don't you think so?'

I laughed, incredulously. 'With the ladies you must have managed well.'

'But not with you?'

'You did not act the character of a gipsy with me.'

'What character did I act? My own?'

'No, some unaccountable one. In short, I believe you have been trying to draw me out – or in. You have been talking nonsense to make me talk nonsense. It is scarcely fair, sir.'

'Do you forgive me, Jane?' he asked, smiling into my eyes.

For weeks now, since our last brief moment – when he had quickly, furtively kissed me – I had yearned to be alone with him, but in the intervening time, seeing what I had seen, learning what I had learnt about his guest, I now felt a shyness in his presence that I had not felt before.

'I will think about it,' I said.

There was a creak outside the door and voices in the corridor. He glanced over my shoulder towards them.

'I should go,' I said, remembering my place. I had already been in here far longer than the others.

'Stay a moment and tell me what the people in the drawing room yonder are doing.'

'Discussing the gipsy, I daresay.'

'Let me hear what they said about me.'

'But I had better not stay long, sir. It must be near eleven o'clock.'

He pulled up the small ottoman next to the armchair and took my hand to lead me to it. So close to him now, so near the warmth of the fire, alone in conspiratorial conversation, I recalled all those heady evenings we had spent before his guests arrived, and I confess the pressing business of asking his permission for leave to visit my aunt went straight out of my head. Instead, I felt a renewed surge of hope. It was all I could to stop myself from sinking into his arms once more.

'What has everyone been doing all day?'

I could hardly recall. I could only stare at his face. 'Well, nothing has happened. Oh, except a stranger has arrived here since you left this morning,' I said.

'A stranger! Well, who can it be? I expected no one. Is he gone?'

'No, not at all. He said he had known you long, and that he could take the liberty of installing himself here till you returned.'

'The devil he did! Did he give his name?'

'His name is Mason, sir, and he comes from the West Indies. From Spanish Town, in Jamaica, I think.'

Mr Rochester was standing near me and had taken my hand, as if to lead me to a chair. As I spoke he gave my wrist a convulsive grip. The smile on his lips froze and a spasm caught his breath.

'Mason! The West Indies!' he said, in the tone one might fancy a speaking automaton to enounce its single words.

'Mason! Here?' he reiterated, now whiter than ashes. He staggered. 'Not Mason. Not now. If Mason is here . . . then we – I – am undone.'

'Do you feel ill, sir?' I inquired.

'Jane, you offered me your shoulder once before, let me have it now.'

'Yes, sir, yes. And my arm. What can I do?'

I took him to the armchair and he sat down heavily, and made me sit beside him. Holding my hand in both his own, he gazed on me with the most troubled look.

'I wish I were on a quiet island with only you. And trouble, and danger, and hideous recollections were far removed from me.'

'Can I help you, sir? I'd give my life to serve you.'

'Jane, if aid is wanted, I'll seek it at your hands, I promise you that. For the others cannot know. They must not know.'

'Tell me what to do. I'll try, at least, to do it,' I said, although in truth I had no idea how I could help him when he was being so agitated and enigmatical.

'Fetch me now, Jane, a glass of wine from the dining room. They will be at supper there. Tell me if Mason is with them and what he is doing.'

I went. I found all the party in the dining room at supper, as Mr Rochester had said. They were not seated at table, as the supper was arranged on the sideboard. Each had taken what he chose, and they stood about here and there in groups, their plates and glasses in their hands. Everyone seemed in high glee. Laughter and conversation were general and animated. Mr Mason stood near the fire, talking to Captain

Dent, and appeared as merry as any of them. I filled a wine glass (I saw Miss Ingram watch me frowningly as I did so – she thought I was taking a liberty, I daresay), and I returned to the library.

Mr Rochester's extreme pallor had disappeared, and he looked once more firm and stern. He took the glass from my hand, swallowed the contents and returned it to me. 'What are they doing, Jane?'

'Laughing and talking, sir.'

'They don't look grave and mysterious, as if they had heard something strange?'

'Not at all. They are full of jests and gaiety.'

'And Mason?'

'He was laughing too.'

He held his forehead in his fingers. I longed to stroke his hair, to soothe him of his anxiety and find out what it was that had made him so agitated.

'You are so good, so pure, Jane. You see only the good intentions in people. But what if all these people came in a body and spat at me, what would you do?'

'Turn them out of the room, sir, if I could.'

He half smiled. 'But if I were to go to them, and they only looked at me coldly, and whispered sneeringly amongst each other, and then dropped off and left me one by one, what then? Would you go with them?'

'I'd rather think not, sir. I should have more pleasure in staying with you.'

'To comfort me?'

'Yes, sir, to comfort you, as well as I could.'

'And if they laid you under a ban for adhering to me?'

'I should care nothing about it.'

He cupped my face with his hand, tenderly looking into my eyes. 'You are my sweet angel,' he said. 'Now, go back into the room, step quietly up to Mason, and whisper in his ear that Mr Rochester is come and wishes to see him. Show him in here and then leave me.'

'Yes, sir.'

I did his behest. The company all stared at me as I passed straight among them. I sought Mr Mason, delivered the message and preceded him from the room. I ushered him into the library, and then I went upstairs.

At a late hour, after I had been in bed some time, I heard the visitors repair to their chambers with much mirth. I distinguished Mr Rochester's voice, and heard him say, 'This way, Mason. This is your room.'

He spoke cheerfully and his gay tones set my heart at ease on one account, but by another I was most vexed. I had not asked for his permission to leave and neither did I want to leave now. Had he not confessed to me himself that he had contrived the situation this evening, disguised himself as a fortune teller, just to be able to talk to me alone?

My heart swelled with pride. I had not been wrong to trust that organ, after all.

FIFTEEN

I had forgotten to draw my curtain, which I usually did, and also to let down my window-blind. The consequence was that when the moon, which was full and bright (for the night was fine), came in her course to that space in the sky opposite my casement, and looked in at me through the unveiled panes, her glorious gaze roused me.

Awaking in the dead of night, I opened my eyes on her disc – silver-white and crystal clear. It was beautiful, but too solemn. I half rose, and stretched my arm to draw the curtain.

Good God! What a cry!

The night – its silence – its rest, was rent in twain by a savage, sharp, shrill sound that ran from end to end of Thornfield Hall.

My pulse stopped. My heart stood still. My stretched arm was paralysed. The cry died, and was not renewed.

It came out of the third storey, for it passed overhead. And overhead – yes, in the room just above my chamber-ceiling – I now heard a struggle. A deadly one it seemed from the noise – and a half-smothered voice shouted, 'Help!

help! help!' three times rapidly. 'Will no one come?' it cried. Then, while the staggering and stamping went on wildly, I distinguished through plank and plaster: 'Rochester! Rochester! For God's sake, come!'

A chamber door opened. Someone ran, or rushed, along the gallery. Another step stamped on the flooring above and something fell. Then there was silence.

I had put on some clothes, though horror shook all my limbs and I crept out from my apartment. The sleepers were all aroused. Terrified murmurs sounded in every room as door after door opened. One looked out and another looked out and soon the gallery filled. Gentlemen and ladies alike had quitted their beds.

'Who is hurt?'

'What has happened?'

'Fetch a light!'

'Is it fire?'

'Are there robbers?'

Voices came through the shadows. But for the moonlight they would have been in complete darkness. They ran to and fro and crowded together in confusion.

'Where the devil is Rochester?' cried Captain Dent. 'I cannot find him in his bed.'

'Here! Here!' was shouted in return. 'Be composed, all of you. I'm coming.'

The door at the end of the gallery opened, and Mr Rochester advanced with a candle. He had just descended from the upper storey. One of the ladies ran to him directly and she seized his arm. It was Miss Ingram.

'What awful event has taken place?' said she. 'Speak! Let us know the worst at once!'

'Don't pull me down or strangle me,' he replied, for the Misses Eshton were clinging about him now.

'All's right. All's right!' he cried. 'It's a mere rehearsal of *Much Ado about Nothing*. Ladies, keep off, or I shall wax dangerous.'

And dangerous he looked. His black eyes darted sparks. Calming himself by an effort, he added, 'A servant has had the nightmare, that is all. She's an excitable, nervous person. She construed her dream into an apparition, or something of that sort, no doubt, and has taken a fit with fright. Now, then, I must see you all back into your rooms, for, till the house is settled, she cannot be looked after.

'Gentlemen, have the goodness to set the ladies the example. Miss Ingram, I am sure you will not fail in evincing superiority to idle terrors. Amy and Louisa, return to your nests like a pair of doves, as you are. My dears,' he added to Lady Fulbright and Miss Dupret, 'you will take cold to a dead certainty, if you stay in this chill gallery any longer.'

And so, by dint of alternate coaxing and commanding, he contrived to get them all once more enclosed in their dormitories. The fact that several – including Lord Ingram, Miss Dupret and Lady Fulbright – were clearly sharing their rooms for the night, was not remarked upon. I did not wait to be ordered back to mine, but retreated unnoticed, as unnoticed I had left it.

Not, however, to go to bed. On the contrary, I dressed myself carefully. The sounds I had heard after the scream, and the words that had been uttered, had probably been heard only by me, for they had proceeded from the room above mine, but they assured me that it was not a servant's dream which had thus struck horror through the house and that the explanation Mr Rochester had given was merely an invention framed to pacify his guests.

I dressed, then, to be ready for emergencies. When dressed, I sat a long time by the window looking out over the silent grounds and silvered fields and waiting for I knew not what. It seemed to me that some event must follow the strange cry, struggle and call.

I had promised I would help Mr Rochester and I felt sure that he would call upon my aid. I felt sure, too, after what had passed between us in the library, he thought of me differently to his guests, and not in an insubordinate way, but as his true equal.

Stillness returned. Each murmur and movement ceased gradually, and in about an hour Thornfield Hall was again as hushed as a desert. It seemed that sleep and night had resumed their empire. Meantime the moon declined. She was about to set. Not liking to sit in the cold and darkness, I thought I would lie down on my bed, dressed as I was. I left the window, and moved with little noise across the carpet. As I stooped to take off my shoes, a cautious hand tapped low at the door.

'Are you up?' asked the voice I expected to hear.

'Yes, sir.'

'And dressed?'

'Yes.'

'Come out, then, quietly.'

I obeyed. Mr Rochester stood in the gallery holding a light.

'I want you,' he said, staring into my eyes. For a second, I thought he meant for himself, then he inclined his head along the corridor. 'Come this way. Take your time, and make no noise.'

My slippers were thin. I could walk the matted floor as softly as a cat. He glided up the gallery and up the stairs, and stopped in the dark, low corridor of the fateful third storey. I had followed and stood at his side.

'Have you a sponge in your room?' he asked in a whisper.

'Yes, sir.'

'Have you any salts? Volatile salts?'

'Yes.'

'Go back and fetch both.'

I returned, sought the sponge on the washstand, the salts in my drawer, and once more retraced my steps. He still waited holding a key in his hand. Approaching one of the small, black doors, he put it in the lock, then he paused, and addressed me again.

'You don't turn sick at the sight of blood?'

'I think I shall not. I have never been tried yet.'

I felt a thrill while I answered him, but no coldness and no faintness.

'Just give me your hand,' he said, 'it will not do to risk a fainting fit.'

I put my fingers into his.

'Warm and steady,' was his remark. Then he turned the key and opened the door.

I saw a room I remembered so vividly the day Mrs Fairfax had showed me over the house and which I had privately revisited since. It was hung with the tapestries I had studied hard – to my shame – but I saw now that one of them was looped up in one part, revealing a door. I was shocked. I had never realized that my private musings might have been so easily discovered.

This door was open and a light shone out of the room within. I heard thence a noise – a heavy panting. Mr Rochester, putting down his candle, said to me, 'Wait a minute,' and he went forward to the inner apartment. A shout of laughter greeted his entrance, noisy at first, and terminating in Grace Poole's own goblin 'Ha! Ha!' He made some sort of arrangement without speaking, though I heard a low voice address him and when he came out, he closed the door quietly behind him.

'Here, Jane!' he said.

I walked round to the other side of a large bed, which with its drawn curtains concealed a considerable portion of the chamber. An easy chair was near the bedhead and a man sat in it, in trousers that were ripped apart at their tops and a torn linen shirt revealing his stomach. His feet were bare. He was still, his head leant back and his eyes were closed. Mr Rochester held the candle over him. I recognized in his pale and seemingly lifeless face the stranger, Mason. I saw too that the linen of his shirt was streaked in blood. Livid bruises were forming around his neck and wrists.

'Hold the candle,' said Mr Rochester, and I took it. He fetched a basin of water from the washstand. 'Hold that,' said he. I obeyed. He took the sponge, dipped it in, and moistened the corpse-like face. Then he asked for my smelling-bottle, and applied it to the nostrils. Mr Mason shortly unclosed his eyes and groaned. Mr Rochester opened the shirt of the wounded man and I saw livid cuts from a birch. I would know them anywhere, having been caned once by my cousin.

He sponged away blood, which was trickling fast down.

'Is there immediate danger?' murmured Mr Mason.

'Pooh! No, a mere scratch. Don't be so overcome, man. Bear up! I'll fetch a surgeon for you now, myself.'

'Take me back to her, Fairfax. Let me go back.'

'Not a chance. You'll be able to be removed by morning, I hope. Jane,' he continued.

'Sir?'

'I shall have to leave you in this room with this gentleman, for an hour, or perhaps two hours. You will sponge the blood as I do when it returns. If he feels faint, you will put the glass of water on that stand to his lips, and your salts to his nose. You will not speak to him on any pretext – and – Richard, it will be at the peril of your life if you speak to her. Open your lips and I'll not answer for the consequences.'

Again the poor man groaned. He looked as if he dared not move. Fear, either of death or of something else, appeared almost to paralyse him. Mr Rochester put the now bloody sponge into my hand, and I proceeded to use it as he had done. He watched me a second, then saying, 'Remember! No conversation,' then he left the room.

I experienced a strange feeling as the key grated in the lock, and the sound of his retreating step ceased to be heard.

Here then I was in the third storey, fastened into one of its mystic cells, night around me, a pale and bloody spectacle under my eyes and hands, a murderess hardly separated from me by a single door. The rest I could bear, but I shuddered at the thought of Grace Poole bursting out upon me.

I stared at the strip of light under the door behind the tapestry, but knew I must keep to my post. I must watch this ghastly countenance – these blue, still lips forbidden to unclose – these eyes now shut, now opening, now wandering through the room, now fixing on me.

I must dip my hand again and again in the basin of blood and water, and wipe away the trickling gore. I must see the light of the candle wane, and the shadows darken on antique tapestries round me and grow black under the hangings of the vast old bed.

Amidst all this, I had to listen as well as watch. To listen for the movements of the wild beast in the den on the other side of the door. But since Mr Rochester's visit I heard but three sounds at three long intervals. A step, a creak and a deep human groan.

Then my own thoughts worried me. What crime was this that lived incarnate in this sequestered mansion, and could neither be expelled nor subdued by the owner? What mystery, that broke out now in fire and now in blood, at the deadest hours of night? What creature was it, that, masked in an ordinary woman's face and shape, uttered the voice, now of a mocking demon, and anon of a carrion-seeking bird of prey?

And this man I bent over, this commonplace, quiet stranger. How had he become involved? What made him seek this quarter of the house at an untimely season, when he should have been asleep in bed? I had heard Mr Rochester assign him an apartment below, so what brought him here! And why, now, was he so tame under the violence or treachery done him? Why did he so quietly submit to the concealment Mr Rochester enforced? And furthermore, why did Mr Rochester enforce this concealment?

His own life on a former occasion had been hideously plotted against, and now this. Both incidents he smothered in secrecy and sank in oblivion! I saw Mr Mason was submissive to Mr Rochester, that the impetuous will of the latter held complete sway over the inertness of the former. The few words which had passed between them assured me of this. As did the conjecture that they had a most complex history. This was surely most apparent in Mr Rochester's dismay when he heard of Mr Mason's arrival? Why had the mere name of this unresisting individual made Mr Rochester react so dramatically?

I could not forget how the arm had trembled which he rested on my shoulder and it was no light matter which could thus bow the resolute spirit and thrill the vigorous frame of Fairfax Rochester.

'When will he come? When will he come?' I cried inwardly,

as the night lingered and lingered and as my bleeding patient drooped, moaned, sickened. Neither day nor aid arrived. I had, again and again, held the water to Mason's white lips and again and again offered him the stimulating salts. My efforts seemed ineffectual. Either bodily or mental suffering, or loss of blood, or all three combined, were fast prostrating his strength. He moaned so, and looked so weak, wild and lost, I feared he was dying, and I was not permitted even to speak to him.

The candle, wasted at last, went out, and as it expired, I perceived streaks of grey light edging the window-curtains. Dawn was then approaching. Presently I heard Pilot bark far below, out of his distant kennel in the courtyard, and hope revived. Nor was it unwarranted. In five minutes more the grating key, the yielding lock, warned me my watch was relieved. It could not have lasted more than two hours, but many a week has seemed shorter.

Mr Rochester entered, and with him the surgeon he had been to fetch.

'Now, Carter, be on the alert,' he said to this last. 'I give you but half an hour for dressing the wound, fastening the bandages, getting the patient downstairs and all.'

'But is he fit to move, sir?'

'No doubt of it. It is nothing serious. He is nervous, his spirits must be kept up. Come, set to work.'

Mr Rochester drew back the thick curtain, drew up the blind, let in all the daylight he could, and I was surprised and cheered to see how far dawn was advanced. What rosy streaks were beginning to brighten the east. Then he approached Mason, whom the surgeon was already handling.

'Now, my good fellow, how are you?' he asked.

'She's done for me, I fear,' was the faint reply. 'I thought she might.'

'Not a whit! Have courage! In a fortnight you'll hardly feel the worse of it. You've lost a little blood, that's all. Carter, assure him there's no danger.'

A dark look passed between the surgeon and Mr Rochester. 'I can do that conscientiously,' said Carter, who had examined the wounds. 'Only I wish I could have got here sooner. He would not have bled so much. But how is this? The flesh on the shoulder is torn as well as cut. This wound was not done with a knife. There have been teeth here!'

'She bit me,' he murmured. 'She worried me like a tigress.'

'You should not have yielded. You should have known better,' said Mr Rochester.

'I know,' he said, shuddering. 'And knew to expect it, but she looked so quiet at first.'

'I warned you,' was his friend's answer. 'I said – be on your guard when you go near her. Besides, you might have waited till tomorrow, and had me with you. It was mere folly to attempt the interview tonight, and alone.'

'I thought it could be as it was. I thought—'

'You thought! You thought! Yes, it makes me impatient to hear you, but, however, you have suffered, and are likely to suffer enough for not taking my advice. So I'll say no more. Carter, man. Hurry! The sun will soon rise, and I must have him off.'

'Directly, sir. I must look to this other wound in the arm and the upper thighs.' A singularly marked expression warped Mr Rochester's countenance almost to distortion, but he only said, 'Come, be silent, Richard, and never mind her gibberish. Don't repeat it.'

'I wish I could forget it,' was the answer. 'I wish I could be free.'

'You will be when you are out of the country. When you get back to Spanish Town. Then you need not think of her at all.'

'But it is impossible to forget this night!'

'It is not impossible. There! Carter has done with you or nearly so. I'll make you decent in a trice. Jane,' he turned to me for the first time since his re-entrance, 'take this key. Go down into my bedroom, and walk straight forward into my dressing room. Open the top drawer of the wardrobe and take out a clean shirt and neck-handkerchief. Bring them here and be nimble.'

I went, sought the repository he had mentioned, found the articles named and returned with them.

'Now,' said he, 'go to the other side of the bed while I order him. But don't leave the room. You may be wanted again.'

I retired as directed, trying not to listen to the audible winces of pain coming from the other side of the curtain.

'Was anybody stirring below when you went down, Jane?' inquired Mr Rochester presently.

'No, sir. All was very still.'

'We shall get you off cannily, Dick. I have striven long to avoid exposure, and I should not like it to come at last.

Here, Carter, help him on with his waistcoat. Where did you leave your furred cloak? You can't travel a mile without that, I know, in this damned cold climate. In your room? Jane, run down to Mr Mason's room, the one next to mine, and fetch a cloak you will see there.'

Again I ran, and again returned, bearing an immense mantle lined and edged with fur.

'Now, I've another errand for you,' said my untiring master. 'You must away to my room again. What a mercy you are shod with velvet, Jane! A clod-hopping messenger would never do at this juncture. You must open the middle drawer of my toilet table and take out a little phial and a little glass you will find there. Quick!'

I flew thither and back, bringing the desired vessels.

'That's well! Now, Doctor, I shall take the liberty of administering a dose myself, on my own responsibility. I got this cordial at Rome, of an Italian charlatan – a fellow you would have kicked, Carter. It is not a thing to be used indiscriminately, but it is good upon occasion, as now, for instance. Jane, a little water.'

He held out the tiny glass, and I half filled it from the water bottle on the washstand.

'That will do. Now wet the lip of the phial.'

I did so. He measured twelve drops of a crimson liquid, and presented it to Mason.

'Drink, Richard. It will give you the heart you lack, for an hour or so.'

Mr Mason obeyed, because it was evidently useless to resist. He was dressed now, but he still looked pale. Mr

Rochester let him sit three minutes after he had swallowed the liquid, then he took his arm.

'Now I am sure you can get on your feet,' he said. 'Try.'

The patient rose.

'Carter, take him under the other shoulder. Be of good cheer, Richard. That's it!'

'I do feel better,' remarked Mr Mason.

'I am sure you do. Now, Jane, trip on before us away to the backstairs and unbolt the side-passage door. Tell the driver of the post-chaise you will see in the yard – or just outside, for I told him not to drive his rattling wheels over the pavement – to be ready. We are coming. And, Jane, if anyone is about, come to the foot of the stairs and hum.'

It was by this time half past five, and the sun was on the point of rising, but I found the kitchen still dark and silent. The side-passage door was fastened and I opened it with as little noise as possible. All the yard was quiet, but the gates stood wide open, and there was a post-chaise, with horses ready harnessed, and driver seated on the box, stationed outside.

I approached him, and said the gentlemen were coming. He nodded, then I looked carefully round and listened. The stillness of early morning slumbered everywhere, the curtains were yet drawn over the servants' chamber windows, and little birds were just twittering in the blossom-blanched orchard trees, whose boughs drooped like white garlands over the wall enclosing one side of the yard. The carriage horses stamped from time to time in their closed stables, but all else was still.

The gentlemen now appeared. Mason, supported by Mr Rochester and the surgeon, seemed to walk with tolerable ease and they assisted him into the chaise. Carter followed.

'Take care of him,' said Mr Rochester to the latter, 'and keep him at your house till he is quite well. I shall ride over in a day or two to see how he gets on. Richard, how is it with you?'

'The fresh air revives me, Fairfax.'

'Leave the window open on his side, Carter, there is no wind. Goodbye, Dick.'

'Fairfax—'

'Well, what is it?'

'Let her be taken care of. Let her be treated as tenderly as may be. Let her—' he stopped and burst into tears.

Mr Rochester went to him and held his head in the most tender and intimate of ways.

'I do my best. You know I have done what has to be done. You know she is mine now. You should not have come back. You know that,' was the answer. Then he kissed Mason on the cheek, shut up the chaise door and the vehicle drove away.

SIXTEEN

After the chaise had departed into the misty lane, Mr Rochester closed and barred the heavy yard gates. This done, he moved with slow step and abstracted air towards a door in the wall bordering the orchard. I, supposing he had done with me, prepared to return to the house. Again, however, I heard him call, 'Jane!'

He had opened a garden door and stood at it, waiting for me.

'Come where there is some freshness, for a few moments,' he said. 'That house is a mere dungeon, don't you feel it so?'

'It seems to me a splendid mansion, sir.'

'The glamour of inexperience is over your eyes,' he answered, 'and you see it through a charmed medium. Now here,' he pointed to the leafy enclosure we had entered, 'all is real, sweet and pure. Just like you.'

He strayed down a walk edged with box, with apple trees, pear trees and cherry trees on one side, and a border on the other full of all sorts of old-fashioned flowers, stocks, sweet-williams, primroses, pansies, mingled with southernwood, sweet-briar and various fragrant herbs.

They were fresh now as a succession of April showers and gleams, followed by a lovely spring morning, could make them. The sun was just entering the dappled east, and his light illumined the wreathed and dewy orchard trees and shone down the quiet walks under them.

'Jane, will you have a flower?'

He gathered a half-blown rose, the first on the bush, and offered it to me.

'Thank you, sir.'

'Do you like this sunrise, Jane? This placid and balmy atmosphere?'

'I do, very much.'

'You have passed a strange night, Jane.'

'Yes, sir.'

'And it has made you look pale. Were you afraid when I left you alone with Mason?'

'I was afraid of someone coming out of the inner room.'

'But I had fastened the door. I had the key in my pocket. I should have been a careless shepherd if I had left a lamb – my pet lamb – so near a wolf's den, unguarded. You were safe.'

'Will Grace Poole live here still, sir?'

'Oh yes! Don't trouble your head about her. Put the thing out of your thoughts.'

'Yet it seems to me your life is hardly secure while she stays.'

'Never fear. I will take care of myself.'

'Is the danger you apprehended last night gone by now, sir?'

'I cannot vouch for that till Mason is out of England. He would not knowingly hurt me but, unintentionally, he might in a moment, by one careless word, deprive me, if not of life, yet for ever of happiness.'

'Tell him to be cautious, sir. Let him know what you fear, and show him how to avert the danger.'

He laughed sardonically, hastily taking my hand.

'Oh, Jane. If I could do that, then everything would be simple. But it is not. Now you look puzzled and I will puzzle you further. You are my little friend, are you not?'

'I like to serve you, sir, and to obey you in all that is right.'

'Precisely. I see that you do. I see genuine contentment in your face, when you are helping me and pleasing me, yet I dare not show you where I am vulnerable, lest, faithful and friendly as you are, you should shun me at once.'

'If you have no more to fear from Mr Mason than you have from me, sir, you are very safe.'

'God grant it may be so! Here, Jane, is an arbour. Sit down.'

The arbour was an arch in the wall, lined with ivy. It contained a rustic seat. Mr Rochester took it, leaving room, however, for me, but I stood before him.

'Sit with me,' he said. 'You don't hesitate, do you? Is that wrong, Jane?'

I answered him by sitting next to him on the seat. The length of his thigh touched mine. He put his hand on my leg and my thigh trembled beneath it. The strangeness of the night seemed like a long-gone dream now that the sunlight was upon us.

'Now, while the sun drinks the dew – while all the flowers in this old garden awake and expand, and the birds fetch their young ones' breakfast out of the Thornfield, and the early bees do their first spell of work – I'll put a case to you. But first, look at me, and tell me you are at ease, and not fearing that I err in detaining you, or that you err in staying.'

'No, sir, I am content.'

'Well then, Jane, suppose you were no longer a girl well reared and disciplined, but a wild boy indulged from childhood upwards. Imagine yourself in a remote foreign land and conceive that you there commit a capital error. No matter of what nature or from what motives, but one whose consequences must follow you through life and taint all your existence. Mind, I don't say a crime. I am not speaking of shedding of blood or any other guilty act, which might make the perpetrator amenable to the law. My word is error. The results of what you have done become in time to you utterly insupportable. You take measures to obtain relief. Unusual measures, but neither unlawful nor culpable.

'Still you are miserable for hope has quitted you. Bitter and base associations have become the sole food of your memory. You wander here and there, seeking rest in exile, happiness in pleasure – I mean in heartless, sensual pleasure – such as dulls intellect and blights feeling.

'Heart-weary and soul-withered, you come home after years of voluntary banishment. You make a new acquaintance

– how or where no matter. You find in this stranger much of the good and bright qualities which you have sought for twenty years, and never before encountered, and they are all fresh, healthy, without soil and without taint.

'Such blissfully innocent society revives and regenerates. You feel better days come back – higher wishes, purer feelings. You desire to recommence your life, and to spend what remains to you of days in a way more worthy of an immortal being. To attain this end, are you justified in overleaping an obstacle of custom – a mere conventional impediment which neither your conscience sanctifies nor your judgment approves?'

He paused for an answer, but what was I to say? What was he suggesting? That he had found in me someone who could regenerate him? That he might sweep aside convention for me? My heart beat so hard, I almost feared he could hear it.

Again Mr Rochester propounded his query.

'Is the wandering and sinful, but now rest-seeking and repentant, man justified in daring the world's opinion, in order to attach to him for ever this gentle, gracious, genial stranger, thereby securing his own peace of mind and regeneration of life?'

I stared at his warm hand on my leg, only inches away from the womanly part of me that ached and throbbed for him.

'Sir,' I answered, 'a wanderer's repose or a sinner's reformation should never depend on a fellow creature. Men and women die, philosophers falter in wisdom, and Christians in goodness. If anyone you know has suffered and erred, let him look higher than his equals for strength to amend and solace to heal.'

'I have myself – I tell it you without parable – been a worldly, dissipated, restless man. And I believe I have found the instrument for my cure in—'

He paused, staring deeply into my eyes, and I felt my cheeks stain pink.

'Yes?' I breathed.

The birds went on carolling, the leaves lightly rustling. I almost wondered they did not check their songs and whispers to catch the suspended revelation, but they would have had to wait many minutes – so long was the silence protracted.

I knew that he thought of me as so innocent, and I longed to disabuse him of the fact and to confess to all that I had seen, to assure him that, though far apart in experience, we were kindred spirits. And yet, as he stared into me, as if searching for an answer, I sensed that to confess this now would be foolish and that to keep up the masquerade would yield greater spoils. He saw in me someone who had the power to reform him and I felt borne up on the giddy heights of his regard for me.

'Oh, who am I to . . .' he said, then he suddenly stood up. Flustered, I watched as he walked a little way away from me and back again.

What had I done to break his mood? His confession – his conviction that I could, that I had already turned his life around – had seemed only moments ago to be tantamount to a proposal. A proposal that he would consider breaking with all convention to be only with me.

But now he seemed to have come to his senses.

'Jane,' said he, in quite a changed tone, while his face changed too, losing all its softness and gravity, and becoming harsh and sarcastic. 'You have noticed my tender penchant for Miss Ingram. Don't you think if I married her she would regenerate me with a vengeance?'

He didn't wait for an answer, but went quite to the other end of the walk, and when he came back he was humming a tune. His confession seemed to have been forgotten, his mood utterly altered. I stared on, feeling utterly bereft. My confidence failed me. My spirits sank. Had his apparent confession not concerned itself with me truly at all?

'Jane, Jane,' said he, stopping before me, 'you are quite pale. Do you curse me for disturbing your rest? For keeping you awake all night?'

How could he possibly think I was pale for that reason? How could he change so suddenly?

'Curse you? No, sir.'

'Shake hands in confirmation of the word. What cold fingers! They were warmer last night when I touched them at the door of the mysterious chamber.'

'I'm glad I could be useful, sir. I would gladly spend every night in your company.'

'Then perhaps you shall again. The night before I am married! I am sure I shall not be able to sleep. Will you promise to sit up with me to bear me company? To you I can talk of my lovely one, for now you have seen her and know her.'

His words felt like daggers in my heart.

'Yes, sir.'

'Come, come,' he said. 'She's a rare one, is she not, Jane?'

'Yes, sir,' I mumbled. I could not bring myself to talk favourably of Miss Ingram. Not now. Not after what had passed between us. Not now he had so nearly changed everything.

'She's a strapper. A real strapper, Jane. Big and buxom. With such womanly endowments a man may delight in. Hair just such as the ladies of Carthage must have had and the breasts and buttocks of—'

'Stop,' I said.

'What is it?' I perceived a narrowing in his eyes. They glittered at me, but I had his full attention now.

'I also . . .' The words would not come easily to me.

'You also what, Jane?'

'I also have such . . .' I swallowed hard, feeling the blood rush through me, '. . . such womanly endowments, that might please you.'

'Do you, Jane?' he said, stepping up close to me. Only this time, as he spoke, his eyes no longer gazed enigmatically at mine, but rather intensified, just as Mason's had, after he had ingested the liquid draught Mr Rochester had administered to revive his spirits.

'Yes,' I whispered, heat still coursing through me.

'I see,' he said, quietly, as he took me in his arms.

I almost swooned as I looked up into his face, which was so close to mine now, but he didn't kiss me. Rather, he held me tight around the waist, staring into my eyes. I beheld in them a challenge, but I didn't surrender. I didn't move away.

After a moment, locked in this exchange, the silence stretching out, filled only with our heightened breathing, I felt his hand rub up my thigh, pulling my skirts with it. I strained towards him, trembling, still not looking away from his gaze.

Then his hand was under my skirt and petticoat. With a deft move, he slid his hand down the front of my drawers, still staring at me, his eyes full of mischief. Yet I could not move away. I wanted him to see for himself – to feel my desire for him.

I gasped as his fingers touched my sex. Holding me still, I felt his fingers slide against my wet crevasse and a whimper escaped me, as the tip of his finger entered my willing tunnel, probing and exploring. I closed my eyes now, surrendering entirely to him. I thought I might faint, such was the longing and desire in my loins.

I could feel him dabbling in my juices, gently stroking me, easily finding my engorged bud, which he gently pinched. My knees trembled, and when I opened my eyes, he was looking at me, raising his eyebrows in acknowledgement of what he was doing to me. I felt a stiffness in his trousers pressing against my thigh.

Then suddenly he stopped, releasing me, and I almost fell back on the path. I stared at him, inhaling back the waves of shock that spread through me, so close had I been to the blissful release my body craved.

He bit his bottom lip, staring at me, his eyes narrowed once more, then he reached out his hand and put the finger he had just placed inside me into my mouth. I tasted my own salty wetness.

'You are a peach, aren't you, Jane.'

I could not look at him. He knew now how much I wanted him.

'Why did you stop?' I asked, but my voice trembled.

He nodded over my shoulder. 'There's Dent and Lynn in the stables! You must go in by the shrubbery, through that wicket. It would not do for my intended to hear of us out here alone.'

He strode off past me, not waiting to see how his words cut me, for they surely did, as mightily as if he had been carelessly throwing sharpened daggers over his shoulder.

'Sir.' The harshness of my tone stopped him. I stood, clasping my hands so he would not see them trembling. I could barely meet his eye, such were the tumultuous emotions raging in my heart, but hearing him talk of the stables had reminded me of Robert Leaven and how he would already be preparing the carriage to take me away.

'Yes? What is it? They approach. You must away.'

'And I shall. I am leaving this morning.'

His demeanour changed. He took a pace back towards me. 'Leaving?'

'With your permission, sir,' I said, not looking at him, 'I wish for an absence for a week or two.'

'To do what? To go where?'

Why did it matter, I thought, when he had declared he would marry Miss Ingram? And yet, I sensed in his tone a new air of genuine concern and upset.

'To see a sick lady who has sent for me.'

'What sick lady? Where does she live?'

'At Gateshead.'

'That is a hundred miles off! Who may she be that sends for people to see her that distance?'

'Her name is Reed, sir. Mrs Reed. Mr Reed was my uncle. My mother's brother.'

'The deuce he was! You never told me that before. You always said you had no relations.'

'None that would own me, sir. Mr Reed is dead, and his wife cast me off.'

'Why?'

'Because I was poor, and burdensome, and she disliked me.'

'And what good can you do her? Nonsense, Jane! I would never think of running a hundred miles to see an old lady who will, perhaps, be dead before you reach her. Besides, you say she cast you off. And you can't travel a hundred miles alone.'

'She has sent her coachman.'

'A person to be trusted?'

'Yes, sir, he has lived ten years in the family.'

Mr Rochester meditated. 'When do you wish to go?'

'This morning, sir. I meant to ask you before.'

'Well, you must have some money. You can't travel without money, and I daresay you have not much. I have given you no salary yet. How much have you in the world, Jane?' he asked.

I drew out my purse. 'Five shillings, sir.' He took the purse, poured the hoard into his palm and chuckled over it as if its scantiness amused him. Soon he produced his pocket book. 'Here,' said he, offering me a note. It was fifty pounds, and he owed me but fifteen. I told him I had no change.

'I don't want change. You know that. Take your wages.'

I declined accepting more than was my due. It felt wrong to accept any money after what had just happened. He scowled at first, then, as if recollecting something, he said, 'Right, right! Better not give you all now. You would, perhaps, stay away three months if you had fifty pounds. There are ten. Is it not plenty?'

'Yes, sir, but now you owe me five.'

'Come back for it, then.'

'Mr Rochester, I may as well mention another matter of business to you while I have the opportunity.'

'Matter of business? I am curious to hear it.'

His ruffled countenance gave me strength. 'You have as good as informed me, sir, that you are going shortly to be married?'

'Yes. What then?'

'In that case, sir, Adèle ought to go to school. I am sure you will perceive the necessity of it.'

'To get her out of my bride's way, who might otherwise walk over her rather too emphatically? There's sense in the suggestion, not a doubt of it. Adèle, as you say, must go to school.'

'I hope so, sir, and I must seek another situation somewhere.'

He looked at me some in alarm, as if this fact had never occurred to him.

'And old Madam Reed, or the Misses, her daughters, will be solicited by you to seek a place, I suppose?'

'No, sir. I am not on such terms with my relatives as would justify me in asking favours of them, but I shall advertise.'

'At your peril you advertise! I wish I had only offered you a sovereign instead of ten pounds. Give me back nine pounds, Jane; I've a use for it.'

'And so have I, sir,' I returned, putting my hands and my purse behind me. 'I could not spare the money on any account.'

'Jane!'

'Sir?'

'Promise me one thing.'

'I'll promise you anything, sir, that I think I am likely to perform.'

'Not to advertise and to trust this quest of a situation to me. I'll find you one in time.'

'I shall be glad so to do, sir, if you, in your turn, will promise that I and Adèle shall be both safe out of the house before your bride enters it.'

'Very well! Very well! I'll pledge my word on it.'

'Now I must go to prepare for the journey.'

'Then you and I must bid goodbye for a little while. And how do people perform that ceremony of parting, Jane? Teach me. I'm not quite up to it.'

He stepped towards me, and once more his eyes were as

they had been when we had been sitting together on the seat. There seemed to be a desperation in them.

'They say, Farewell, or any other form they prefer.'

'Then say it.'

'Farewell, Mr Rochester, for the present.'

'What must I say?'

'The same, if you like, sir.'

'Farewell, Miss Eyre, for the present. Is that all?'

'Yes?'

'I should like something else. A little addition to the rite. A kiss perhaps?'

Another kiss? After what he had just done? After what he had just said? I wanted to refuse him – to punish him. I wanted to demand – no – to force him to forsake all thoughts and consideration of Blanche Ingram, the woman he did not love.

I glanced over in the direction of the stables and folded my hands in front of me, but he quickly stepped up to me and lifted my chin. Then softly, lovingly, he kissed me on my lips.

'Farewell, my Jane,' he said in a voice that was so tender it wrenched my heartstrings.

As I appeared from the bower, I wished the gentlemen and their horses good morning. I walked calmly inside the house, then, once safely out of view, pressed my back against the kitchen door and closed my eyes, a silent tear escaping down my cheek.

He loved me. I knew it and he knew it. He loved me and yet he lied to himself and would marry another. But could

I surrender all hope? No, even as I shuddered, I dried my eyes. He could not truly give me up, could he? The cruel hand of separation would be the timely test needed to make him follow his heart. Yet I knew the severance would cut as deeply as a knife.

SEVENTEEN

Mr Rochester had given me but one week's leave of absence, and yet a month elapsed before I quitted Gateshead. I wished to leave immediately after the funeral of my Aunt Reed, who had professed on her deathbed to keeping news of distant relations and their fortune from me, although the details and my exact claim upon any inheritance were unknown. However, a rich relative had been in touch with Mrs Reed seeking my whereabouts, and it was this fact that had caused a last-minute crisis of conscience on her part.

Her confession left me cold. The fact that there might have been an alternative path which my life could have taken, should I have called upon this branch of my family, hardly, in retrospect, seemed to matter. Because without my aunt's dismissal from her house, I would never have gone to Lowood and been in a position to apply for the job at Thornfield Hall. If I had never been to Thornfield Hall, I would never have met Mr Rochester. And it was Mr Rochester who filled my every waking thought in those dull, grey, gloom-filled days.

My two cousins, Georgiana and Eliza, were both feeble-minded and selfish. I found their company bland and their lamentations detestable. They pretended to know how to be ladies in polite society, and yet compared to the ladies I had known at Thornfield Hall, they were insipid and pathetic in both their musings and actions.

However, both entreated my aid in their separate ways, and quite without enough of an obligation in their eyes to leave at a time of family bereavement, I was prevented from making my own plans until Georgiana had departed for London and Eliza to the Continent, where she was intent upon joining a nunnery in Lisle. She wanted to embrace the life she perceived she would find there – to be quiet and unmolested. Her fear of all things carnal or of the flesh was no surprise, having grown up with the strictures of her repressed mother, yet I found her calling less noble than she would have liked. I neither expressed surprise at this resolution nor attempted to dissuade her from it. 'The vocation will fit you to a hair,' I thought. 'Much good may it do you!'

As I shall not have occasion to refer either to her or her sister again, I may as well mention here, that Georgiana made an advantageous match with a wealthy worn-out man of fashion, and that Eliza actually took the veil, and is at this day superior of the convent where she passed the period of her novitiate, and which she endowed with her fortune.

I, for my part, was glad to be rid of the whole business. Although I tried, I could not grieve for my aunt. She had been a cold, cruel woman in life and had hardly softened towards me on her deathbed, despite calling me to her. I was glad when Robert Leaven escorted me into the horse and trap to take me to the stagecoach.

How people feel when they are returning home from an absence, long or short, I did not know, as I had never experienced the sensation. I had known what it was to come back to Gateshead when a child after a long walk, to be scolded for looking cold or gloomy. I also knew what it was like to come back from church to Lowood, longing for a plenteous meal and a good fire, and to be unable to get either. Neither of these returnings was very pleasant or desirable. No magnet drew me to a given point, increasing in its strength of attraction the nearer I came. The return to Thornfield was yet to be tried.

My journey seemed tedious – very tedious. Fifty miles one day, a night spent at an inn, fifty miles the next day. During the first twelve hours I thought of Mrs Reed in her last moments. I saw her disfigured and discoloured face, and heard her strangely altered voice. I mused on the funeral day, the coffin, the hearse, the black train of tenants and servants, the notably small number of relatives, the gaping vault, the silent church, the solemn service.

Then I thought of Eliza and Georgiana and beheld one of them in a ballroom, the other the inmate of a convent cell. I dwelt on and analysed their separate peculiarities of person and character. Yet, as my journey went on, it scattered these thoughts, and night gave them quite another turn. As I laid down on my traveller's bed, my mind became preoccupied with Thornfield and Mr Rochester with an intensity that seemed greater the closer I got.

I was going back to Thornfield, but how long was I to stay there? Not long – of that I was sure. I had heard from Mrs Fairfax in the interim of my absence. The party at the hall was dispersed and Mr Rochester had left for London three weeks ago, but he was then expected to return in a fortnight.

Mrs Fairfax surmised that he was gone to make arrangements for his wedding, as he had talked of purchasing a new carriage. She said the idea of his marrying Miss Ingram still seemed strange to her, but from what everybody said, and from what she had herself seen, she could no longer doubt that the event would shortly take place.

For my own part, I could not believe that the event would take place. I felt sure that there was more to be played out between Mr Rochester and myself, especially after what had passed between us on the morning I had left. Each time I thought of him touching me so intimately, every sinew in my body ached for him. And each time I thought of our parting kiss, my heart ached even more.

Yet I knew not, in truth, how our relationship could now progress. I had deliberated for the past month over each and every possibility as to a possible path out of this agony of not knowing, until I felt like a spider caught in the middle of my own web of supposing.

In the bleakest of these avenues, I dreamt of Miss Ingram closing the gates of Thornfield against me and pointing me out another road. I saw Mr Rochester coming up behind her, kissing her neck, exposing her naked breasts. Then I imagined her gown falling away and him spreading her buttocks and taking her against the gates, as she held onto the bars and pressed back against him. I awoke in a hot sweat.

And then there was the question of Mr Mason and the strange night I had spent tending him and his wounds. In retrospect, though he was injured, it seemed to me stranger than ever that he had not berated Mr Rochester for Grace Poole's wicked behaviour, or that Mr Rochester had once again failed to do anything about his dangerous servant. I remembered his torn trousers and shirt, the birch marks across his chest.

Mr Rochester had rather implied that Mr Mason had brought his injuries upon himself and he alone was to blame. Mason seemed to go along with this theory, and had been resigned to his injuries – deserving of them, almost – and had seemed bereft that he had to leave Thornfield. I could not fathom the exchange between the two men and Mr Rochester's heightened emotions towards his old friend, before, during or after that night.

My own part in the proceedings as a bystander had only served to perplex me more. After the charades I had witnessed, I realized that Mr Rochester and his guests had naturally operated in two guises of behaviour. One in private, that I had secretly witnessed – where they eschewed all common codes of what society dictated was decent and instead embraced carnality, nudity and lust – and one in public, in front of the staff.

Mr Rochester clearly considered me to be ignorant of the private proceedings between him and his guests, which is why, I supposed, he had considered it safe for me to tend to Mr Mason. I felt, however, privy to a conversation operating from the private side of Mr Rochester's affairs, which I almost understood, but the fact of it remained elusive to me and I found my own ignorance increasingly frustrating.

I had not notified to Mrs Fairfax the exact day of my return, for I did not wish either car or carriage to meet me at Millcote. I proposed to walk the distance quietly by myself. After leaving my box in the ostler's care, I slipped away from the George Inn, about six o'clock of a June evening, and took the old road to Thornfield. It was a road which lay chiefly through fields, and was now little frequented.

It was a bright and splendid summer evening, both fair and soft. The haymakers were at work all along the road and the sky was mild and blue, and its cloud strata high and thin.

I stopped after a long climb up the hill, feeling the warm breeze across my skin, as I shaded my eyes. The path on which I walked wound its way down a hilly green field in which the labourers had finished their toil, the hay stacks dotting the fields.

Quite sure that I was alone, I unbuttoned my bodice, pulling at the front of it for a moment to cool the perspiration that glistened on my cleavage. So near to home, I felt a new sense of arousal and, as I thought of my proximity to Mr Rochester, I felt my nipples involuntarily swell and stiffen.

I sat down on the grass, pulling at a piece to chew it and taking a moment to savour the view of the fertile valley below. The sun was now glowing on the horizon and I slipped off my shoes, pulling up my skirts. I felt the warm sun on my thighs above my stockings and, as a breath of wind caught my skin, I thought of Rochester again and the way he had touched me, and I remembered the way he had put his rough finger between my lips.

I put my own finger there now, and, keen to recreate the memory with a physical impulse, I took my finger from my mouth and slipped it down my drawers, feeling beneath and finding myself warm, open and wet. I thought of my master's face as he had felt this for himself, and ached for more.

Then, hearing the labourers on the road in the distance, I lowered my skirts and got to my feet. Yet the wetness, the pulsing between my legs did not diminish, but rather grew greater still as I took each step.

A gladness and a heightened joy of both mind and body filled me as the road before me shortened. So glad was I, that I stopped once to ask myself what that joy meant. I had to remind myself that it was not to my home I was going, or to a permanent resting place, or to a place where fond friends looked out for me and waited my arrival. 'Mrs Fairfax will smile you a calm welcome, to be sure,' I said, 'and little Adèle will clap her hands and jump to see you, but you know very well you are thinking of another than they, and that he is not thinking of you.'

But it was Mr Rochester I wanted to see again most and my heart said, 'Hurry! Hurry. Be with him while you may, but a few more days or weeks, at most, and you are parted from him for ever!' And then a new-born agony rose up – a deformed thing which I could not persuade myself to own and rear – and I quashed it and ran on.

They are making hay, too, in Thornfield meadows, or rather, the labourers are just quitting their work, and returning home with their rakes on their shoulders, now, at the hour I arrive. I have but a field or two to traverse, and then I shall cross the road and reach the gates. How full the hedges are of roses!

But I have no time to gather any as I want to be at the house. I pass a tall briar, shooting leafy and flowery branches across the path, and I see the narrow stile with stone steps. And then I see – oh, and my heart thumps like a drum – Mr Rochester sitting there, a book and a pencil in his hand. He is writing.

Well, he is not a ghost, yet every nerve I have is unstrung. For a moment I am beyond my own mastery. What does it mean? I did not think I should tremble in this way when I saw him, or lose my voice or the power of motion in his presence. I will go back as soon as I can stir. I need not make an absolute fool of myself. I know another way to the house. But it does not matter if I knew twenty ways, for he has seen me.

'Hello!' he cries. He puts up his book and his pencil. 'There you are! Come on. Come here!'

I suppose I do come on, though in what fashion I know not, being scarcely cognizant of my movements, and solicitous only to appear calm. And, above all, to control the working muscles of my face – which I feel rebel insolently against my will, and struggle to express what I had resolved to conceal.

'And this is Jane Eyre? Are you coming from Millcote, and on foot? Yes – just like one of your tricks not to send for a carriage, and to come clattering over street and road like a common mortal, but to steal into the vicinity of your home along with twilight, just as if you were a dream or a shade. What the deuce have you done with yourself this last month? Where have you been?'

The urgency of his tone, the way he now touched my arm, made my knees shake. He had missed me. His words could not convey that which his eyes now told me to be true. He looked over not only my face, but my body too, although only quickly and I wondered whether, with his uncanny divining powers, he knew that I had been lying in the grass feeling aroused only minutes before with thoughts of him.

'I have been with my aunt, sir, who is dead.'

'A true Janian reply! Good angels be my guard! She comes from the other world – from the abode of people who are dead, and tells me so when she meets me alone here in the gloaming!' He smiled at me, then added, 'Absent from me a whole month, and forgetting me quite, I'll be sworn!'

I knew there would be pleasure in meeting my master again, even though broken by the fear that he was so soon to cease to be my master, and by the knowledge that I was nothing to him. But there was ever in Mr Rochester (so at least I thought) such a wealth of the power of communicating happiness, that to taste but of the crumbs he scattered to stray and stranger birds like me, was to feast genially. His last words were balm. They seemed to imply that it imported something to him whether I forgot him or not. And he had spoken of Thornfield as my home. Would that it were my home!

He did not leave the stile, and I dared not ask to go by, as it would mean my body would have to press against his. I inquired soon if he had not been to London.

'Yes. I suppose you found that out by second sight.'

'Mrs Fairfax told me in a letter.'

As he met my gaze, the throbbing between my legs had become all but overpowering.

'And did she inform you what I went to do?'

'Oh, yes, sir! Everybody knew your errand.'

'You must see the carriage, Jane, and tell me if you don't think it will suit Mrs Rochester exactly. And whether she won't look like Queen Boadicea, leaning back against those purple cushions. I wish, Jane, I were a trifle better adapted to match with her externally. Tell me now, fairy as you are – can't you give me a charm, or something of that sort, to make me a handsome man?'

How could he taunt me like this? How could he pretend that nothing had happened between us the last time we had met? How could I reprove him and yet show him that I cared for him still?

'It would be past the power of magic, sir,' and, in thought, I added, 'A loving eye is all the charm needed, to such you are handsome enough, or rather your sternness has a power beyond beauty.'

Mr Rochester had sometimes read my unspoken thoughts with an acumen to me incomprehensible. In the present instance he took no notice of my abrupt vocal response, but he smiled at me with a certain smile he had of his own, and which he used but on rare occasions. He seemed to think it too good for common purposes. It was the real sunshine of feeling and he shed it over me now. I tried to bask in it, yet my heart ached, for he had spoken of Blanche Ingram, his betrothed, in the very same breath as he had smiled at me.

'Pass, sweet Jane,' said he, making room for me to cross the stile. 'Go up home, and stay your weary little wandering feet at a friend's threshold.'

All I had now to do was to obey him in silence. There was nothing more for me to say. Yet as I passed over the stile, I felt his hand upon my waist for a moment, guiding me, and, close to him now as I could be, I turned and quite on impulse said, 'Thank you, Mr Rochester, for your great kindness. I am strangely glad to get back again to you. You see, wherever you are is my home. My only home.'

I slipped out of his grasp and walked on so fast that even he could hardly have overtaken me had he tried. Little Adèle was half wild with delight when she saw me. Mrs Fairfax received me with her usual plain friendliness and Leah smiled. This was very pleasant. There is no happiness like that of being loved by your fellow creatures, and feeling that your presence is an addition to their comfort. And Mr Rochester was here, I reminded myself. Here and alone, and quite happy to see me too.

I shut my eyes resolutely against the future. I stopped the

voice that kept warning me of near separation and coming grief. When tea was over and Mrs Fairfax had taken her knitting, and I had assumed a low seat near her, and Adèle, kneeling on the carpet, had nestled close up to me, and a sense of mutual affection seemed to surround us with a ring of golden peace, I uttered a silent prayer that we might not be parted far or soon.

As we thus sat, Mr Rochester entered, and looking at us, seemed to take pleasure in the spectacle of a group so amicable. He said he supposed the old lady was all right now that she had got her adopted daughter back again, and added that he saw Adèle was 'prête à croquer sa petite maman Anglaise'.

I half ventured to hope that he would, even after his marriage, keep us together somewhere under the shelter of his protection, and not quite exiled from the sunshine of his presence.

EIGHTEEN

Much to my dismay, that evening and for the whole of the next morning, nothing was said of the master's marriage, and I saw no preparation going on for such an event. I asked Mrs Fairfax if she had yet heard anything decided and her answer was always in the negative. She said she had actually put the question to Mr Rochester as to when he was going to bring his bride home, but he had answered her only by a joke and one of his queer looks, and she could not tell what to make of him.

One thing specially surprised me over the coming days. There were no journeyings backward and forward or visits to Ingram Park. It was twenty miles off, on the borders of another county, but what was that distance to an ardent lover? To so practised and indefatigable a horseman as Mr Rochester, it would be but a morning's ride.

When his soft look met mine, I began to cherish hopes I had no right to conceive. I convinced myself that the match was broken off and that rumour had been mistaken or that one or both parties had changed their minds. I used to look at my master's face to see if it were sad or fierce, but I could not remember the time when it had been so uniformly clear of clouds or evil feelings. Never had he called me more frequently to his presence, never been kinder to me and never had I loved him so well. And never had I been so willing to forget that he had ever taunted me with the prospect of his marriage to another, or so hopeful that it had been some kind of test or game, which I had won. For all the times I had mused on my homecoming, I had never thought that it could be as blissful as this.

My heart raced each time he spoke to me and my mind strayed incessantly to the time he had touched me so intimately and the other times he had kissed me. Once, on the night of the fire in his room, and then again on his return with his guests to Thornfield, and that last time, before I had gone to Mrs Reed's. Three times, I supposed, he must have taken leave of his senses – or, I reasoned, some inner, more truthful part of himself had taken over.

I was not to mistake those kisses for promises. I knew that in my heart of hearts. A man such as Mr Rochester could still do as he pleased and could change his mind at any time. But even so, being so near him now and seeing him in such good humour brought the fact of them to the forefront of my mind. Had he forgotten what had occurred between us? Even though a month had passed, I felt increasingly sure, in each look that he gave me, that he had not.

At night, I lay in the moonlight of my room, staring at the ceiling, quite unable to sleep with longing, my ears straining to hear the sound of his door opening. He would come to me, I told myself. He would come. Something inside felt sure. And if he did? What then?

A splendid midsummer shone over England. Skies so pure, suns so radiant as were then seen in long succession, such that seldom favour our wave-girt land. It was as if a band of Italian days had come from the South, like a flock of glorious birds. The hay was all got in, the fields round Thornfield were green and shorn, the roads white and baked. The trees were in their dark prime, and hedge and wood, full-leaved and deeply tinted, contrasted well with the sunny hue of the cleared meadows between.

On midsummer eve, Adèle, weary with gathering wild strawberries in Hay Lane half the day, had gone to bed with the sun. I watched her drop asleep, and when I left her, I sought the garden.

It was now the sweetest hour of the twenty-four, where the sun had gone down in simple state – pure of the pomp of clouds. Soon the purple sky would boast the moon, but she was yet beneath the horizon.

I walked a while on the pavement, but a subtle, well-known scent – that of a cigar – stole from some window and I saw that the library casement window was open. I knew that I might be watched from there by others than the one I desired, if Mr Rochester still had visitors, but still I walked past, hoping to catch a glimpse of him, so that he might see I was alone.

I turned off the path opposite the library window into the orchard. No nook in the grounds was more sheltered and more Eden-like. It was full of trees all in bloom with flowers. A very high wall shut it out from the court on one side, and on the other, a beech avenue screened it from the lawn.

At the bottom was a sunk fence, its sole separation from the fields beyond. A winding walk, bordered with laurels terminated in a giant horse chestnut, circled at the base by a seat, led down to the fence. While such honeydew fell, such silence reigned, such gloaming gathered, I felt as if I could haunt such shade for ever in waiting, but my step slowed – halted once more by a warning fragrance – and my heart soared.

Sweet-briar and southernwood, jasmine, pink and rose have long been yielding their evening sacrifice of incense. This new scent is neither of shrub nor flower, it is Mr Rochester's cigar, but just as sweet to me. It could only mean that he had seen me and followed me.

I look round and I listen. I see trees laden with ripening fruit. I hear a nightingale warbling in a wood half a mile off. No moving form is visible, no coming step audible, but that perfume increases. I make for the wicket leading to the shrubbery, and I see Mr Rochester entering.

I step aside into the ivy recess. If I sit still he will never see me. For, in truth, dear reader, now that I have seen him, a sudden nervousness has overtaken me. I know I cannot risk an encounter, my emotions heightened as they are. He is betrothed to another, I remind myself. His heart will never be mine and that is why we must not be alone together, for I cannot trust myself not to betray the feelings that pump through me with my blood.

But it seems that this eventide is as pleasant to him as to me, and this antique garden as attractive, and he strolls on, now lifting the gooseberry-tree branches to look at the fruit, large as plums, with which they are laden, now taking a ripe cherry from the wall, now stooping towards a knot of flowers, either to inhale their fragrance or to admire the dew beads on their petals. A great moth goes humming by me. It alights on a plant at Mr Rochester's foot. He sees it, and bends to examine it.

'Now, he has his back towards me,' I thought, 'and he is occupied too. Perhaps, if I walk softly, I can slip away unnoticed.'

I trod on the edging of turf so that the crackle of the pebbly gravel might not betray me. He was standing among the beds at a yard or two distant from where I had to pass, the moth apparently still engaging him.

'I shall get by very well,' I thought to myself.

Yet, as I crossed his shadow, thrown long over the garden by the moon, not yet risen high, I looked at the smooth line of his back and buttocks as he bent over, and I accidentally scuffed my toe against the stones, and I heard him say, without turning, 'Jane, come and look at this fellow.'

I had made so little noise, so how had he known it was me? Did his shadow possess feelings? Or had he known my hiding place all along?

Blushing, I approached him.

'Look at his wings,' he said, 'he reminds me rather of a West Indian insect. One does not often see so large and gay a night-rover in England. There! He has flown.'

The moth roamed away. I was sheepishly retreating also, but Mr Rochester followed me, and when we reached the wicket, he said, 'Turn back. On so lovely a night it is a shame to sit in the house and surely no one can wish to go to bed while sunset is thus at meeting with moonrise.'

It is one of my faults, that though my tongue is sometimes prompt enough at an answer, there are times when it sadly fails me in framing an excuse, and always the lapse occurs at some crisis, when a facile word or plausible pretext is specially wanted to get me out of painful embarrassment. And so it was that I could not find a reason to allege for leaving him.

I followed with lagging step, and thoughts busily bent on discovering a means of extrication, but he himself looked so composed and so grave also, I became ashamed of feeling any confusion. The evil – if evil existent or prospective there was – seemed to lie with me only. His mind was unconscious and quiet.

'Jane,' he recommenced, as we entered the laurel walk, and slowly strayed down in the direction of the sunk fence and the horse chestnut, 'Thornfield is a pleasant place in summer, is it not?'

'Yes, sir.'

'You must have become in some degree attached to the house?'

'I have indeed.'

'And though I don't comprehend how it is, I perceive you have acquired a degree of regard for that foolish little child Adèle, too. And even for simple dame Fairfax?'

'Yes, sir. In different ways, I have an affection for both.'

'And would be sorry to part with them?'

'Yes.'

'Pity!' he said, and sighed and paused. 'It is always the way of events in this life,' he continued presently. 'No sooner have you got settled in a pleasant resting place, than a voice calls out to you to rise and move on, for the hour of repose is expired.'

'Must I move on, sir?' I asked. 'Must I leave Thornfield?'

'I believe you must, Jane. I am sorry, but I believe indeed you must.'

This was a blow, but I did not let it prostrate me, although a sharp ache started in my chest. I reminded myself that in all those dull days at Mrs Reed's bedside, I had prepared myself for this moment and yet, now it was here, I felt my self-control slipping away from me.

'Well, sir, I shall be ready when the order to march comes.'

'It is come now. I must give it tonight.'

'Then you are going to be married, sir?'

'Exactly. With your usual acuteness, you have hit the nail straight on the head.'

'Soon, sir?'

'Very soon. You'll remember, Jane, the first time I, or Rumour, plainly intimated to you that it was my intention to put my old bachelor's neck into the sacred noose, to enter into the holy estate of matrimony – to take Miss Ingram to my bosom, in short (she's an extensive armful, but that's not to the point – one can't have too much of such a very excellent thing as my beautiful Blanche). Well, as I was saying

. . . listen to me, Jane! You're not turning your head to look after more moths, are you? That was only a ladybird flying away home.

'I wish to remind you that it was you who first said to me that in case I married Miss Ingram, both you and little Adèle had better trot forthwith. I pass over the sort of slur conveyed in this suggestion on the character of my beloved. Indeed, when you are far away, Jane, I'll try to forget it. I shall notice only its wisdom, which is such that I have made it my law of action. Adèle must go to school and you, Miss Eyre, must get a new situation.'

'Yes, sir, I will advertise immediately. And meantime, I suppose—' I was going to say, 'I suppose I may stay here, till I find another shelter to go to,' but I stopped, feeling it would not do to risk a long sentence, for my voice was not quite under command.

'In about a fortnight I hope to be a bridegroom,' continued Mr Rochester, 'and in the interim, I shall myself look out for employment and an asylum for you.'

'Thank you, sir. I am sorry to give—'

'Oh, no need to apologize! I consider that when a dependent does her duty as well as you have done yours, she has a sort of claim upon her employer for any little assistance he can conveniently render her. Indeed I have already, through my future mother-in-law, heard of a place that I think will suit. It is to undertake the education of the five daughters of Mrs Dionysius O'Gall of Bitternutt Lodge, Connaught, Ireland. You'll like Ireland, I think. They're such warm-hearted people there, they say.'

'It is a long way off, sir.'

'No matter – a girl of your sense will not object to the voyage or the distance.'

'Not the voyage, but the distance. And then the sea is a barrier—'

'From what, Jane?'

'From England and from Thornfield and . . .'

'Well?'

'From you, sir.'

I said this almost involuntarily, and, with as little sanction of free will, my tears gushed out. I did not cry so as to be heard, however. I avoided sobbing. The thought of Mrs O'Gall and Bitternutt Lodge struck cold to my heart and colder the thought of all the brine and foam, destined, as it seemed, to rush between me and the master at whose side I now walked, and coldest the remembrance of the wider ocean – wealth, caste, custom intervened between me and what I naturally and inevitably loved.

'It is a long way,' I again said.

'It is, to be sure, and when you get to Bitternutt Lodge, Connaught, Ireland, I shall never see you again, Jane. That's certain. I never go over to Ireland, not having myself much of a fancy for the country. We have been good friends, Jane, though, have we not?'

'Yes, sir.'

'And when friends are on the eve of separation, they like to spend the little time that remains to them close to each other. Come! We'll talk over the voyage and the parting quietly half an hour or so, while the stars enter into their shining life up in heaven yonder. Here is the chestnut tree. Here is the bench at its old roots. Come, we will sit there in peace tonight, though we should never more be destined to sit there together.'

He seated me and himself.

'It is a long way to Ireland, Jane, and I am sorry to send my little friend on such weary travels, but if I can't do better, how is it to be helped? Are you anything akin to me, do you think, Jane?'

I could risk no sort of answer by this time.

'Because,' he said, 'I sometimes have a queer feeling with regard to you, especially when you are near me, as you are now. It is as if I had a string somewhere under my left ribs, tightly and inextricably knotted to a similar string situated in the corresponding quarter of your little frame. And if that boisterous Channel, and two hundred miles or so of land come broad between us, I am afraid that cord of communion will be snapped. And then I've a nervous notion I should take to bleeding inwardly. As for you – you'd forget me.'

'That I never should, sir . . .' But it was impossible to proceed.

'Jane, do you hear that nightingale singing in the wood? Listen!'

In listening, I sobbed convulsively, for I could not repress what I endured any longer. I was obliged to yield, and I was shaken from head to foot with acute distress. When I did speak, it was only to express an impetuous wish that I had never been born, or never come to Thornfield.

'Because you are sorry to leave it?'

The vehemence of emotion, stirred by grief and love within me, was claiming mastery, and struggling for full sway, and asserting a right to predominate, to overcome, to live, rise and reign at last, yes, to speak.

'I grieve to leave Thornfield. I love Thornfield. I love it, because I have lived in it a full and delightful life – momentarily at least. I have not been trampled on. I have not been petrified. I have not been buried with inferior minds, and excluded from every glimpse of communion with what is bright and energetic and high. I have talked, face to face, with what I reverence, with what I delight in – with an original, a vigorous, an expanded mind. I have known you, Mr Rochester, and wanted you with my body and soul, and it strikes me with terror and anguish to feel I absolutely must be torn from you for ever. I see the necessity of departure and it is like looking on the necessity of death.'

'Where do you see the necessity?' he asked suddenly.

'Where? You, sir, have placed it before me.'

'In what shape?'

'In the shape of Miss Ingram. A noble and beautiful woman. Your bride.'

'My bride! What bride? I have no bride!'

'But you will have.'

'Yes. I will! I will!'

'Then I must go. You have said it yourself.'

'No. You must stay!'

'I tell you I must go!' I retorted, roused to something like passion. 'Do you think I can stay to become nothing to you?

Do you think I am an automaton? A machine without feelings? Do you think I can bear to have my morsel of bread snatched from my lips, and my drop of living water dashed from my cup? Do you think, because I am poor, obscure, plain and little, I am soulless and heartless? You think wrong! I have as much soul as you, and full as much heart! And if God had gifted me with some beauty and much wealth, I should have made it as hard for you to leave me, as it is now for me to leave you. You have chosen Miss Ingram because she can give you sweet pleasures of the flesh, but all the time I have been waiting to give myself to you, if you would only have me.'

'Is that really true, Jane?'

'Of course it's true. You know it to be true. But that aside, I am not talking to you now through the medium of custom, conventionalities, nor even of mortal flesh. It is my spirit that addresses your spirit. Just as if both had passed through the grave, and we stood at God's feet, equal, as we are!'

'As we are!' repeated Mr Rochester. 'So,' he added, enclosing me in his arms, gathering me to his breast, pressing his lips on my lips. 'So, Jane!'

'Yes, so, sir,' I rejoined. 'And yet not so. For you are a married man – or as good as a married man – to one with whom you have no sympathy – whom I do not believe you truly love. For I have seen and heard you sneer at her. I would scorn such a union. Therefore I am better than you. So let me go!'

I pushed him away, angrily.

'Where, Jane? To Ireland?'

'Yes, to Ireland. I have spoken my mind, and can go anywhere now.'

'Jane, be still. Don't struggle so, like a wild frantic bird that is rending its own plumage in its desperation.'

'I am no bird and no net ensnares me. I am a free human being with an independent will, which I now exert to leave you.'

Another effort set me at liberty, and I stood erect before him.

'And your will shall decide your destiny,' he said. 'I offer you my hand, my heart and a share of all my possessions.'

'You play a farce, which I merely laugh at.'

'I ask you to pass through life at my side – to be my second self, and best earthly companion.'

'For that fate you have already made your choice, and must abide by it.'

'Jane, be still a few moments. You are over-excited. I will be still too.'

A waft of wind came sweeping down the laurel walk, and trembled through the boughs of the chestnut. The nightingale's song was then the only voice of the hour. In listening to it, I again wept. Mr Rochester sat quiet, looking at me gently and seriously. Some time passed before he spoke. He at last said, 'Come to my side, Jane, and let us explain and understand one another.'

'I will never again come to your side. I am torn away now, and cannot return.'

'But, Jane, I summon you as my wife. It is only you I intend to marry.'

I was silent. I thought he mocked me.

'Come, Jane. Come hither.'

'Your bride stands between us.'

He rose, and with a stride reached me.

'My bride is here,' he said, again drawing me to him, 'because my equal is here, and my likeness. Jane, will you marry me?'

Still I did not answer, and still I writhed myself from his grasp, for I was still incredulous.

'Do you doubt me, Jane?'

'Entirely.'

'You have no faith in me?'

'Not a whit.'

'Am I a liar in your eyes?' he asked passionately. 'Little sceptic, you shall be convinced. What love have I for Miss Ingram? None. And that you know. What love has she for me? None. As I have taken pains to prove. I caused a rumour to reach her that my fortune was not a third of what was supposed, and after that I presented myself to see the result. It was coldness both from her and her mother. I knew then that I would not – I could not – marry Miss Ingram. You strange, you almost unearthly thing! I love as my own flesh. You, poor and obscure, and small and plain as you are, I entreat to accept me as a husband.'

'Me?' I gasped.

'You, Jane, I must have you for my own. Entirely my own. Will you be mine? Say yes, quickly.'

'Mr Rochester, let me look at your face. Turn to the moonlight.'

'Why?'

'Because I want to read your countenance. Turn!'

'There! You will find it scarcely more legible than a crumpled, scratched page. Read on. Only make haste, for I suffer.'

His face was very much agitated and very much flushed, and there were strong workings in the features, and strange gleams in the eyes.

'Oh, Jane, you torture me!' he exclaimed. 'Say, Edward. Give me my name. Edward, I will marry you.'

'Are you in earnest? Do you truly love me? Do you sincerely wish me to be your wife?'

'I do. And if an oath is necessary to satisfy you, I swear it.'

My heart leapt. 'Then, sir, I will marry you.'

'Edward, my little wife!'

'Dear Edward!'

'Come to me. Come to me entirely now,' said he, and added, in his deepest tone, speaking in my ear as I fell into his arms and his cheek pressed against mine, 'Make my happiness. I will make yours.'

He took me in his arms then and kissed me with an ardour I had never known. Just as it had been on the night of the fire in his bedroom, my body surrendered to his. I grabbed his hair, and my lips pressed against his, as if my whole life depended on clinging on to him.

'Oh, Jane,' he breathed. 'I want you. Oh Jane, my love.'

I felt his hand straying beneath my shawl, feeling my breast which strained towards him, as he kissed me more passionately than ever, his breath hot on my wet face.

'Will you really give yourself to me? Do you mean it?'

'Yes, yes,' I breathed, as he kissed my neck. 'Now we are betrothed, I will give myself completely.'

'We shall be married soon, for it was for you and me that I made arrangements in the church, praying as I did so that you would reveal your heart to me.'

'Oh, sir,' I gasped, laughing and crying now.

'But whom do I need to consult?'

'There is no one to meddle, sir. I have no kindred to interfere.'

'No, that is the best of it,' he said.

And if I had loved him less I should have thought his accent and look of exultation savage, but, as he sat down on the bench, he positioned me so that I was sitting astride him. I felt afloat, borne up, roused from the nightmare of parting and called to the paradise of union, and I thought only of the bliss given me to drink in so abundant a flow.

Again and again he said between kisses, 'Are you happy, Jane?' And again and again I answered, 'Yes.'

Roughly, he pulled apart the buttons of my dress, my hair becoming loose, as his face pressed against my skin, freeing my breasts to kiss and nuzzle them. I gasped, as he held my erect nipple in his teeth, igniting a fire within me until my body was aching for his. I was lost in a passion that seemed at last to bring my soul together with my flesh, the whole universe shrinking only to him and me.

'Here,' he said, taking my hand and placing it on the hard bulge in his breeches. I momentarily thought of the maid and butler I had spied, and, trying to act with a confidence I did not possess, I began to unbutton him.

He moaned as I touched his flesh, tentatively at first, but then he pulled his member free and, as it sprang forth, I held him in my grasp. It was thick and hard and long and my hand delighted at the contrast of smoothness and strength. I had long wanted to marvel at the intricacies of the male body, but there was no time. An urgency was upon us both. An urgency that had swept us away.

In a moment, I had slid off him, hastily stepping out of my undergarments and lifting up my dress.

'Oh, Jane, Jane,' he breathed, grabbing my hand and clasping it once more around his quivering erection.

I sat astride him now, hitching up my skirts, just as the maid had done, but I no longer cared. I was borne away and my need for him to be inside me, to fill me, fuse with me, felt greater to me at that moment than even drawing breath.

He lifted me up for a moment, guiding himself with a practised skill so that he was grazing against the wet groove between my legs. And then, my mouth open against his, our gasps mingling, he stared into my eyes, moving slowly until I felt him enter me a little way. I strained against him, knowing only that I wanted him to fill me.

'You want more?' he asked. 'Are you sure?'

'Yes, yes,' I breathed, utterly undone, my body melting against his, knowing that I could never go back, only go forward one tantalizing new second at a time, that life itself from this point on was all new and everything was unknown.

Pain, ecstasy, delight, fear, crashed in unison through me, as he held my hips, parting me, guiding me, moving me up and down on him, taking me, owning and possessing me, breaking through my virginity, until I cried out, clawing at his shoulders, rocking back on him, feeling the whole of him fill me, utterly and completely.

Then I was cascading into an avalanche of pleasure, my mind breaking into a million dazzling pieces as I sobbed with relief. Then, when I opened my eyes, I saw him gasp and felt him tense and spasm inside me. And as he did so, he let out a primal cry that made the rooks take off from the lawn.

Afterwards, we stayed together, joined so thoroughly, it felt as if we could never be apart. I felt as if something magical had taken place and when I told him so, he whispered that I had bewitched him. Then he kissed me again, long and hard, his tongue dancing again with mine, and still I felt his manhood twitch inside me, as much a part of me, it now seemed, as it was of him.

But what had befallen the night? The moon was not yet set, and we were all in shadow. I could scarcely see my master's face, near as I was. And what ailed the chestnut tree? It writhed and groaned, while wind roared in the laurel walk, and came sweeping over us.

'We must go in,' said Mr Rochester. 'The weather changes. I could have been with thee till morning, Jane.'

'And so,' thought I, 'could I with you.' I should have said so, perhaps, but a livid, vivid spark leapt out of a cloud at which I was looking, and there was a crack, a crash, and a close rattling peal, and I thought only of hiding my dazzled eyes against Mr Rochester's shoulder.

The rain rushed down. Gathering up my cast-off garments, he hurried me up the walk, through the grounds and into the house, but we were quite wet before we could pass the threshold. He was taking off my shawl in the hall, and shaking the water out of my loosened hair, when Mrs Fairfax emerged from her room. I did not observe her at first, nor did Mr Rochester. The lamp was lit. The clock was on the stroke of twelve.

'Hasten to take off your wet things,' said he, 'my darling!'

He kissed me repeatedly. When I looked up, on leaving his arms, there stood the widow, pale, grave and amazed. I only smiled at her, and ran upstairs. 'Explanation will do for another time,' I thought.

Still, when I reached my chamber, I felt a pang at the idea she should even temporarily misconstrue what she had seen. But joy soon effaced every other feeling. As loud as the wind blew, as near and deep as the thunder crashed, fierce and frequent as the lightning gleamed, cataract-like as the rain fell, I experienced no fear because Mr Rochester was mine and that was strength for anything.

I lay in my room, wide awake, lightning filling up my room, as I gasped with delight and trembled with wonder. My mind could not comprehend what had happened and I guessed that I must have fallen into a deep sleep, for the next thing I knew, it was morning and all was tranquil and calm, the birds singing at the window.

Before I left my bed, little Adèle came running in to tell me that the great horse chestnut at the bottom of the orchard had been struck by lightning in the night, and half of it split away.

NINETEEN

As I rose and dressed, I thought over what had happened the night before, and wondered if it were a dream. I could not be certain of the reality till I had seen Mr Rochester again, and heard him renew his words of love and his promise.

While arranging my hair, I looked at my face in the glass, and felt it was no longer plain. There was hope in its aspect and life in its colour, and my eyes seemed as if they had beheld the fount of fruition, and borrowed beams from the lustrous ripple. I had often been unwilling to look at my master, because I feared he could not be pleased at my look, but I was sure I might lift my face to his now, and not cool his affection by its expression. I took a plain but clean and light summer dress from my drawer and put it on. It seemed no attire had ever so well become me, because none had I ever worn in so blissful a mood.

I was not surprised, when I ran down into the hall, to see that a brilliant June morning had succeeded to the tempest of the night, and to feel, through the open glass door, the breathing of a fresh and fragrant breeze.

Mrs Fairfax surprised me by looking out of the window with a sad countenance, and saying gravely. 'Miss Eyre, will you come to breakfast?'

During the meal she was quiet and cool, but I could not undeceive her then. I must wait for my master to give explanations and so must she. I ate what I could, and then I hastened upstairs. I met Adèle leaving the schoolroom.

'Where are you going? It is time for lessons.'

'Mr Rochester has sent me away to the nursery.'

'Where is he?'

'In there,' pointing to the apartment she had left, and I went in, and there he stood.

'Come and bid me good morning,' he said.

I gladly advanced, running the last few steps across the green carpet and, with a smile, he wrapped me into his embrace and kissed me. It seemed so natural, to be so well loved, so caressed by him.

'Jane, you look blooming, and smiling, and pretty,' he said, tenderly stroking my hair. 'Is this truly my pale little elf?'

'It is Jane Eyre, sir,' I said, with a curtsey.

'Soon to be Jane Rochester,' he added. 'In a fortnight and not a day more. Do you hear that?'

I did, and I could not quite comprehend it. It made me giddy. The feeling, the announcement sent through me, was something stronger than was consistent with joy – something that smote and stunned. It was, I think, almost fear.

'You blushed, and now you are white, Jane. Why?'

'Because you gave me a new name – Jane Rochester. It seems so strange.'

'Yes, Mrs Rochester,' he said. 'Young Mrs Rochester. Fairfax Rochester's girl-bride.'

'It can never be, sir. It does not sound likely. Human beings never enjoy complete happiness in this world. I was not born for a different destiny to the rest of my species. To imagine such a lot befalling me is a fairy tale.'

'Which I can and will realize. I shall begin today. This morning I wrote to my banker in London to send me certain jewels he has in his keeping, heirlooms for the ladies of Thornfield. In a day or two I hope to pour them into your lap, for every privilege, every attention shall be yours that I would accord a peer's daughter, if about to marry her.'

'Oh, sir! Never rain jewels! Jewels for Jane Eyre sounds unnatural and strange. I would rather not have them.'

'I will myself put the diamond chain round your neck, and the circlet on your forehead, which it will become, for nature, at least, has stamped her patent of nobility on this brow, Jane. And I will clasp the bracelets on these fine wrists,' he said, kissing my wrists, 'and load these fairy-like fingers with rings. I will behold you naked, yet covered in jewels.'

'No, no, sir! Don't address me as if I were a beauty. I am your plain, Quakerish governess.'

The colour rose in my cheeks, as I remembered him adorning Blanche Ingram in the manner he had described, when he had been dressed as an Eastern mogul in the charade I had witnessed. I remembered, too, the bored disinterest with which he had beheld her when she was covered in jewels. As if reading my thoughts, he lifted my face to look at him.

'You are a beauty in my eyes, and a beauty just after the desire of my heart,' he said.

'You are dreaming, sir.'

'I was not dreaming last night, when you revealed yourself to me. To know that it was only the beginning makes my heart beat all the faster. You are beautiful, my Jane, and I will make the world acknowledge your beauty, too,' he went on. 'I will attire my love in satin and lace, and she shall have roses in her hair and I will cover the head I love best with a priceless veil.'

'And then you won't know me, sir, as I shall not be your Jane Eyre any longer, but a jay in borrowed plumes.'

He pursued his theme, however, without noticing my deprecation. 'This very day I shall take you in the carriage to Millcote, and you must choose some dresses for yourself and for the wedding day.'

'Can it really be so soon?'

'There is surely no need to wait? I have arranged for the wedding to take place quietly, in the church down below yonder, and then I shall waft you away at once to town. After a brief stay there, I shall bear my treasure to regions nearer the sun. To French vineyards and Italian plains, where she shall see whatever is famous in old story and in modern record, and she shall taste, too, of the life of cities and she shall learn to value herself by just comparison with others.'

'Shall I travel? With you, sir?' I gasped with surprise and pleasure.

'You shall sojourn at Paris, Rome and Naples. At Florence, Venice and Vienna too. All the ground I have wandered over shall be re-trodden by you. Wherever I stamped my hoof, your sylph's foot shall step also. Ten years since, I flew through Europe half mad, with disgust, hate and rage as my companions, but now I shall revisit it healed and cleansed, with a very angel as my comforter.'

I laughed at him as he said this. 'I am not an angel,' I asserted. 'Mr Rochester, you must neither expect nor exact anything celestial of me, for you will not get it, any more than I shall get it of you, which I do not at all anticipate.'

'I never met your likeness. Jane, you please me, and you master me – you seem to submit, and I like the sense of pliancy you impart, and while I am twining the soft, silken skein round my finger, it sends a thrill up my arm to my heart.' He smiled at me. 'Oh yes, and other more secret places too.'

And with this, he took my hand and pressed it hard against the buttons of his breeches, which sprang up to attention, as though some great sea serpent were attempting to rise up and break free from the deep.

'You see, I am influenced and conquered, and the influence is sweeter than I can express, and the conquest I undergo has a witchery beyond any triumph I can win.'

He kissed me again, but as his kiss became more rousing I felt the hardness in his breeches firming like a bough of seasoned wood, and I felt my own sex responding. I knew desire could at any moment overtake us both. Withdrawing my hand with great haste, I held him at arm's length.

'No, sir. Stop. We must stop. There is too much to discuss. Too much I want to ask you. And there is the matter of

Adèle and the servants. They must not witness this impropriety of ours.'

'Then ask me something now, Jane, the least thing. I desire to be entreated.'

'Indeed I will, sir. I have my petition all ready.'

I stepped away from him, smoothing my hair and pressing my lips together. I clasped my hands in front of me, still so conscious of the tingling below them, between my legs. I cleared my voice, ignoring his penetrating stare.

'This is what I have to ask,' I said. 'Why did you take such pains to make me believe you wished to marry Miss Ingram?'

'I will confess,' he said, with a small laugh, 'even although I should make you a little indignant, Jane – and I have seen what a fire-spirit you can be when you are indignant. You glowed in the cool moonlight last night, when you mutinied against fate, and claimed your rank as my equal. Jane, by the bye, it was you who made me the offer.'

'Of course I did. But to the point if you please, sir. Miss Ingram?'

'Well, I feigned courtship of Miss Ingram, because I wished to render you as madly in love with me as I was with you and I knew jealousy would be the best ally I could call in for the furtherance of that end.'

'It was a burning shame and a scandalous disgrace to act in that way. Did you think nothing of Miss Ingram's feelings, sir?'

'Her feelings are concentrated in one – pride. And that needs humbling. Were you jealous, Jane?'

'Never mind, Mr Rochester. It is in no way interesting to you to know that. Answer me truly once more. Do you think Miss Ingram will not suffer from your dishonest coquetry? Won't she feel forsaken and deserted?'

'Impossible! When I told you how she, on the contrary, deserted me. The idea of my insolvency cooled, or rather extinguished, her flame in a moment.'

'But you were . . .' it pained me to go on. 'You were lovers, were you not? Does that not place you under some obligation? I am afraid your principles on some points are eccentric.'

'My principles were never trained, Jane. They may have grown a little awry for want of attention. As for Miss Ingram and our union, it was of no import to me and little to her. I suspect and I have no doubt I will soon be replaced.'

'Say it seriously, sir, so I may enjoy the great good that has been vouchsafed to me, without fearing that anyone else is suffering the bitter pain I myself felt a while ago.'

'That you may, my good little girl. There is not another being in the world has the same pure love for me as yourself – for I lay that pleasant unction to my soul, Jane, a belief in your affection.'

He came to me and held me from behind and I turned my lips to the hand that lay on my shoulder. I loved him very much – more than I could trust myself to say – more than words had power to express.

'Ask something more,' he said presently, rubbing himself seductively across my behind. I could feel the urgency of his hardness pressing against me though the cloth of my skirt and it was all I could do not to lean back against him. 'It is my delight to be entreated, and to yield.'

I jumped away again, all too aware that the servants were about and could catch us at any moment. Again, I smoothed myself down, but I was blushing.

'Communicate your intentions to Mrs Fairfax, sir. She saw me with you last night in the hall, and she was shocked. Give her some explanation before I see her again. It pains me to be misjudged by so good a woman.'

'Go to your room, and put on your bonnet,' he replied. 'I mean you to accompany me to Millcote this morning, and while you prepare for the drive, I will enlighten the old lady's understanding. Did she think, Jane, you had given the world for love, and considered it well lost?'

'I believe she thought I had forgotten my station, and yours, sir.'

'Station! Station! Your station is in my heart.'

I went to my room and dressed, and when I heard Mr Rochester quit Mrs Fairfax's parlour, I hurried down to it. The old lady had been reading her morning portion of Scripture and her Bible lay open before her, and her spectacles were upon it. Her occupation, suspended by Mr Rochester's announcement, seemed now forgotten.

Seeing me, she roused herself. She made a sort of effort to smile, and framed a few words of congratulation, but the smile expired, and the sentence was abandoned unfinished. She put up her spectacles, shut the Bible and pushed her chair back from the table.

'I feel so astonished,' she began, 'I hardly know what to say to you, Miss Eyre. Can you tell me whether it is actually true that Mr Rochester has asked you to marry him? Don't laugh at me. But I really thought he came in here five minutes ago, and said that in a fortnight you would be his wife.'

'He has said the same thing to me,' I replied.

'He has! Do you believe him? Have you accepted him?'

'Yes.'

She looked at me bewildered. 'I could never have thought it. He is a proud man. All the Rochesters were proud and his father, at least, liked money. He, too, has always been called careful. He means to marry you?'

'He tells me so.'

She surveyed my whole person. In her eyes I read that they had there found no charm powerful enough to solve the enigma.

'It passes me!' she continued. 'But no doubt, it is true since you say so. Equality of position and fortune is often advisable in such cases and there are twenty years of difference in your ages. He might almost be your father.'

'No, indeed, Mrs Fairfax!' I exclaimed. 'He is nothing like my father! No one, who saw us together, would suppose it for an instant. Mr Rochester looks as young, and is as young, as some men at five-and-twenty.'

'Is it really for love he is going to marry you?' she asked.

I was so hurt by her coldness and scepticism, that the tears rose to my eyes.

'I am sorry to grieve you,' pursued the widow, 'but you

are so young, and so little acquainted with men, I wished to put you on your guard. It is an old saying that "all is not gold that glitters", and in this case I do fear there will be something found to be different to what either you or I expect.'

'Why? Am I a monster?' I said. 'Is it impossible that Mr Rochester should have a sincere affection for me?'

'No. You are very well and much improved of late and Mr Rochester, I daresay, is fond of you. I have always noticed that you were a sort of pet of his. There are times when, for your sake, I have been a little uneasy at his marked preference, and have wished to put you on your guard, but I did not like to suggest even the possibility of wrong. I knew such an idea would shock, perhaps offend you, and you were so discreet, and so thoroughly modest and sensible, I hoped you might be trusted to protect yourself. Last night I cannot tell you what I suffered when I sought all over the house, and could find you nowhere, nor the master either and then, at twelve o'clock, saw you come in with him.'

'Well, never mind that now,' I interrupted impatiently. 'It is enough that all was right.'

'I hope all will be right in the end,' she said, 'but believe me, you cannot be too careful. Try and keep Mr Rochester at a distance. Distrust yourself as well as him. Gentlemen in his station are not accustomed to marry their governesses.'

I was growing truly irritated, but happily, Adèle ran in.

'Let me go. Let me go to Millcote too!' she cried. 'Mr Rochester won't, though there is so much room in the new carriage. Beg him to let me go, Mademoiselle.'

'That I will, Adèle,' I said, and I hastened away with her, glad to quit my gloomy monitress.

The carriage was ready. They were bringing it round to the front, and my master was pacing the pavement, Pilot following him backwards and forwards.

'Adèle may accompany us, may she not, sir?'

'I told her no. I'll have no brats! I'll have only you.'

'Do let her go, Mr Rochester, if you please. It would be better.'

'What is the matter?' he asked. 'All the sunshine is gone. Do you really wish the bairn to go? Will it annoy you if she is left behind?'

'I would far rather she went, sir,' I said. I had no wish to tell him the real reason for my dampened spirits was Mrs Fairfax's gloomy warning.

'Then off for your bonnet, and back like a flash of lightning!' cried he to Adèle, and she obeyed him, running off at speed. Then to me, he added with a theatrical flourish, 'Now my Boadicea, your new carriage awaits.'

The hour spent at Millcote was a somewhat harassing one to me. Mr Rochester obliged me to go to a certain silk warehouse where I was ordered to choose half a dozen dresses. I hated the business, I begged leave to defer it, but he insisted it should be gone through with now.

By dint of entreaties expressed in energetic whispers, I reduced the half-dozen to two. These, however, he vowed he would select himself. With anxiety I watched his eye rove over the gay stores. He fixed on a rich silk of the most brilliant amethyst dye, and a superb pink satin. I told him in a new series of whispers, that he might as well buy me a gold gown and a silver bonnet at once. I should certainly never venture to wear his choice. With infinite difficulty, for he was stubborn as a stone, I persuaded him to make an exchange in favour of a sober black satin and pearl-grey silk.

'It might pass for the present,' he said, but I knew that he would yet see me glittering like a queen. 'And when we are in Paris,' he added. 'I will buy you the finest silk underwear to go under your gowns. You will have to dress as I dictate when we are married, Jane.'

I was about to contradict him and tell him how I would continue to dress as I pleased, yet he took my wrist suddenly, and as the soft leather of his glove contracted around it, trapping me, I was forced to look at him. My stomach lurched as I met his dark gaze and as I saw how serious he was about this matter. I confess, a small shimmer of fear darted through me, so I smiled meekly and let the matter pass.

I was glad to get him out of the silk warehouse, and then out of a jeweller's shop. The more he bought me, the more my cheek burned.

'You need not treat me this way,' I said, on our return to Thornfield. 'If you do, I'll wear nothing but my old Lowood frocks to the end of the chapter. I'll be married in this lilac gingham. I only want an easy mind, sir, not crushed by crowded obligations. Do you remember what you said of Céline Varens? Of the diamonds, the cashmeres you gave her? I will not be your English Céline Varens. I shall continue to act as Adèle's governess and by that I shall earn my board and lodging, and thirty pounds a year besides. I'll furnish my own wardrobe out of that money, and you shall give me nothing but—'

'Well, but what?'

'Your regard.' My eye roved towards Adèle, who was dozing in the far corner of the carriage as we entered through the gates. I would not talk of what I was going to give him in front of his ward, but the amusement on his face at my confliction only made me feel more flustered.

'You can have my regard, for now. But shortly I mean to claim you. Your thoughts, conversation and company – for life.'

With these words, he leant in and kissed me deeply and slipped his hand between my legs over my skirts.

'If Adèle was not here, I swear I would have you again right at this moment.'

I laughed, trying to silence him.

'You are insatiable, sir,' I said.

'Of that you are entirely correct. And tonight, you shall be mine again. Prepare yourself, Jane.'

'For what?'

His dark eyes bored into mine and set my heart fluttering. He said nothing, but took my hand so that I could step down from the carriage.

TWENTY

He duly summoned me to his presence in the evening. As I entered the drawing room, my tread was hesitant, so full was I with nerves and trepidation, but as Mr Rochester rose from his chair by the fire and came towards me, I saw that his face was kind and compassionate, his full falcon-eye flashing, and tenderness and passion in every lineament.

A shadow passed over the ceiling, but then I assured myself that we were alone in the room. Perhaps my mind had only invented the shadows because I had been a spy myself behind those curtains, but Adèle was in the nursery and Mrs Fairfax in her room. It must only be my guilty conscience making me suspicious. I quailed momentarily, then I rallied.

He continued to smile at me, as he locked the door softly, then walked over to the day bed, which was surrounded by candles. His dark eyes lured me towards him as he lay down and patted the bed next to him. He poured me some wine and handed the glass to me.

I approached and took the heavy crystal glass from him and took a long draught. I was not used to wine, but then,

I was not used to being alone in such a manner with my master, either. Although we had been intimate the night before and had spent the day together, seeing him in a supine position, waiting for me, felt like yet another step into the unknown. Yet, I could not back away now, nor did my heart desire it.

'Are you nervous, Jane? You need not be afraid.' He touched my forearm, sending a shimmer of desire through me.

'I am not afraid of you, sir, only of my own inadequacy.'

'Inadequacy? You could never be inadequate to me.'

'But I have no experience.'

He inclined his head. 'As I noted by your virginity. You have no regrets, I hope?'

'None at all.'

'Then what troubles you? I can read every thought so clearly upon your brow.' As he said this, he reached up and traced my brow with his fingertip.

I thought back to the last time I had seen this room in candlelight on the night of the charades. Dare I tell him what I knew? What I had seen? I longed to confess everything to him, to reveal every secret, to lay out the details of my obsession before him. Yet, seeing the love shining in his eyes, and how tenderly he touched me, my pride would not allow my conscience to speak, for fear of his regard for me waning.

And yet, my conscience did break through, regardless of my censure, for I found myself saying, 'It is only that I wonder, sir, when you have often confided in me that you consider my virtue to be my best and most redeeming asset and the means with which to rejuvenate your ailing spirits, that your opinion of me may now perhaps have altered? Now that my virtue is gone, do you think less of me?'

My voice started to tremble as I said this and he took me in his arms, until I was lying beside – and partly below – him, yet his weight upon me felt like a deeper solace than I had ever known. His face filled my vision as he stroked my cheek in the candlelight.

'You still have your virtue. When pleasure is given with love, it is raised up and exulted, delivered from the base to the beautiful.'

'Yet you have known pleasure with so many others.'

'But you are different in every way. Because you will be my wife – you are already my wife in my heart, for I married you last night in our pagan ritual beneath that great and noble tree. At least I thought it so. Did you not?'

I nodded.

'There will be no more wanting or roving for me, for with you, I will be faithful and pure.'

His words were heavenly to my ears and I reached up to kiss him. Then I pressed myself against him, my arms around his neck. He was mine and my heart rejoiced.

'I want to know how to please you,' I whispered, after a long time in his embrace. 'Like she did.'

'Who? Blanche?'

'You spoke of her lustrous hair and bosoms and buttocks.'

'That I did, that I did.' He sighed and turned over onto his back to look at me, his arms folded behind his head. 'I can share my experience with you, if you wish.'

'I do wish it. I wish to know every detail of every woman you have ever been with. I see no reason to stop being your confessor now.'

He smiled, clearly surprised, as I sat up beside him. 'You would hear about the other women? Would that not make you jealous.'

'Why would I be jealous? I simply wish to know you fully, sir. I want to know your past – the good and the bad. And perhaps in that way, you can start afresh and I may be able to yet rejuvenate and reform you.'

He had an enigmatic look on his face and he glanced at me askance, as if seeing me in a new light. Then he rubbed his thick eyebrows.

'Perhaps. Well, in the case of Miss Ingram, in between the sheets, she was a vixen, but she was cold, too.' He reached up, pulling me back down on top of him. 'I never held her like this. I never kissed her like I kiss you. I never loved her, like I love you.'

He kissed me fully then, and lying in his arms in that beautiful, sensual room, I felt faint with happiness, because I knew it was true.

'But even so, I feel inadequate. I wish you to teach me. To show me what to do.'

He sighed. 'Then I shall. I shall start with . . .' he paused, as if he had just had an idea. His eyes flashed at me, as he quickly lay me back down and alighted from the day bed.

I sat up again, watching him and, for a second, I thought I saw a movement in the corner of the room again. My eyes shot towards the large painting on the far wall – the one showing the naked bodies running amongst the trees – which I now saw, in the low candlelight, was as explicit as I had first suspected. Perhaps even more so, in fact. Now that my eyes were fully opened, I saw that the leaves of the painting hardly masked the copulating couples. How had I not realized what it depicted, when I had first beheld the great painting? I felt as if Mr Rochester had opened my eyes and I was seeing for the first time, not in black and white, but in wondrous colour.

Mr Rochester walked to the fireplace, where the fire was roaring, although it was not necessary on such a balmy June night.

'Why don't you take your dress off?' he said, without turning round. He took the poker and stirred the fire.

Nervously, I knelt up and unbuttoned my summer gown. He turned and watched me, although I could not read his gaze.

'That's it,' he instructed, 'take it off. We have no need of it tonight.'

I knelt in my white undergarments, my drawers, stockings and corset top.

Mr Rochester took a red ornament off the mantelpiece and came towards me.

'The first Japanese girl I ever knew gave me a collection of these,' he said, bringing over one of the glass objects.

'She liked to use ones like these to pleasure herself.'

I felt a blush rising to my cheek as I took the ornament from him. It felt heavy in my hand, but I now saw from the shape of it, that it was shaped like a man's appendage. I was amazed that Mrs Fairfax had supervised the cleaning of this room so often and that little Adèle had played in here, pointing out these objects, never knowing their true purpose.

'I have found that women often like to pleasure themselves.' He stared at me, his eyes dancing in the candlelight. 'I wonder, have you ever pleasured yourself, Jane?'

I avoided his question, as I weighed the red phallus in my palm. I felt too overwhelmed to admit how many times I had pleasured myself, imagining myself with him. I thought of the first night we had met and how I had not been able to stop my wild imagination casting him in the role of the sea god I had studied in the tapestry on the third floor.

He smiled when he saw how my cheeks pounded.

'You will learn to find pleasure in all manner of ways, Jane,' he whispered, sitting next to me on the bed and kissing my neck. 'That is where my experience will benefit you the most. I will raise you up to new heights. Would you like that?'

He kissed me more and more, kissing along my collar bone and expertly unhooking the laces at the front, until my corset fell away. I closed my eyes, tipping my head back, lost once again in desire.

Eventually, my breast was exposed and he flicked his tongue over my erect nipples, sending darts of exquisite agony all over me.

'I will know your body. Every part of it.'

I felt feverish and hot at his words. I had not considered that my body would be his plaything, or that he would be so serious about my pleasure.

'Fear not,' he said. 'These lessons will come in time. So. To start at the beginning. Here. If you wish to please me, I will show you how.'

He reached over and dipped the red ornament into his wine and then proffered it to me, his dark eyes dazzling me. I extended my tongue and licked the droplet from the end as I stared at him.

'Very good,' he said. 'Take it.'

I took the heavy red ornament, my heart stuttering at his dictates.

'Take it in your mouth,' he said, studying me closely.

I did as he told me, my mouth filling with the warm hard glass.

'And now to compare,' he said, unbuttoning himself and withdrawing his throbbing member. My loins ached at the sight of him. I knelt forward, licking the tip of him, as I had licked the droplet from the glass.

'That's it,' he said, as I took him further into my mouth, delighting in the unfamiliar salty taste of him.

I felt him shuddering, holding my head as I moved up and down the length of him. It made me feel at once submissive and powerful, and his moans of pleasure only lit up my own desire, like a flame.

'Wait,' I said, sensing his ardour was mounting perilously close to its summit. Remembering how I had observed the maid and everything she had said, I shuffled away from him, pulling down my drawers to expose myself. I felt immense power, as I knelt before him, spreading my legs.

'Oh, Jane,' he breathed heavily. 'Oh, Jane, my beauty.'

Then he entered me, slowly – tantalizingly slowly – as if he was easing into the very core of my soul. And just like I had been under the tree, I was lost.

Afterwards, we lay half dressed in each other's arms as we talked softly. I traced the soft hair of his chest, marvelling at every mark on his skin, devouring him, poring over him in the magnifying glass of my attention. Yet soon, the wine, the candles, the heavy feeling of deep satisfaction, made my eyelids heavy. I longed to spend the night in his arms, sleeping on that magical bed in that beautiful room, but before long, he jogged me awake, asserting that we would have to wait until after the wedding to sleep together.

After he had bidden me goodnight, with a chaste kiss in the corridor, I fell into my bed and into a delicious sleep, delirious with tiredness. I thought I heard a door opening above me on the third floor and laughter, but I was too tired to pay any attention, my body and mind exhausted.

Thus, a pattern emerged over the following days and nights. When Mr Rochester and I were in other people's presence I was, as formerly, deferential and quiet, any other line of conduct being uncalled for. It was only in the evening conferences I could be myself with him. He continued to send for me punctually the moment the clock struck seven and I never knew what lesson he would have prepared for me.

Sometimes, he had no such honeyed terms as 'love' and 'darling' on his lips. The best words at my service were 'provoking puppet', 'malicious elf', 'sprite', 'changeling'. Then at other times, he gave me the tenderest of caresses.

One night I went into the drawing room to find the bed strewn with books that I recognized to be the ones from the top shelves of the locked library cupboards. When Mr Rochester entreated me to join him and look, I saw that they contained the most fantastical engravings and etchings. I remembered how his guests had studied these books, but seeing them for the first time myself took my breath away.

I had gazed upon the tapestries in the third floor, as you know, dear reader, but there the images had been blurred and difficult to discern, but these were so clear, it was as if I were watching the lustful scenes myself.

As I flicked over the pages, I felt Mr Rochester observing me closely, and reader, shocked as you may be, let me assure you, it was harder to conceal my own astonishment.

'Have you done these things?' I asked, my voice no more than a husky whisper.

'Never with you.'

'What about this?' I asked, pointing to a picture of two men with a woman.

My finger trembled. I remembered my fantasy when I had cast myself as Céline Varens with Mr Rochester and the vicomte. I had had no way of imagining where I could take such a longing, but here it was before me, drawn in black and white. Two naked men, holding their erect members above the woman's open mouth. Her sex was showing as she crouched down, her breasts standing proud, but the look in her eye as she stared up at the two men was all-powerful.

I felt Mr Rochester observing me keenly. He was, at the time, massaging my bare foot, his fingers slipping in between my toes. He had, in his exploration of my naked body, taught me to appreciate the erotic zones of this particular area.

I turned over the page. Now I saw something that made my breath catch in my throat. The woman in the picture was standing over a man, who seemed to be tied to a bed. A blindfold covered his eyes. He had a hard erection proud against his stomach. The woman, depicted from the back and side, had ample buttocks and bosoms and a whip was flexed in her hand. She stood beside the bed, one foot pressing down on her captive's chest.

'What is this?' I asked.

Mr Rochester had a strange look on his face.

'Why? How does it make you feel?'

The blood pulsed in my loins, but now colour rose to my cheeks.

'I don't know,' I said. 'Fearful for the man. Why has she tied him up?'

'She is a dominatrix.'

'A dominatrix? What kind of woman is that?' I asked, having never heard the word.

'Some men liked to be controlled by a woman. It gives them pleasure.'

I was incredulous. 'But the woman? The woman with the whip. Will he readily submit to her?' I looked harder at the image, seeing that his wrists and ankles were bound to the bed. 'He does not look happy, or as if it is giving him any pleasure.'

'Ah, but there is nothing readily about it. The man's submission is borne of compulsion.'

His words were measured, as if testing me out for a reaction. Suddenly, I remembered the chair in the charades I had seen. How Blanche Ingram had pretended to chain his ankles and wrists. I felt the blood pounding in my cheeks. Then, without warning, the words I had been holding back slipped from my lips.

'Sir, I saw your friends. I saw the game of charades you played.'

His hand stopped on my foot.

'You were spying, Jane?'

My heart stuttered, my blurted confession filling the space around me. I stared at him in horror as I looked up from the book.

'And what did you think? Were you repelled?'

'No, sir,' I said quickly. 'Not repelled exactly. Only fascinated.'

'I see,' he said. 'Then I may have to educate you less than I thought.'

I wanted to ask him more, for him to explain whether he liked to be dominated too, whether this was part of his dark experience, but instead, he made me lie in front of him on my side on the bed, the books before me. I felt him fondling me with his fingers. My heart relaxed, thrilled that he was not angry with me at my confession.

'Look at the pictures, Jane,' he whispered in my ear. 'Tell me which images you like the best.'

I confess I hardly looked at the pages as he pleasured me, so lost was I in his embrace, his nimble fingers making my pleasure mount and mount. But at length, he made me flick over the pages, until I chanced upon a vivid picture of two women together. Then, still pleasuring me with his fingers, I felt him ease inside me, his throbbing manhood slowly entering me, and, as his fingers quickened, I was quite overcome and cried out at the intensity of my pleasure.

He studied the picture over my shoulder. 'Ah, I see. It is one of my favourite images too. You like the women together, Jane?' he asked, his look so searching that I wondered if he knew everything in my experience. 'You need not be ashamed,' he said. 'It is natural and most encouraging. A delight in the female form is something else that we share in common.'

Yet it was his form I treasured the most and I told him so with fervent kisses.

Indeed, it was a theme I happily pursued, until later that night, I entreated him to let me draw him. I was not satisfied with the results, but to capture his naked form in my rudimentary charcoal strokes gave me more pleasure than I could express.

As for my duties during the day, I was neglectful of Adèle. I sensed that our relationship had changed upon her discovery that I was to be betrothed to her Mr Rochester. At first, I expected her to be jealous, but her delight was quite infectious and her willingness to co-operate in my slackened regime was a secret relief to me. If she noted my drowsiness, my heavy-lidded happiness, she did not express any dissatisfaction.

And sleepy I was, dear reader, as I was fast discovering that Mr Rochester was a hard man to satisfy. He had insatiable energy, although it was he who chastised me for accosting him. Quite often he affirmed in front of Mrs Fairfax at breakfast, that I was wearing him to skin and bone, and threatened awful vengeance for my present conduct at some period fast coming. I laughed in my sleeve, delighting to share in his secret code. Mrs Fairfax for her part said nothing, and I was too delirious with happiness to wish to indulge her in her obvious disapproval by paying heed to it.

One morning, I awoke early, anxious that I should catch him before he had to go to Millcote on business. In those days, he was more occupied than ever in getting his affairs in order before our wedding. I stole quickly out of bed, hoping to surprise him with a morning kiss, before the servants awoke.

The dawn had just broken when, as I approached his chamber, I was halted by the distant sound of singing. Stopping and straining my ears, I realized the sound was coming from Mr Rochester's chamber. Smiling to myself, I listened at the door, and when the deep baritone stopped, I knocked softly on the wooden panel.

'Come in, John, the door is open,' he called.

I stepped inside, to find that Mr Rochester was in a large bathtub by the fire. His beard was covered in white soap suds and a large cut-throat razor was in his hand.

He stopped when he saw me, his eyes widening.

'Oh. It is you.'

I must confess, reader, that I laughed, thrilled to catch him in so uncompromising a position at such an unexpectedly early hour of the morning. I confess that everything about him had become an obsessive fascination to me: the click of his riding boots, the smell of his cape, the objects in his pockets, the dent in his pillow, the contents of his papers – each detail filled me with joy, and so to come upon him thus was a treasured find.

'Come in,' he said quickly, glancing out into the corridor. 'No one has seen you?'

I shook my head and slipped inside, shutting the door and turning the key in the lock. I noted, not for the first time, that every lock in Thornfield seemed to be silent, each key securing the latch with hardly a sound.

'Well, my little wife-to-be, how are you feeling today?'

I smiled and kissed him, getting soap on my chin. We had been intimate on that delicious daybed every evening for the past week, until my legs felt permanently weak and I could hardly stand, yet this felt different. A blissful prelude to our future life together.

'You have never seen a man in a bathtub, I take it?' he said. 'You see, I am quite compromised.'

I smiled at him, touching the rivulets of water running through the dark hair on his chest.

'Do you wish to shave me?' he asked, handing me the razor.

'I don't know how,' I said, laughing with surprise.

'Here. It is easy. I will show you. I like it when a woman shaves me.'

I had asked him to teach me how to please him and entreated him to tell me about his experiences, the number and variety of which I had found shocking, although I had striven not to show it. Another woman may have found his talk of his past conquests upsetting, or might have succumbed to jealousy, but, as I have said before, I was not jealous. I was enraptured, clamouring for more and more details, certain that in sharing his secret life with me, he was making us closer.

I took the razor as he showed me how to hold his skin taut with my fingertips, and I shaved away his whiskers beneath the soap. I found the razor passing his throat at once terrifying and exhilarating. I was amazed that he trusted me so.

'So which of your paramours was the one to shave you?' I asked, tilting my head to finish the long stroke.

'In Paris. I had a lover. The one before Céline. She was a fine creature, Jane. A dancer. Her name was Emmanuelle and she was from Rio de Janeiro in Brazil.'

'She sounds exotic.'

'She was exotic, that was true enough. She let me shave her too.'

'Her hair?' I asked, stopping to stare into his eyes. They twinkled with amusement.

'Below. She said it made everything more sensual.'

'What a thought.'

'Would you like to be a Brazilian girl tonight?' he asked.

'I don't know—' I stumbled, but I could see from the dark menace in his eyes that he had made up his mind.

'Oh, I think I should insist. Now you have mentioned it, I must see you that way. Come. Take off your gown and sit on the tub.'

'No, sir. I can't.'

'You yourself have locked the door, so nobody will find us.'

'But—'

'Jane,' he said, in that tone that made me quail, for the fear of displeasing him. 'You said you trusted me, that you wanted to do what pleases me. Well, this pleases me, as it will please you. Come. Let us be equals in all things. I have not disappointed you yet, have I?'

I shivered as I sat on the edge of the tub, my bare feet in the water, my body tingling with terror.

Slowly, he took the soap from the bath and, forming a lather, spread it across the dark hair between my legs.

'Hold still,' he said, as he took the razor, examining me, but my thighs quivered as the blade touched them.

'Be still, my little bird. Do not tremble so. Trust me.'

I closed my eyes as he shaved me, not daring to look. Then afterwards, he rinsed me with water, and how the sensation made me quiver. I felt naked, utterly laid bare before him.

'Now then,' he said, and I saw that he was studying me, like an artist might assess his own work.

Leaning forward, he ran his tongue across the smooth skin where he had expertly shaved the hair away, leaving only a thin line of down above my puckering bud. A deep moan escaped my throat, for the desire within my loins seemed unstoppable. The fear I had felt had somehow only increased my longing. When I looked down into his face, I sensed that perhaps he knew this and wondered whether it had brought him a kind of pleasure too.

'That is all,' he said in a gruff tone, and I gasped with shock as he withdrew. 'You must leave me. And when you come to me tonight, I want to know how you have felt all day. I daresay you will be weak with longing by then.'

I watched him stand in the bath, his body glistening with water. His erection stood firm and proud, and I reached for it, hoping to take it once more in my mouth, but he ducked out of my way.

'You cannot touch. If you do, I will be forced to punish you and tie you to my bed. Would you like that, Jane?'

He stared at me and then at my shaven sex, and for a second, I thought that he may well overpower me and take me to his bed. And, reader, I would have submitted. I was lost in his power, such was the strength of my carnal desire for him.

My future husband was becoming to me my whole world, and more than the world, almost my hope of heaven. He stood between me and every thought of religion, as an eclipse intervenes between man and the broad sun. I could not, in those days, see God for His creature: of whom I had made an idol.

TWENTY-ONE

The fortnight of courtship had gone and its very last hours were being numbered. There was no putting off the day that advanced – the bridal day and all preparations for its arrival were complete. It was to be a simple affair, and for my part, I was glad that Mr Rochester had decided that there should be no guests. It seemed to me fitting that our wedding, much like our liaisons with each other, should be intensely private.

I, at least, had nothing more to do. There were my trunks, packed, locked, corded, ranged in a row along the wall of my little chamber. Tomorrow, at this time, they would be far on their road to London, and so should I – or rather, not I, but one Jane Rochester, a person whom as yet I knew not. The cards of address alone remained to nail on. They lay, four little squares, in the drawer.

Mr Rochester had written them himself, yet I could not persuade myself to affix them, or to have them affixed. Mrs Rochester! She did not exist. She would not be born till tomorrow, some time after eight o'clock in the morning, and

I would wait to be assured she had come into the world alive before I assigned to her all that property.

It was enough that in yonder closet, opposite my dressing table, garments said to be hers had already displaced my black stuff Lowood frock and straw bonnet. There, hanging up, was the pearl-coloured wedding robe and veil, which at this evening hour –nine o'clock – gave out certainly a most ghostly shimmer through the shadow of my apartment. 'I will leave you by yourself, white dream,' I said. 'I am feverish. I hear the wind blowing. I will go out of doors and feel it.'

It was not only the hurry of preparation that made me feverish. Not only the anticipation of the great change – the new life which was to commence tomorrow, both of these circumstances had their share, doubtless, in producing that restless, excited mood which hurried me forth at this late hour into the darkening grounds, but a third cause influenced my mind more than they.

I had at heart a strange and anxious thought. Something had happened which I could not comprehend. No one knew of or had seen the event but myself. It had taken place the preceding night.

Mr Rochester that night was absent from home, nor was he yet returned. Business had called him to a small estate of two or three farms he possessed thirty miles off – business he had to settle in person, before his departure from England. I waited now for him to return, eager to disburden my mind, and to seek of him the solution of the enigma that perplexed me. Stay till he comes, reader, and, when I disclose my secret to him, you shall share the confidence.

I sought the orchard, driven to its shelter by the wind, which all day had blown strong and full from the south, without, however, bringing a speck of rain. It was not without a certain wild pleasure I ran before the wind, delivering my trouble of mind to the measureless air-torrent thundering through space.

Descending the laurel walk, I faced the wreck of the chestnut tree. It stood up black and riven, the trunk split down the centre, although the cloven halves were not broken from each other, for the firm base and strong roots kept them un-sundered below.

'You did right to hold fast to each other,' I said, as if the monster-splinters were living things, and could hear me. 'I think, scathed as you look, and charred and scorched, there must be a little sense of life in you yet, rising out of that adhesion at the faithful, honest roots. You will never have green leaves more – never more see birds making nests and singing idylls in your boughs, but you are not desolate. Each of you has a comrade to sympathize with him in his decay.'

I looked up and saw the moon appearing from a cloud.

'How late it grows!' I said. 'I will run down to the gates. I can see a good way on the road in the moonlight. He may be coming now, and to meet him will save some minutes of suspense.'

The wind roared high in the great trees which embowered the gates, but the road as far as I could see, to the right hand and the left, was all still and solitary, save for the shadows of clouds crossing it at intervals as the moon looked out, it was but a long pale line, unvaried by one moving speck.

A puerile tear dimmed my eye while I looked – a tear of disappointment and impatience. Ashamed of it, I wiped it away.

'I wish he would come! I wish he would come!' I exclaimed, seized with hypochondriac foreboding. I had expected his arrival before tea, but now it was dark. What could keep him? Had an accident happened?

The event of last night again recurred to me. I interpreted it as a warning of disaster. I feared my hopes were too bright and that I had enjoyed so much bliss lately that my fortune had passed its meridian, and must now decline.

'Well, I cannot return to the house,' I thought. 'Better tire my limbs than strain my heart. I will go forward and meet him.'

I set out, but before long, I heard the tramp of hoofs and a horseman came on in full gallop and a dog ran by his side. Away with evil presentiment! It was Mr Rochester on Mesrour, followed by Pilot. He saw me, for the moon had opened a blue field in the sky, and rode in it watery bright. He took his hat off, and waved it round his head. I now ran to meet him.

'There!' he exclaimed, as he stretched out his hand and bent from the saddle. 'You can't do without me, that is evident. Step on my boot-toe. Give me both hands and mount!'

I obeyed. Joy made me agile and I sprang up before him. A hearty kissing I got for a welcome, and some boastful triumph, which I swallowed as well as I could. He checked himself in his exultation to demand, 'But is there anything the matter, Jane, that you come to meet me at such an hour? Is there anything wrong?'

'No, but I thought you would never come. I could not bear to wait in the house for you, especially with this rain and wind.'

'Rain and wind, indeed! Yes, you are dripping like a mermaid. Pull my cloak round you. Here, you will be more comforted inside. Put your leg over the saddle. That's it.' I did ask he asked, sitting astride Mesrour in front of Mr Rochester. 'I ask again, my love, is there anything the matter?'

'Nothing now. I am neither afraid nor unhappy.'

'Then you have been both?'

'Rather, but I'll tell you all about it by and by, sir, and I daresay you will only laugh at me for my pains.'

I sank back against him, feeling his warmth, enveloped by the manly scent of his coat, and swooning with relief.

'Oh my pretty one,' he said, kissing my ear. 'I can no longer be apart from you, as you from me.'

And it was then, beneath his cloak, that I felt his hands find mine and transfer the reins into them.

'I know not how to ride, sir.'

'Mesrour needs no guidance,' said Mr Rochester. 'He is more than familiar with this terrain.'

I felt my master shuffling in the saddle behind me, and pushing up in the stirrups to raise himself. A fumbling occurred behind my back and then, as Mr Rochester resumed his seated position, I felt his hands stroking my thighs and hitching my skirt up higher.

'But, sir,' I whispered, incredulous now I had realized his plan, 'surely we cannot here?'

'All is possible, Jane, if there is but sufficient will.'

And with that, dear reader, he cupped his strong hands beneath my buttocks and raised me, as though I weighed no more than a bird, and simultaneously employed his fingertips to sweep my undergarments aside. In that private area between his body and mine and the soft leather of Mesrour's saddle, all was warm and intimate and I gasped as every nerve ending and every fibre of my attention went there. His length was so great and so rigid that he had to raise me higher still, before slowly lowering me onto the moist tip of his member.

Powerless, and indeed unwilling to resist, I gripped the reins tighter in my fists, the wind in my hair, as Mr Rochester dipped his throbbing end inside me, over and over, each time a little deeper – opening me wider – until, finally, he impaled me fully upon its entire wide length, with a exultant sigh, and my trembling buttocks rested in that sweet seat comprising his stomach and his thighs.

Aching with pleasure myself, I now wished to give pleasure in return, and attempted to raise my hips such as I might begin to move my eager, wet sex up and down his.

'No, Jane,' he commanded me. 'Be still. Allow Mesrour to do all the work. Give a flick of the reins, just so. That's it.'

Mesrour began to walk on and, as he did so, Mr Rochester's arms wrapped around me once more. His right hand slid between the buttons of my dress, first cupping my breast, then pinching my nipple hard between his forefinger and thumb, so that I cried out, thus startling Mesrour, who gave a whinney and broke into a trot.

Mr Rochester's left hand delved deeper between my legs, and there began to caress and fondle me.

'Faster,' he urged, spurring Mesrour now into a canter, as Pilot barked in excitement, running alongside.

With each powerful fall of Mesrour's hooves now upon the moonlit ground, I found myself effortlessly sliding up and down my master's manhood, secured from at any time being removed from it completely by its prodigious hard length.

We were galloping now, with the wind and rain in my face and now my naked breast and sex exposed to its cool caress too. And then, as we made it up the final hill and saw the yellow lights of Thornfield glowing welcomingly in the valley below, a final burst of speed from Mesrour brought me shuddering back against my master, lost in a shivering ecstasy that burst a cry of unadulterated pleasure from my lips.

At Thornfield, we lingered for a moment in the shadows, as Mr Rochester raised me up one last, exquisite time, before finally withdrawing from me. Adjusting our garments, so as to make ourselves once more decent, we rode on to the house, where he landed me on the pavement.

As John took his horse, Mr Rochester followed me into the hall and told me to make haste and put something dry on, and then return to him in the library. He stopped me, as I made for the staircase, to extort a promise that I would not be long. Nor was I long. In five minutes I rejoined him. I found him at supper.

'Take a seat and bear me company, Jane. Please God, it is the last meal but one you will eat at Thornfield Hall for a long time.'

I sat down near him, but told him I could not eat. 'Is it because you have the prospect of a journey before you, Jane? Is it the thought of going to London that takes away your appetite?'

'I cannot see my prospects clearly tonight, sir, and I hardly know what thoughts I have in my head. Everything in life seems unreal.'

'Except me. I am substantial enough. Here touch me.'

'You, sir, are the most phantom-like of all. You are a mere dream.'

He held out his hand, laughing. 'Is that a dream?' said he, placing his thumb on my lips. He had a rounded, muscular and vigorous thumb, and he pressed it inside my mouth.

I grabbed his hand. 'Though I touch it, it is a dream,' I said, putting his thumb fully in my mouth, running my tongue along the underside of it.

He grunted in a way that set my stomach dancing, but I remembered my purpose.

'Sir, have you finished supper?' I asked, removing his thumb and kissing it lightly on the end, before placing his hand back on his chair.

'Yes, Jane.'

I rang the bell and ordered away the tray. When we were again alone, I stirred the fire.

'Come here,' he said, patting his knee, and I sat on his lap.

'It is near midnight,' I said.

'Yes, but remember, Jane, you promised to wake with me the night before my wedding.'

'I did and I will keep my promise, for an hour or two at least. I have no wish to go to bed.'

'Are all your arrangements complete?'

'All, sir.'

'And on my part likewise,' he returned. 'I have settled everything and we shall leave Thornfield tomorrow, within half an hour after our return from church.'

'Very well, sir.'

'With what an extraordinary smile you uttered those words – "very well", Jane! What a bright spot of colour you have on each cheek! And how strangely your eyes glitter! Are you quite well? Tell me what you feel.'

'I could not, sir. No words could tell you what I feel. I wish this present hour would never end. Who knows with what fate the next may come charged?'

I looked up at him to read the signs of bliss in his face.

'Relieve your mind of any weight that oppresses it, by imparting it to me. What do you fear? That I shall not prove a good husband?' He brushed a loose strand of hair tenderly from my forehead.

'It is the idea farthest from my thoughts.'

'Are you apprehensive of the new sphere you are about to enter? Of the new life into which you are passing?'

'No.'

'Mrs Fairfax has said something, perhaps? Or you have overheard the servants talk? Your sensitive self-respect has been wounded?'

'No, sir.' It struck twelve. I waited till the timepiece had concluded its silver chime, and the clock in the hall its hoarse, vibrating stroke, and then I proceeded.

'All day yesterday I was very busy, and very happy in my ceaseless bustle, for I am not, as you seem to think, troubled by any haunting fears about the new sphere I am about to enter. I think it a glorious thing to have the hope of living with you, because I love you. No, sir, don't caress me now – let me talk undisturbed.'

I removed myself from his lap and sat by his feet on the small stool there, staring up at him. He shifted in the great chair, listening intently.

'Yesterday it was a fine day, if you recollect. The calmness of the air and sky forbade apprehensions respecting your safety or comfort on your journey. I walked a little while on the pavement after tea, thinking of you, and I beheld you in imagination so near me, I scarcely missed your actual presence. I thought of the life that lay before me – your life, sir – with me – an existence more expansive and stirring than I could have ever imagined might happen.'

He smiled down at me, his eyes soft in the firelight.

'Just at sunset, the air turned cold and the sky cloudy. I went in and Leah called me upstairs to look at my wedding dress, which they had just brought, and under it in the box I found your present. The veil which, in your princely extravagance, you sent for from London, resolved, I suppose, since

I would not have jewels, to cheat me into accepting something as costly. I smiled as I unfolded it, and devised how I would tease you about your aristocratic tastes, and your efforts to masque your plebeian bride in the attributes of a peeress.

'I thought how I would carry down to you the square of unembroidered blond I had myself prepared as a covering for my low-born head, and ask if that was not good enough for a woman who could bring her husband neither fortune, beauty, nor connections. I saw plainly how you would look and heard your impetuous republican answers, and your haughty disavowal of any necessity on your part to augment your wealth, or elevate your standing, by marrying either a purse or a coronet.'

'How well you read me!' interposed Mr Rochester, laughing, 'but what did you find in the veil besides its embroidery? Did you find poison, or a dagger, that you look so mournful now?'

'No, no, sir. Besides the delicacy and richness of the fabric, I found nothing save Fairfax Rochester's pride, which did not scare me, because I am used to the sight of it.'

'True enough.'

'But, sir, as it grew dark, the wind rose. I wished you were at home. I came into this room, and the sight of the empty chair and fireless hearth chilled me. For some time after I went to bed, I could not sleep. A sense of anxious excitement distressed me. The gale still rising, seemed to my ear to muffle a mournful under-sound, whether in the house or abroad I could not at first tell, but it recurred, doubtful yet doleful at every lull. It seemed to be calling my name.

'My dreams were feverish and disturbing and several times, I cried out. Then once, after the third most terrible dream, I woke up with a gleam dazzling my eyes. I thought, "Oh, it is daylight!" But I was mistaken. It was only candlelight.

'There was a light in the dressing table, and the door of the closet, where, before going to bed, I had hung my wedding dress and veil, stood open. I heard a rustling there. Presuming Mrs Fairfax or Leah had come in, I asked, "What are you doing?"

'No one answered, but a form emerged from the closet. It took the light, held it aloft and surveyed the garments pendent from the portmanteau. "Leah! Leah!" I again cried, but still it was silent. I had risen up in bed, and I went forward. First surprise, then bewilderment came over me, and then my blood crept cold through my veins. Mr Rochester, this was not Leah, it was not Mrs Fairfax. It was not – no, I was sure of it, and am still – it was not even that strange woman, Grace Poole.'

'It must have been one of them,' interrupted my master.

'No, sir, I solemnly assure you to the contrary. The shape standing before me had never crossed my eyes within the precincts of Thornfield Hall before. The height, the contour were new to me.'

'Describe it, Jane.'

'It seemed, sir, a woman, tall and shapely, with thick and dark hair hanging long down her back. I know not what dress she had on. It was red and shaped around her.'

'Did you see her face?'

'Not at first. But presently she took my veil from its place.

She held it up, gazed at it long, and then she threw it over her own head, and turned to the mirror. At that moment I saw the reflection of the visage and features quite distinctly in the dark oblong glass.'

'And how were they?'

'Oh, sir, I never saw a face like it! She had fine, dark skin and huge green eyes. She looked as if she might have stepped out of a painting, such was her expression of haughty grandeur.'

'Ghosts are usually pale, Jane. But what did it do?'

'Sir, it removed my veil from its gaunt head, and rent it in two parts, flinging both on the floor with a flourish.'

'And afterwards?'

'It drew aside the window-curtain and looked out. Perhaps it saw dawn approaching, for, taking the candle, it retreated to the door. Just at my bedside, the figure stopped. The fiery eyes glared upon me and she thrust up her candle close to my face, and extinguished it under my eyes, her breath and the smoke filling my nostrils. I was aware of her lurid visage flaming over mine, with a hunger in her eyes I could not fathom, but at that point, I lost consciousness, for the second time in my life – only the second time that I became insensible from terror.'

'Who was with you when you revived?'

'No one, sir, but the broad day. I rose, bathed my head and face in water, drank a long draught. I felt that though enfeebled I was not ill, and determined that to none but you would I impart this vision. Now, sir, tell me who and what that woman was?'

'The creature of an over-stimulated brain, that is certain. I must be careful of you, my treasure. Nerves like yours were not made for rough handling.'

'Sir, depend on it, my nerves were not in fault. The thing was real. The transaction actually took place.'

'Jane, the day is already commenced which is to bind us indissolubly, and when we are once united, there shall be no recurrence of these mental terrors, I guarantee that.'

'Mental terrors, sir! I wish I could believe them to be only such. I wish it more now than ever since even you cannot explain to me the mystery of that awful visitant.'

'And since I cannot do it, Jane, it must have been unreal.'

'But, sir, when I said so to myself on rising this morning, and when I looked round the room to gather courage and comfort from the cheerful aspect of each familiar object in full daylight, there on the carpet I saw the veil, torn from top to bottom in two halves!'

I felt Mr Rochester start and shudder. He hastily leant forward and flung his arms round me. 'Thank God!' he exclaimed. 'That if anything malignant did come near you last night, it was only the veil that was harmed. Oh, to think what might have happened!'

He drew his breath short, and strained me so close to him, I could scarcely pant. After some minutes' silence, he continued, cheerily, 'Now, Jane, I'll explain to you all about it. It was half dream, half reality. A woman did, I doubt not, enter your room. And that woman was – must have been – Grace Poole. You call her a strange being yourself. From all you know, you have reason so to call her. Remember what she did to me? To Mason? In a state between sleeping and waking, you noticed her entrance and her actions, but feverish, almost delirious as you were, you ascribed to her an appearance different from her own. I see you would ask why I keep such a woman in my house. When we are married, I will tell you, but not now. Are you satisfied, Jane? Do you accept my solution of the mystery?'

I reflected, and in truth it appeared to me the only possible one. Satisfied I was not, but to please him I endeavoured to appear relieved. I answered him with a contented smile.

'And now, no more sombre thoughts. Chase dull care away, Jane. Don't you hear to what soft whispers the wind has fallen? There is no more beating of rain against the window panes. Look here,' he said, getting up and walking towards the window. He lifted up the curtain. 'It is a lovely night!'

It was. Half heaven was pure and stainless. The clouds, now trooping before the wind, which had shifted to the west, were filing off eastward in long, silvered columns. The moon shone peacefully. I stood and joined him, staring out at the silvery lawns.

'I know how to ease your mind,' he said, kissing my neck in a way I now knew was a prelude to his ardour. 'Here, the room is warm now,' he continued in that beguiling low tone of his that made me do his bidding. 'Lie naked with me in front of the hearth. Let me kiss you in the soft light.'

He locked the door quietly. I remembered how he had pretended to be a fortune teller in this room and how he had gazed upon me. He quietly, softly undressed me and I was meek in his embrace, compliant in his wishes. I had only need for his comfort, but as he lay me down in the glow of the fire, peppering my stomach with kisses, his tongue darting below and into my sex itself, he awoke the fire within me.

He stayed down low, his head between my legs, but would not rise and enter me, even though I begged him until he had lapped so thoroughly at me, I felt molten, as if I was dissolving. Then, just as I was tipping over a precipice, he stretched upwards and entered me fully with his huge, hot member. To be so suddenly filled made me gasp and shudder. Then, still scaling the ever-emerging climactic heights to which he was entreating me, I felt him pumping hard inside me, staring down at me, the sweat on his brow as his eyes became foggy, his breath ragged.

Then he was still, pressed hard inside me, and I clenched around him, my limbs holding him tight.

He gathered me in his arms, his enormous hardness still filling me.

'Well,' said Mr Rochester, gazing inquiringly into my eyes, 'how is my Jane now?'

'The night is serene, sir, and so am I.'

'And you will not dream of separation and sorrow tonight, but of happy love and blissful union, for I will never tire of my union with you.'

'Or I with you.'

Much comforted, some time afterwards, I went to bed. I did not indeed dream of sorrow, but as little did I dream of joy, for I never slept at all. I knew that our wedding the following morning was a mere formality, as I had already given Mr Rochester my body and heart, and yet I could not shake the strange sense of foreboding that had now returned.

Alone and awake, I wondered what Mr Rochester would tell me after our wedding, in order to make sense to me of the vision I had seen the previous night. I grasped for possible explanations in the dark, but none came to me.

As the room began to lighten with the coming dawn, I reflected that this would be the last time I would sleep alone in this chamber, for from now on, I would share Mr Rochester's. Then I remembered that I was leaving Thornfield Hall, bound for a hotel in London, and a shudder of fear passed through me.

I had told Mr Rochester I was not afraid of the new sphere I was entering, but it was not strictly true. Mr Rochester had expressed his desire to show me off, but now I remembered the guests he had entertained at Thornfield Hall and how dismissive of me they had been. Would society readily accept me, as he had told me they would? And what if we happened upon the likes of Lady Fulbright or Miss Dupret, or Captain Dent? Mr Rochester had assured me he was shunning his old life only to be with me, but breaking his old ties might not be as easy as he thought, when I could never be truly one of them.

I was pleased when the door opened and little Adèle – terrified by some nightmare of her own – crept into my arms. I watched the slumber of childhood, so tranquil, so passionless, so innocent, and waited for the coming day.

All my life was awake and astir in my frame and as soon as the sun rose I rose too. I remember Adèle clung to me as I left her. I remember I kissed her as I loosened her little hands from my neck and I cried over her with strange emotion, and quitted her because I feared my sobs would break her still sound repose. She seemed the emblem of my past life, and here I was now to array myself to meet the dread, but adored, type of my unknown future day.

CHAPTER TWENTY-TWO

Mrs Fairfax came at seven to dress me. She was very long indeed in accomplishing her task. So long that Mr Rochester, grown, I suppose, impatient of my delay, sent up to ask why I did not come. She was just fastening my veil (the plain square of blond after all) to my hair with a brooch and I hurried from under her hands as soon as I could.

'Stop!' she cried. 'Look at yourself in the mirror. You have not taken one peep.'

So I turned at the door. I saw a robed and veiled figure, so unlike my usual self that it seemed almost the image of a stranger.

'Jane!' called a voice, and I hastened down. I was received at the foot of the stairs by Mr Rochester.

'Lingerer!' he said. 'My brain is on fire with impatience, and you tarry so long!'

He took me into the dining room, surveyed me keenly all over, pronounced me 'fair as a lily, and not only the pride of his life, but the desire of his eyes,' and then telling me he would give me but ten minutes to eat some breakfast, he rang the bell. One of his lately hired servants, a footman, answered it.

'Is John getting the carriage ready?'

'Yes, sir.'

'Is the luggage brought down?'

'They are bringing it down, sir.'

'Go you to the church. See if Mr Wood (the clergyman) and the clerk are there. Return and tell me.'

The church, as the reader knows, was but just beyond the gates and the footman soon returned.

'Mr Wood is in the vestry, sir, putting on his surplice.'

'And the carriage?'

'The horses are harnessing.'

'We shall not want it to go to church, but it must be ready the moment we return. All the boxes and luggage arranged and strapped on, and the coachman in his seat.'

'Yes, sir.'

'Jane, are you ready?'

I rose. There were no groomsmen, no bridesmaids, no relatives to wait for or marshal. None but Mr Rochester and I. Mrs Fairfax stood in the hall as we passed. I would have liked to have spoken to her, but my hand was held by a grasp of iron and I was hurried along by a stride I could hardly follow. To look at Mr Rochester's face was to feel that not a second of delay would be tolerated for any purpose. I wonder what other bridegroom ever looked as he did – so bent up to a purpose, so grimly resolute. Or who, under such steadfast brows, ever revealed such flaming and flashing eyes.

I know not whether the day was fair or foul. In descending the drive, I gazed neither on sky nor earth. My heart was with my eyes and both seemed migrated into Mr Rochester's frame. I wanted to see the invisible thing on which, as we went along, he appeared to fasten a glance fierce and fell. I wanted to feel the thoughts whose force he seemed breasting and resisting.

At the churchyard wicket he stopped. He discovered I was quite out of breath. 'Am I cruel in my love?' he said. 'Delay an instant. Lean on me, Jane.'

And now I can recall the picture of the grey old house of God rising calm before me, of a rook wheeling round the steeple, of a ruddy morning sky beyond. Mr Rochester was earnestly looking at my face from which the blood had, I daresay, momentarily fled, for I felt my forehead dewy, and my cheeks and lips cold. When I rallied, which I soon did, he walked gently with me up the path to the porch. I noticed two figures – both gentlemen, judging from their attire – watching us from the other side of the graveyard, although Mr Rochester paid no attention to them.

We entered the quiet and humble temple. The priest waited in his white surplice at the lowly altar, the clerk beside him. Our place was taken at the communion rails. Hearing a cautious step behind me, I glanced over my shoulder. A stranger – a gentleman, evidently – was advancing up the chancel.

The service began. The explanation of the intent of matrimony was gone through and then the clergyman came a step further forward, and, bending slightly towards Mr Rochester, went on.

'I require and charge you both (as ye will answer at the dreadful day of judgment, when the secrets of all hearts shall be disclosed), that if either of you know any impediment why ye may not lawfully be joined together in matrimony, ye do now confess it. For be ye well assured that so many as are coupled together otherwise than God's Word doth allow, are not joined together by God, neither is their matrimony lawful.'

He paused, as the custom is. When is the pause after that sentence ever broken by reply? Not, perhaps, once in a hundred years. And the clergyman, who had not lifted his eyes from his book, and had held his breath but for a moment, was proceeding, his hand was already stretched towards Mr Rochester, as his lips unclosed to ask, 'Wilt thou have this woman for thy wedded wife?' – when a distinct and near voice said, 'The marriage cannot go on. I declare the existence of an impediment.'

The clergyman looked up at the speaker and stood mute. The clerk did the same. Mr Rochester moved slightly, as if an earthquake had rolled under his feet. Taking a firmer footing, and not turning his head or eyes, he said, 'Proceed.'

Profound silence fell when he had uttered that word, with deep but low intonation. Presently Mr Wood said, 'I cannot proceed without some investigation into what has been asserted, and evidence of its truth or falsehood.'

'The ceremony is quite broken off,' subjoined the voice behind us. 'I am in a condition to prove my allegation. An insuperable impediment to this marriage exists.'

Mr Rochester heard, but heeded not. He stood stubborn

and rigid, making no movement but to possess himself of my hand.

Mr Wood seemed at a loss. 'What is the nature of the impediment?' he asked. 'Perhaps it may be got over? Explained away?'

'Hardly,' was the answer. 'I have called it insuperable, and I speak advisedly.'

The speaker came forward and leaned on the rails. He continued, uttering each word distinctly, calmly, steadily, but not loudly, 'It simply consists in the existence of a previous marriage. Mr Rochester has a wife now living.'

My nerves vibrated to those low-spoken words as they had never vibrated to thunder. My blood felt their subtle violence as it had never felt frost or fire. Yet I was collected and in no danger of swooning. I looked at Mr Rochester. I made him look at me. His whole face was colourless rock, his eye was both spark and flint. He disavowed nothing. In fact, he seemed as if he would defy all things. Without speaking, without smiling, without seeming to recognize in me a human being, he only twined my waist with his arm and riveted me to his side.

'Who are you?' he asked of the intruder.

'My name is Briggs, a solicitor of Bow Street, London.'

'And you would thrust on me a wife?'

'I would remind you of your lady's existence, sir, which the law recognizes, if you do not.'

Mr Briggs calmly took a paper from his pocket, and read out in a sort of official, nasal voice, '"I affirm and can prove that on the 20th of October A.D. (a date of fifteen years back), Edward Fairfax Rochester, of Thornfield Hall, England, was married to my cousin, Bertha Antoinetta Mason, daughter of Jonas Mason, merchant, and of Antoinetta his wife, a Creole, at the church in Spanish Town, Jamaica. The record of the marriage will be found in the register of that church – a copy of it is now in my possession. Signed, Richard Mason."'

'That – if a genuine document – may prove I have been married, but it does not prove that the woman mentioned therein as my wife is still living.'

'She was living six weeks ago,' returned the lawyer. 'I have a witness to the fact. He is here. Mr Mason, have the goodness to step forward.'

Mr Rochester, on hearing the name, set his teeth. He experienced, too, a sort of strong convulsive quiver. Near to him as I was, I felt the spasmodic movement of fury or despair run through his frame.

The second stranger, who had hitherto lingered in the background, now drew near and I saw a pale face looking over the solicitor's shoulder. And yes, it was Mason himself.

Mr Rochester turned and glared at him. His eye, as I have often said, was a black eye. His face flushed, his olive cheek and hueless forehead received a glow as from spreading, ascending heart-fire and he stirred, lifting his strong arm as if he could have struck Mason, dashed him on the church floor. But Mason shrank away, and cried faintly, 'Good God!'

Contempt fell cool on Mr Rochester. His passion died as if a blight had shrivelled it up. He only asked, 'What have you to say?'

An inaudible reply escaped Mason's white lips.

'The devil is in it if you cannot answer distinctly. I again demand, what have you to say?'

'Sir, sir,' interrupted the clergyman, 'do not forget you are in a sacred place.' Then addressing Mason, he inquired gently, 'Are you aware, sir, whether or not this gentleman's wife is still living?'

'Courage,' urged the lawyer. 'Speak out.'

'She is now living at Thornfield Hall,' said Mason, in more articulate tones. 'I saw her there recently. She entreated me to stop the marriage.'

'At Thornfield Hall!' said the clergyman. 'Impossible! I am an old resident in this neighbourhood, sir, and I never heard of a Mrs Rochester at Thornfield Hall.'

I saw a grim smile contort Mr Rochester's lips, and he muttered, 'No, by God! I took care that none should hear of it. Or of her under that name.' He mused for a moment, holding counsel with himself. Then he seemed to form his resolve, and announced it.

'Enough! There will be no wedding today.' Mr Rochester continued, hardily and recklessly, 'Bigamy is an ugly word! I meant, however, to be a bigamist, but fate has out-manoeuvred me, or Providence has checked me, more likely. I am little better than a devil at this moment and, as my pastor there would tell me, deserve no doubt the sternest judgments of God, even to the quenchless fire and deathless worm.

'Gentlemen, my plan is broken up. What this lawyer and his client say is true. You say you never heard of a Mrs Rochester at the house up yonder, Wood, but I daresay you have many a time inclined your ear to gossip about the mysterious person kept there under watch and ward. Some have whispered to you that she is my bastard half-sister, some, my cast-off mistress, no doubt. I now inform you that she is my wife, whom I married fifteen years ago. Bertha Mason by name, cousin of this resolute personage, who is now, with his quivering limbs and white cheeks, showing you what a stout heart men may bear.

'Cheer up, Dick! Never fear me! I'd almost as soon strike a woman as you. Bertha Mason is not like other women, as you will find out for yourself, which is why I shut her up and keep her out of society, for her conduct would surely ruin me and my fortunes. But exist she does. This girl,' he continued, looking at me, 'knew no more than you, Wood, of the shameful secret. She thought all was fair and legal and never dreamt she was going to be entrapped into a feigned union with a defrauded wretch like me. Come. I'll show you. Then you'll understand.'

Still holding me fast, he pushed past the others and left the church, and I ran by his side, hardly able to keep up, or to draw my breath, let alone speak. At the front door of the hall we found the carriage.

'Take it back to the coach house, John,' said Mr Rochester coolly, 'it will not be wanted today.'

At our entrance, Mrs Fairfax, Adèle and Leah advanced to meet and greet us.

'Away with your congratulations!' cried Mr Rochester. 'Who wants them? Not I! They are fifteen years too late!'

He passed on and ascended the stairs. Still holding my

watching you in the drawing room. You have done well.' Then her eyes flashed back at Mr Rochester. 'But now you must be punished for your disobedience.'

I saw Grace Poole now in the doorway to the far chamber. A dark look of anguish was on her face as she stared at her mistress. Then her eyes flashed at me. They were filled with scorn and jealousy.

But I had no time to consider the magnitude of her role in my deception as there was a noise behind us and Mason burst in.

'I am still here. I am still yours,' he said to the woman breathlessly, tearing his shirt open to bare his scars and falling to his knees. 'I have done your bidding, now do with me what you will, Bertha. Anything. I beg of you. Please.'

I bolted, using the distraction of Mason to slip from Mr Rochester's grasp. I ran downstairs, not stopping to hear more, although Mr Rochester was protesting and calling after me. I heard the familiar cackle of the woman I had now seen for the second time, and the crack of a whip, as well as shouting from Mason.

I covered my ears and ran to my room, shut myself in, fastened the bolt that none might intrude and proceeded to cover my ears with my pillow. When I finally heard footsteps retreating, I got up and mechanically took off my wedding dress and changed into my old dress from yesterday.

I did not weep. My shock was too great. That everything I thought Mr Rochester had done for me, he had done at this creature's bidding, made me feel as if I had walked through a door into a different world. One where nothing was familiar.

As I fastened my buttons with a shaking hand, I realized that nothing had smitten me, or scathed me, or maimed me. And yet where was the Jane Eyre of yesterday? Where was her life? Where were her prospects?

Jane Eyre, who had been an ardent, expectant woman – almost a bride, was a cold, solitary girl again. Her life was pale. Her prospects were desolate. I looked at my love. That feeling which was my master's – which he alone had created, shivered in my heart, like a suffering child in a cold cradle. Sickness and anguish had seized it, but it could not seek Mr Rochester's arms or derive warmth from his breast.

Oh, never more could it turn to him, for faith was blighted and all confidence destroyed! Mr Rochester was not to me what he had been and from his presence I must go. That I perceived well.

Real affection, it seemed, he could not have for me. It had been only fitful passion, with another motive I could scarce comprehend, but only knew I balked at. Oh, how blind had been my eyes! How weak my conduct!

The whole consciousness of my life lorn, my love lost, my hope quenched, my faith death-struck, swayed full and mighty above me in one sullen mass. 'That I am not Edward Rochester's bride is the least part of my woe,' I alleged. 'That I have wakened out of most glorious dreams, and found them all void and vain, is a horror I could bear and master, but that I must leave him decidedly, instantly, entirely, is intolerable.'

I knew where to find in my drawers some linen, a locket, a ring. In seeking these articles, I encountered the beads of a pearl necklace Mr Rochester had forced me to accept a few days ago. I left that. It was not mine. It was the visionary bride's who had melted in air. The other articles I made up in a parcel. My purse, containing twenty shillings (it was all I had), I put in my pocket. I tied on my straw bonnet, pinned my shawl, took the parcel and my slippers, which I would not put on yet, and stole from my room.

I stumbled over an obstacle in the doorway and an outstretched arm caught me. I looked up. I was supported by Mr Rochester, who sat in a chair across my chamber threshold.

'Five minutes more of that death-like hush, and I should have forced the lock like a burglar. Well, Jane! Not a word of reproach? Nothing bitter, nothing poignant? Nothing to cut a feeling or sting a passion? You regard me with a weary, passive look.

'Let me pass. I must have some water.'

He caught my arm and I saw such remorse in his eye, such true pity in his tone, such manly energy in his manner, and besides, there was such unchanged love in his whole look as he said, 'Oh Jane, I never meant to wound you thus.'

My heart was torn. He looked like the Edward Rochester I had loved – still loved.

'You know I am a scoundrel?'

'That is obvious, sir.'

'Then tell me so roundly and sharply. Don't spare me.'

'I cannot. I must leave.'

I remembered last night and how we had lain together by the fire, but it felt as if I was recalling a dream, a fragment of another life. Yet the fact of it remained and stung me. I had given myself to him. I was his, no matter what these new circumstances had revealed. I could not go back and claim my virtue. It had long gone.

And yet, a steadfast part of me remained. I had not lost everything. Still a shred of self-preservation remained.

He stooped towards me as if to kiss me, but I remembered caresses were now forbidden. I turned my face away and put his aside.

'What! How is this?' he exclaimed hastily. 'Oh, I know! You won't kiss the husband of Bertha Mason? You consider my arms filled and my embraces appropriated?'

'That, she has made obvious. At any rate, there is neither room nor claim for me, sir.'

'If you think so, you must have a strange opinion of me. You must regard me as a plotting profligate. A base and low rake who has been simulating disinterested love in order to draw you into a snare deliberately laid, and strip you of honour and rob you of self-respect.'

He had often told me – proved to me – that he could read my mind, and in this regard, he had been entirely accurate. He tried to kiss me again, but I whipped my face away. 'Do not,' I said, but my unsteady voice warned me to curtail my sentence, for everything he had said was true.

I did consider myself drawn into a terrible and horrible snare. She had admitted as much. That he really could have tricked me so completely still defied belief. Still, I thought he must have affection for me, perhaps not the mirror image of my own for him, as I had thought, but at least some regard. I could not comprehend still the scene I had witnessed upstairs and what it might mean.

I cleared and steadied my voice to reply. 'Everything has changed, sir.'

'It hasn't. She is nothing to me. She stays out of sight because she is a mad woman. She is nothing like you, Jane. You are the one I love.'

'I have no choice. I must leave you.'

'Jane! Do not talk so. Will you not hear reason?'

I felt an inward power, a sense of influence, which supported me. The crisis was perilous, but not without its charm. Such as the Indian, perhaps, feels when he slips over the rapid in his canoe.

'Jane! Jane!' he said again, in such an accent of bitter sadness it thrilled along every nerve I had, 'You don't love me, then? It was only my station, and the rank of my wife, that you valued? Now that you think me disqualified to become your husband, you recoil from my touch.'

These words cut me, yet what could I do or I say? I ought probably to have done or said nothing, but I was so tortured by a sense of remorse at thus hurting his feelings, I could not control the wish to drop balm where I had wounded.

'I do love you,' I said, 'more than ever, but I must not show or indulge the feeling and this is the last time I must express it. I am leaving you.'

He shook his head. 'This is madness, this talk of parting from me. You cannot do that. You are already bound to me.

Your body is already mine. You may claim a new existence, but only as part of me. You shall be Mrs Rochester – both virtually and nominally. You shall go to a place I have in the south of France. It's a whitewashed villa on the shores of the Mediterranean. There you shall live a happy, and guarded, and most innocent life. Never fear that I wish to lure you into error or to make you my mistress, for when I am with you, we shall be as husband and wife, as we have been these past weeks. Why did you shake your head? Jane, you must be reasonable, or in truth I shall again become frantic.'

His voice and hand quivered, his large nostrils dilated, his eye blazed, but still I dared to speak.

'Sir, your wife is living. That is a fact acknowledged this morning by yourself. If I lived with you as you desire, I should then be your mistress. To say otherwise is a lie. And I do not – cannot – understand how I could be under the same roof as her, for the danger I had thought was up there, is so much worse than I could ever have conceived.'

'You disapprove of me. I see that clearly, although I have never lied to you about my wild taste in women. You yourself have entreated me to tell you of my mistresses. And given time, I can explain the circumstances of my attachment to Bertha Mason and our history, in a way you will understand too. For sympathy, Jane, is your gift.'

I closed my eyes briefly, his words scalding me. It was true that I had asked him of his past conquests and sexual adventures, only hoping that his recollections might deflect from my own inadequacy. Yet I had never sought to understand the context of his lovers, only the details of the physical acts between them. And I had become aroused as he had shared the details, but now shame washed over me.

'Don't you understand? You are my sympathy, my better self, my good angel. I am bound to you with a strong attachment. I think you good, gifted, lovely. A fervent, a solemn passion is conceived in my heart. It leans to you, draws you to my centre and spring of life, wraps my existence about you, and, kindling in pure, powerful flame, fuses you and me in one.'

I was experiencing an ordeal. A hand of fiery iron grasped my vitals. It was he who thus loved me, and whom I absolutely worshipped, and I must renounce my love and idol.

'Mr Rochester, I will not be yours. Ever again.'

Another long silence.

'Jane!' recommenced he, with a gentleness that broke me down with grief. 'Jane, do you mean to go one way in the world, and to let me go another?'

'I do.'

'Jane' (bending towards and embracing me), 'do you mean it now?'

'I do.'

'And now?' softly kissing my forehead and cheek, cupping my breast with his hand. Then he put his hand between my legs, over my skirt. My sex throbbed, still roused by fidelity to him.

'I do,' extricating myself from restraint rapidly and completely.

'Oh, Jane, this is bitter! This is wicked. It would not be wicked to love me.'

'It would to obey you.'

'Then you snatch love and innocence from me? You fling me back on lust for a passion and vice for an occupation?'

'Mr Rochester, I no more assign this fate to you than I grasp at it for myself. You will forget me before I forget you.'

'That is not true. Will never be true. Why can you not stay? No man is being injured by these circumstances. For you have neither relatives nor acquaintances whom you need fear to offend by living with me? Nobody need ever know about her.'

This was true and while he spoke my very conscience and reason turned traitors against me, and charged me with crime in resisting him. They spoke almost as loud as Feeling, and that clamoured wildly. 'Oh, comply!' it said. 'Think of his misery, think of his danger. Look at his state when left alone. Soothe him. Save him. Love him. Tell him you love him and will be his. Who in the world cares for you? Or who will be injured by what you do? You are already his. Can you forsake the ecstasy that your body delights in with his?'

Still indomitable was the reply. 'I care for myself. I will hold to the principles received by me when I was sane, and not mad as I am now.' For I could not, would not live with him knowing that another woman had dominated him – and may still.

She certainly held some power over Mason. I knew that now. I had sat with Mason after he had been wounded by her and now I thought back to his demeanour as I tended him. His exhaustion I now knew was the exhaustion of ecstasy. He had travelled halfway across the world to be with Bertha Rochester. Which is why he had never questioned her treatment of him, or railed against Rochester for the injuries he had suffered.

It had been Mason who had interrupted our wedding, still clearly in the thrall of this woman and intent on doing her bidding. And once again, Rochester had hardly chastised him for such a heinous act. It was this which convinced me that she dominated Rochester too.

I remembered now the way she had stared at me as she had blown the candle out in my face. It was the look of an all-powerful dominatrix – like those I had seen in Mr Rochester's books, tying up their man-slaves, whipping them in punishment and yet having them submit and return for more.

Mr Rochester had crushed my innocence, intoxicating me with carnal knowledge that I had devoured with a hunger I did not know I possessed. Yet that was the reason I had to leave. Because I could only sink further and further down now, into the depths that had no bottom.

His faith that I could elevate him beyond the quagmire of sin he had experienced before me was misplaced. I could not. No human being complicit in his actions as I had become could be his redeemer.

'I am going, sir.'

'You cannot.'

'Do you not think I heard the words that she said?' I

spat, fury rising up in me, that he could not see the position he had put me in. I recalled her terrible pronouncement, 'You were first to "train her, to strip her of her innocence, to make her pliant and then to bring her to me",' I reminded him.

Mr Rochester looked beaten. Tears filled his eyes. He could no longer look me in the face.

'Yes, my sweet, sweet Jane. I promised her that. How could I not promise to do her bidding, when her threats were so terrible? She threatened to ruin me.'

I turned to leave, but he grabbed my dress, making me turn.

'But I would have disobeyed her. And once I grew to know you, once I realized that I was no longer training you for her, but for myself . . . then I knew I must leave this place with you and thereby break her spell. And that is why I tried to leave today.'

'I am not your dog to be trained,' I said, whipping my skirt out of his hands, my mind now made up. Even though I could see how much he loved me, I would not submit to his manipulations any further, as he had so readily submitted to hers.

I made for the stairs, but Mr Rochester, seeing me go, let out a yell, his fury wrought to the highest. I saw then the red ruby stain of that charlatan's cure on his lips. I had long ago heard tales of men becoming enthralled to such medicines. Was this part of the witch's power over him too?

He crossed the floor and seized my arm and grasped my waist. He seemed to devour me with his flaming glance.

Physically, I felt, at the moment, powerless as stubble exposed to the draught and glow of a furnace. Mentally, I still possessed my soul, and with it the certainty of ultimate safety. The soul, fortunately, has an interpreter – often an unconscious, but still a truthful interpreter – in the eye. My eye rose to his and while I looked in his fierce face I gave an involuntary sigh. His grasp was painful, and my over-taxed strength almost exhausted.

'Never,' said he, as he ground his teeth, 'never was anything at once so frail and so indomitable. A mere reed she feels in my hand!' He shook me with the force of his hold. 'I could bend her with my finger and thumb, but what good would it do if I bent, if I tore, if I crushed her? Consider that eye. Consider the resolute, wild, free thing looking out of it, defying me, with more than courage – with a stern triumph. Whatever I do with its cage, I cannot get at it – that savage, beautiful creature! If I tear, if I rend the slight prison, my outrage will only let the captive loose. Conqueror I might be of the house, but the inmate would escape to heaven before I could call myself possessor of its clay dwelling place.

'And it is you, spirit – with will and energy, and virtue and purity – that I want. Not just your brittle frame. Of yourself you could come with soft flight and nestle against my heart. If you wanted to, you could live by my side in peace and joy. But if I seize you against your will, you will elude my grasp like an essence and will vanish even before I inhale your fragrance. Oh! Come, Jane, come!'

As he said this, he released me from his clutch, and only

looked at me. The look was far worse to resist than the frantic strain. Only an idiot, however, would have succumbed now. I had dared and baffled his fury and now I must elude his sorrow.

I walked once more away from him.

'You are really going, Jane?'

'I am going, sir.'

'You are leaving me?'

'Yes.'

'You will not come? You will not be my comforter, my rescuer? My deep love, my wild woe, my frantic prayer, are all nothing to you?'

What unutterable pathos was in his voice! How hard it was to reiterate firmly, 'I am going.'

I put my head down, resolute, gathering my bag and heading for the stairs.

'Jane!' he shouted. 'Oh, Jane! My hope, my love, my life!' broke in anguish from his lips. Then came a deep, strong sob.

'Farewell!' was the cry of my heart as I left him. Despair added, 'Farewell for ever!'

I knew what I had to do, and I did it mechanically and quickly. Downstairs, I sought the key of the side door in the kitchen. I got some water, I got some bread, for perhaps I should have to walk far and my strength, sorely shaken of late, must not break down. All this I did without one sound. I opened the door, passed out, shut it softly. Dim dawn glimmered in the yard. The great gates were closed and locked, but a wicket in one of them was only latched. Through that I departed. It, too, I shut, and now I was out of Thornfield.

A mile off, beyond the fields, lay a road which stretched in the contrary direction to Millcote. It was a road I had never travelled, but often noticed, and wondered where it led, and thither I bent my steps. No reflection was to be allowed now, not one glance was to be cast back, not even one forward. Not one thought was to be given either to the past or the future.

I longed to be his. I panted to return. It was not too late. I could yet spare him the bitter pang of bereavement. I could go back and be his comforter, his redeemer from misery, perhaps from ruin. I could take him away from her. In the midst of my pain of heart and frantic effort of principle, I abhorred myself. I had no solace from self-approbation, none even from self-respect. I had injured, wounded and left my master. I was hateful in my own eyes. Still I could not turn, nor retrace one step. I could not, would not submit. God must have led me on.

I was weeping wildly as I walked along my solitary way. Fast, fast I went like one delirious. A weakness, beginning inwardly, extending to the limbs, seized me, and I fell. I lay on the ground some minutes, pressing my face to the wet turf. I had some fear, or hope, that here I should die, but I was soon up, crawling forwards on my hands and knees, and then again raised to my feet, as eager and as determined as ever to reach the road.

When I got there, I was forced to sit to rest me under the hedge and while I sat, I heard wheels, and saw a coach come on. I stood up and lifted my hand. It stopped. I asked where it was going. The driver named a place a long way off, and where I was sure Mr Rochester had no connections. I asked for what sum he would take me there. He said thirty shillings and I answered that I had but twenty and he would try to make it do. He further gave me leave to get into the inside, as the vehicle was empty. I entered, and was shut in.

Gentle reader, may you never feel what I then felt! May your eyes never shed such stormy, scalding, heart-wrung tears as poured from mine. May you never appeal to heaven in prayers so hopeless and so agonized as in that hour left my lips, for never may you, like me, dread to be the instrument of evil to what you wholly love. Judge me if you will, but there was no other choice: reader, I left him.